CHARLES DICKENS AND
LITERARY DIALECT

CHARLES DICKENS AND LITERARY DIALECT

OSAMU IMAHAYASHI

KEISUISHA

Hiroshima, Japan

2006

First published in August 2006

Imahayashi, Osamu, 1964 -
    Charles Dickens and Literary Dialect / Osamu Imahayashi
    Includes bibliographical references and index
    ISBN 4-87440-938-5 C3082

Copyright © 2006 Osamu Imahayashi

All rights reserved. No part of this publication may be reproduced, stored in a retrieval system, or transmitted, in any form, or by any means, electronic, mechanical, photocopying, recording or otherwise, without the prior permission in writing of Keisuisha Publishing Company.

Published in Japan by
Keisuisha Co., Ltd., 1-4 Komachi, Naka-ku, Hiroshima 730-0041

Printed in Japan

PREFACE

The main aim of this little volume is to appreciate Dickens's literary art on the representation of English provincial dialects and Americanisms from the viewpoint of stylistics and philology. This book is based upon my doctoral dissertation, by which I received a doctorate degree in literature at the Graduate School of Letters, Hiroshima University on the 23rd of March, 2006. Some of the material in this book has also formed the basis of two research papers read at the International Conference of the Poetics and Linguistics Association (PALA): one is "'A Word to the Reader': Dickens on the use of Literary Dialect" (2005), read at Huddersfield University, England and the other is "A Stylistic Approach to Pip's Class-consciousness" (2006) at Joensuu University, Finland.

In sending forth this monograph I take the welcome opportunity of tendering my sincere thanks to Michio Kawai, Professor Emeritus at Hiroshima University and Toshiro Tanaka, Professor Emeritus at Hiroshima University, both of whom have guided me into the unbeaten forests of English language and literature. I wish to acknowledge my indebtedness to Professor Akiyuki Jimura, Graduate School of Letters at Hiroshima University, who has constantly encouraged me to complete and publish this book, and whose academic suggestions have been of great value. To Professor Ken Nakagawa, Yasuda Women's University, I am greatly indebted for encouraging me to read the papers at the PALA conference. I would like to express my gratitude to Professor Yoshiyuki Nakao, Graduate School of Education at Hiroshima University, who has given me constant advice on English linguistics. My hearty thanks are also due to Professor Kensuke Ueki, Graduate School of Letters at Hiroshima University, who has given me invaluable academic suggestions on literary criticism since I was an undergraduate student. I have been much obliged to the members of the English Research Association of Hiroshima for giving me invaluable suggestions at the annual meeting.

I have much benefitted from the discussions with sociologists at my university, especially with Professor Masami Takahashi, Professor Hideaki Wakuda, and Professor Kenji Katou.

I wish to thank Itsushi Kimura, President of Keisuisha Publishing Co., Ltd. for his hearty cooperation and assistance in publishing this book. I would also like to express my hearty thanks to William Shang, Associate Professor at Kibi International University, who has carefully checked my English and given me some useful suggestions; and to Ms. Tomoko Oshimo and Ms. Emi Maeda, postgraduates at Kibi International University, both of whom have spared no pains to proofread my rough draft. All the remaining errors in this book are, of course, my own.

Last, but not least, I would like to express my hearty thanks to my wife and family for their devoted support.

Okayama
July 2006

Osamu Imahayashi

CONTENTS

Preface	v
Table of abbreviations	ix
List of tables	xii
INTRODUCTION	1
CHAPTER I PROVENANCE AND SOURCE	9
1.1 *Nicholas Nickleby*	9
1.2 *David Copperfield*	10
1.3 *Hard Times*	12
1.4 *American Notes* and *Martin Chuzzlewit*	15
1.5 *Great Expectations*	17
CHAPTER II SPOKEN AND WRITTEN	19
2.1 Phonetic Spelling	20
2.2 *Paraarer, parearer*, or *paroarer*?	21
2.3 *Nighbut, nighbout*, or *nighb't*?	23
CHAPTER III CHARACTERISATION AND EXPERIMENT	25
3.1 Conventional use of phonetic spellings	26
3.2 Conventional use of apostrophes	29
3.3 Experimental use of capital letters	31
3.4 Experimental use of italics	33
3.5 Experimental use of hyphens	34
3.6 Experimental use of diacritic marks	39
3.7 Dickens's linguistic experiments	39
3.8 Dickens's linguistic characterisation	40
CHAPTER IV REALISM AND VERISIMILITUDE	45
4.1 Dickens's natural gift and pursuit for dialect materials	46
4.2 Heroic speech and dialect suppression	49
4.3 Linguistic stigmatisation in *Hard Times*	52

CHAPTER V STYLISTICS AND SOCIOLINGUISTICS 71
5.1 Omniscient narrator as a dialect glossarist 71
5.2 Visual effect and the point of view 75
5.3 Regional dialect and class dialect 78
5.4 American English and British English 82

CHAPTER VI PROVINCIALISMS AND AMERICANISMS 101
6.1 Yorkshire provincialisms in *Nicholas Nickleby* 101
6.2 Lancashire provincialisms in *Hard Times* 105
6.3 East Anglia provincialisms in *David Copperfield* 118
6.4 Kentish provincialisms in *Great Expectations* 129
6.5 Americanisms in *American Notes* and *Martin Chuzzlewit* 132

CONCLUSION 165

Select Bibliography 171
Index 183

TABLE OF ABBREVIATIONS

A. The works of Charles Dickens
AN	American Notes	(1842)
BH	Bleak House	(1852-53)
BR	Barnaby Rudge	(1841)
CB	Christmas Books	(1843-48)
DC	David Copperfield	(1859-50)
DS	Dombey and Son	(1846-48)
ED	The Mystery of Edwin Drood	(1870)
GE	Great Expectations	(1860-61)
HT	Hard Times	(1854)
LD	Little Dorrit	(1855-57)
MC	Martin Chuzzlewit	(1843-44)
MHC	Master Humphrey's Clock	(1840-41)
NN	Nicholas Nickleby	(1838-39)
OCS	The Old Curiosity Shop	(1840-41)
OMF	Our Mutual Friend	(1864-65)
OT	Oliver Twist	(1837-39)
PP	The Pickwick Papers	(1836-37)
SB	Sketches by Boz	(1833-36)
TTC	A Tale of Two Cities	(1859)
UT	Uncommercial Traveller	(1860)

B. The letters of Charles Dickens
Let. I	The Letters of Charles Dickens, Vol. I	(1820-39)
Let. II	The Letters of Charles Dickens, Vol. II	(1840-41)
Let. III	The Letters of Charles Dickens, Vol. III	(1842-43)
Let. V	The Letters of Charles Dickens, Vol. V	(1847-49)
Let. VI	The Letters of Charles Dickens, Vol. VI	(1850-52)
Let. VII	The Letters of Charles Dickens, Vol. VII	(1853-55)
Let. IX	The Letters of Charles Dickens, Vol. IX	(1859-61)
Let. XI	The Letters of Charles Dickens, Vol. XI	(1865-67)

C. References
Century	The Century Dictionary
DA	A Dictionary of Americanisms
DAE	A Dictionary of American English

Charles Dickens and Literary Dialect

EDD   *The English Dialect Dictionary*
EDG   *The English Dialect Grammar*
Forby   *The Vocabulary of East Anglia*
GLD   *A Glossary of the Lancashire Dialect*
MEG   *A Modern English Grammar*
MEU   *A Dictionary of Modern English Usage*
Moor   *Suffolk Words and Phrases*
MW   *The Miscellaneous Works Tim Bobbin, Esq.*
OED   *The Oxford English Dictionary*
SUE   *A Dictionary of Slang and Unconventional English*
Webster *Webster's Third International Dictionary of the English Language*

D. List of counties and places

Abd.	Aberdeen	Lakel.	Lakeland
Ant.	Antrim	Lan.	Lancashire
Bch.	Buchan	Lei.	Leicester
Bck.	Bucks	Lin.	Lincoln
Bdf.	Bedford	Lth.	Lothian
Brks.	Berks	Midl.	Midlands
Cai.	Caithness	Nhb.	Northumberland
Chs.	Cheshire	Nhp.	Northampton
Cmb.	Cambridge	Not.	Nottingham
Cor.	Cornwall	Nrf.	Norfolk
Cum.	Cumberland	Or.I.	Orkney Isles
Der.	Derby	Oxf.	Oxford
Dev.	Devon	Peb.	Peebles
Dnb.	Denbigh	Per.	Perth
Dor.	Dorset	Rut.	Rutland
Dur.	Durham	Sc.	Scotland
e.An.	East Anglia	Sh.I.	Shetland Isles
Edb.	Edinburgh	Shr.	Shropshire
Eng.	England	Som.	Somerset
Ess.	Essex	Stf.	Stafford
Flt.	Flint	Suf.	Suffolk
Frf.	Forfar	Sur.	Surrey
Glo.	Gloucester	Sus.	Sussex
Hmp.	Hampshire	Uls.	Ulster
Hnt.	Huntingdon	Wal.	Wales
Hrf.	Hereford	War.	Warwick
Hrt.	Hertford	Wil.	Wiltshire
I.Ma.	Isle of Man	Wm.	Westmoreland
Inv.	Inverness	Wor.	Worcester
Irel.	Ireland	Wxf.	Wexford
Kcb.	Kirkcudbright	Yks.	Yorkshire
Ken.	Kent		

TABLE OF ABBREVIATIONS

E. Miscellanies

adj.	adjective	No.	Number
adv.	adverb	nom.	nominative
Amer.	America, American	nw.	north-west
&	and	obj.	objective
aux.	auxiliary	obs.	obsolete
conj.	conjunction	obsol.	obsolescent
cons.	consonant	OE.	Old English
dial.	dialect, -al	OF	Old French
CD	Charles Dickens	orig.	originally
Ch.	Chapter	pers.	person, personal
Cy.	country	pl.	plural
e.	east	pp.	past participle
em.	east-mid	ppl. a.	participial adjective
esp.	especially	poss.	possessive
fem.	feminine	pr., pres.	present
fn.	footnote	prep.	preposition
Fr.	French	pret.	preterite
gen.	generally	pron.	pronoun
hist.	historical	prov.	provincial
indef.	indefinite	rel.	relative pronoun
indic.	indicative	Rom.	Romanic, Romance
inf.	infinitive	s.	south
Ir.	Irish	sb.	substantive
It.	Italian	se.	south-east
L.	Latin	sing.	singular
lit.	literary	sm.	south-mid
m.	mid	sn.	south-north
masc.	masculine	snw.	south-north-west
ME.	Middle English	Sc.	Scotland, Scottish
me.	mid-east	Sp.	Spanish
Midl.	Midland	s.v.	sub verbo
mod.	modern	sw.	south-west
Mod.E	Modern English	U.S.	The United States
ms.	mid-south	v.	verb
n.	north	w.	west
ne.	north-east	wm.	west-mid
NE.	New English		

LIST OF TABLES

Table 1	The regional dialects in Dickens	18
Table 2	Reduction of vowels and consonants	59
Table 3	Short vowels	65
Table 4	Long vowels	67
Table 5	Diphthongs	68
Table 6	Consonants	70
Table 7	Flat adverbs	99
Table 8	Yorkshire provincialisms in *Nicholas Nickleby*	104
Table 9	Lancashire provincialisms in *Hard Times*	116
Table 10	East Anglia provincialisms in *David Copperfield*	127
Table 11	Kentish provincialisms in *Great Expectations*	132
Table 12	Americanisms I	139
Table 13	Americanisms II	145
Table 14	Americanisms III	148
Table 15	Americanisms IV	150
Table 16	Americanisms V	160

INTRODUCTION

The term "dialect" refers to one of the varieties of language related to a group of people with common geographical identity or common social identity.[1] The former is called regional or provincial dialect, and the latter class or social dialect.

While many provincial dialects have rapidly vanished since the appearance of the broadcasting system, urban dialects have become so distinctive and flourished. In order to record the disappearing regional dialects in Britain, Harold Orton and Eugen Dieth published *Survey of English Dialects* from 1962 to 1971 in 13 volumes from the University of Leeds. During the second half of the last century sociolinguistics had been applied to the study of urban dialects. William Labov's elaborate work, *The Social Stratification of English in New York City*, published in 1966 from Center for Applied Linguistics, is one of the most famous and influential contributions of this kind. The linguistic surveys carried out by Orton and Dieth, or Labov are called "dialectology."

The basic academic method for the study of the present volume is not "dialectology," but "dialectism," which was first

---

[1] The definition of this term is based on the following studies: G. L. Brook (1978) *English Dialects*, the third edition, pp. 17-18; R. Chapman (1973) *Linguistics and Literature*, p. 18; and K. Wales (2001) *A Dictionary of Stylistics*, the second edition, p. 105.

introduced and defined as "the borrowing of features of socially or regionally defined dialects" by Geoffrey Leech[2]. While dialectology is based on the direct survey of the speech of people in a particular area by questionnairing or interviewing them, "dialectism" is the "use" of a dialect by writers for the purpose of putting some "reality" into the literary text. Some of the Victorian authors know the dialect directly like Elizabeth Gaskell (Lancashire dialect), Charlotte, Emily, Anne Brontë (Yorkshire dialect), George Eliot (Warwickshire dialect) and Thomas Hardy (Dorsetshire dialect); and others like Dickens do not have a first-hand knowledge of the dialect. So "literary dialect" we shall discuss in this book is the dialect used by the author in the literary text for the purpose of linguistic characterisation[3].

As is said above, "dialect" is to be divided into two large categories: regional dialect and class dialect. The primary concern in this book lies in the regional dialects employed by Dickens in his literary works. It is, however, inadequate to discuss only his use of regional dialects because the characters he creates belong to a lower-class order as well as a rural community.

First of all we should evaluate the present study on Dickens's use on literary dialect as objectively as possible by probing the preceding studies concerning this kind historically. Not a few studies on the regional dialects rendered by Charles Dickens in his writings have been published since 1889, when German philologist Wilhelm Franz contributed "Die Dialekt-

---

[2] G. N. Leech (1968) *A Linguistic Guide to English Poetry*, p. 49.
[3] We shall discuss Dickensian Characterisation later in Chapter III.

sprache bei Ch. Dickens"[4] to *Englische Studien*[5]. He made scientific research into Dickens's use of London dialect, i.e. Cockney, especially from the phonological point of view.

In 1927 Louise Pound, American philologist, first attempted to research into Dickens's portrayal of American English in her "The American Dialect of Charles Dickens."[6] Her general view on his description of Americans is that "Dickens tends to picture our countrymen as offensive, conceited, bad-mannered, and ignorant, but he does so humorously."[7] Her close reading of his letters from the United States to John Forster as well as *American Notes* and *Martin Chuzzlewit* made it possible to reveal his linguistic view on the English language in America clearly. Her study penetrated far into phonology, morphology, grammar, and vocabulary.

K. J. Fielding[8] convincingly claimed that Dickens's main source for East Anglia words and phrases found in the speech of Mr. Peggotty's Yarmouth family[9] in *David Copperfield* was Edward Moor's *Suffolk Words and Phrases* (1823), which he carefully compared with another possible source, Robert Forby's *The Vocabulary of East Anglia* (1830). His reference

---

[4] Sanki Ichikawa benefitted from this research when he wrote "Dickens to Zokugo no Kenkyu" in *Studies in English Grammar*, (Kenkyusha: Tokyo, 1912, 1948, pp. 246-311).

[5] Vol. XII, pp. 197-244.

[6] *American Speech*, XXII, No. 2, 1927, pp. 124-130.

[7] L. Pound (1927) "The American Dialect of Charles Dickens," p. 126.

[8] "*David Copperfield* and Dialect," *The Times Literary Supplement*, 30 April 1949, p. 288.

[9] Nina Burgis summarised Dickens's treatment for East Anglia vocabulary in "Introduction" to the Clarendon Edition of *David Copperfield*, The Clarendon Press: Oxford, 1981, pp. xxiii-xxiv.

to the dialect was concentrated mainly on vocabulary, so other linguistic fields, pronunciation, grammar, syntax, and so on, were out of his scope.

Just one year after the publication of Fielding's article, Tadao Yamamoto's elaborated work, *Growth and System on the Language of Dickens* was published, in which he devoted himself to the analysis of the linguistic growth in Dickens's use of colloquial idioms by regarding them as "delimitable units" in parallel with his growth as a novelist. In chapter XII, entitled "Journeys," he brought up Dickens's use of regional dialects en bloc for philological discussions for the first time.

One of the most strenuous and essential contributions to the phonological studies on the substandard speech of all the Dickensian characters is undoubtedly Stanley Gerson's *Sound and Symbol in the Dialogue of the Works of Charles Dickens*[10], in which he tried to examine "the methods used by Dickens in his novels, tales, and journalist works, to suggest pronunciations that did not conform to the educated norm of his day."[11] In "Chapter 6 Some Conclusions" Gerson energetically discussed Dickens's treatment of Yorkshire and Lancashire dialect[12], and in "Appendix 11"[13] he made a brief biographical sketch of "Dickens and dialect" from the very early period of his career.

---

[10] This work was published by Almqvist & Wiksell, Stockholm in 1967 as No. XIX of "Stockholm Studies in English" series.

[11] S. Gerson (1967) *Sound and Symbol*, p. xvii.

[12] Dickens's treatment of Yorkshire dialect, which was represented mainly by John Browdie in *Nicholas Nickleby*, is studied in pp. 337-39, and that of Lancashire dialect, which was represented chiefly by Stephen Blackpool in *Hard Times*, is discussed in pp. 339-40.

[13] S. Gerson (1967) *Sound and Symbol*, pp. 366-372.

The monumental achievement on the study of the language of Charles Dickens is George Leslie Brook's *The Language of Dickens*, published by André Deutsch as one of "The Language Library" series in 1970 in commemoration of the centenary of the death of this great novelist. He was the founder of Lancashire Dialect Society and had deep interest in regional dialects as well as Cockney. This encouraged him to spare one chapter for the study of regional dialects and one more for substandard speech. He made survey of Dickens's use of three English regional dialects, East Anglia, Yorkshire, and Lancashire dialect, and American English from the phonological, morphological, syntactical, and lexical point of view, comparing them almost always with his use of Cockney.

Toshiro Tanaka made philological contributions to the regional dialect used in the speech of Joe Gargery[14] and Abel Magwitch[15] in *Great Expectations*. He pointed out that the speech of Joe and Magwitch is very similar to that of low-life London characters.

Norman Page first published *Speech in the English Novel* from Longman in 1973[16], in which he used "the novels of Dickens as a major source of exemplification throughout."[17] In his *Speech*, he made a brief sketch of Dickens's use of the

---

[14] T. Tanaka (1972) "Regional and Occupational Dialect of Joe Gargery," *Literature and Language of Dickens*, edited by Michio Masui and Masami Tanabe, Sanseido: Tokyo, pp. 153-187.

[15] T. Tanaka (1973) "Regional Dialect of Abel Magwitch". *Eibungaku-Ronshu*. No. 11. The English Literary Society of Kansai University: Osaka. 44-59.

[16] The second edition, published by Macmillan in 1988, included additional examples and the enlarged bibliography.

[17] N. Page (1988) *Speech in the English Novel*, p. x.

dialect in *Nicholas Nickleby* and *David Copperfield*[18], and discussed his use of Lancashire dialect in *Hard Times*[19] in comparison with Mrs. Gaskell's industrial novels, *Mary Barton* and *North and South*. He first pointed out Dickens's reference to The Rev. William Gaskell's *Two Lectures on the Lancashire Dialect*[20], and he argued some linguistic peculiarities of American English[21] which he introduced into *American Notes* and *Martin Chuzzlewit*.

In response to Page's reference to Dickens's use of Gaskell's *Lectures*, Angus Easson, one of the eminent Gaskell scholars, contributed "Dialect in Dickens's *Hard Times*" to *Notes and Queries*.[22] In this article he first demonstrated that the major source of Dickens's use of Lancashire words and phrases was John Collier's *The Miscellaneous Works of Tim Bobbin, Esq.*, published in 1818.

Now let us turn into the present study on Dickens's use of literary dialect. Primarily the scope of this book will focus on his use of regional dialects described in *Nicholas Nickleby* (Yorkshire dialect), *David Copperfield* (East Anglia dialect), *American Notes* and *Martin Chuzzlewit* (American dialect), *Hard Times* (Lancashire dialect), and *Great Expectations* (Kentish dialect). However, we will never let class dialect be

---

[18] N. Page (1988) *Speech in the English Novel*, p. 64.

[19] N. Page (1988) *Speech in the English Novel*, p. 68-69.

[20] The Lectures were reprinted in the fifth edition of *Mary Barton* by Chapman and Hall.

[21] N. Page (1988) *Speech in the English Novel*, p. 159-60.

[22] No. 23, 1976, pp. 412-413. It is very sorry for Patricia Ingham not to refer to this article in her "Dialect as 'Realism': *Hard Times* and the Industrial Novel," *The Review of English Studies*, No. 37, 518-27.

ignored, which almost always appear in these novels.[23]

The present small volume consists of six chapters: Chapter I Provenance and Source, Chapter II Spoken and Written, Chapter III Characterisation and Experiment, Chapter IV Realism and Verisimilitude, Chapter V Stylistics and Sociolinguistics, and Chapter VI Provincialisms and Americanisms.

The first chapter of this volume will show the provenance and glossarial sources of the regional dialect used in the novels and who uses the dialect in them.

The linguistic problem which lies between spoken and written language will be dealt with in Chapter II. The first section of this chapter treats phonetic spelling which represent dialectal deviation. The other two will make it clear that Dickens took great pains to adopt appropriate spellings into the text.

The first half of Chapter III will point out the two sides of his use of dialects: one is the conventional use of them (the conventional use of phonetic spellings and apostrophes); and the other the experimental use of them (the experimental use of capital letters, italics, hyphens, and diacritic marks). The latter half will deal with his linguistic characterisation.

It is the problem lying between realism and verisimilitude that every novelist has to be face with. It is our chief concern in Chapter IV. Firstly we shall have a look at the relation between his keen ear as a natural gift and collecting dialect materials for making the speech and description in the novels true to life, secondly stop to think about "heroic speech" in *Great Expectations*, and lastly analyse why some critics

---

[23] We shall examine the relationship between regional and class dialect in Section 5.3 of Chapter V.

stigmatise his rendering Lancashire dialect in *Hard Times*.

In Chapter V we shall attempt to make stylistic and sociolinguistic approaches to Dickens's use of dialects, putting some stress on the point of view, the relation between class and regional dialect, and British English and American English.

In the last chapter we shall have a close look at English provincialisms in *Nicholas Nickleby, Hard Times, David Copperfield,* and *Great Expectations,* and Americanisms in *American Notes* and *Martin Chuzzlewit.*

CHAPTER I

Provenance and Source

It is our chief concern in this chapter to make it clear where the dialect is used; who speaks the dialect; and how Dickens obtains the knowledge of the dialect by consulting the provincial and dialect dictionaries and references shown in "Select Bibliography" below. Let us begin with *Nicholas Nickleby*.

1.1 *Nicholas Nickleby*
Nicholas Nickleby is the first provincial novel in which Dickens set its main scene outside of London and was published in monthly instalments from April 1838 to October 1839. Dickens set its scene in the North Riding of Yorkshire. It was one of his main aims of this novel that he exposed the notorious Yorkshire schools and their scandalous ill-treatment for their pupils.[1] Just before he started writing the novel, he made a trip with H. K. Browne, "Phiz," whose role was to sketch the visual background, to north Yorkshire for one week from 30th January 1838[2], so as to collect the materials for his new work. They

---

[1] Dickens explained this aim in the "Preface" to the original edition, 1839 (Penguin Classics edition edited by M. Ford, 1999, pp. 3-5).

[2] As for their trip to Yorkshire, see E. Johnson (1952) *Charles Dickens: His Tragedy and Triumph*, Simon and Schuster: New York, pp. 218-19, and the letter to his wife, dated 1 Feb. 1838 (*Let. I*, 365-66).

stayed at the New Inn at Greta Bridge on the second night. The next morning they went to an academy kept by William Shaw at Bowes. This academy is considered the original for Dotheboys Hall and this schoolmaster one of the model for Wackford Squeers. Then the investigators stretched their legs to Barnard Castle, about four miles away from Greta Bridge, where they investigated some of the schools. That night Dickens succeed in drawing some information of Yorkshire schools from Richard Barnes, a native attorney there, who is reckoned to be the original for John Browdie, who is the chief contributor to the dialect. There are a few examples of the dialect in the speech of the guard on the stage-coach which takes Nicholas and Squeers to Yorkshire.

1.2 David Copperfield

For writing the next first person story, which was eagerly recommended by John Forster[3], Dickens made a short trip to Yarmouth with his friends, John Leech, illustrator and Mark Lemon, private theatricals from 7th to 10th January 1849.

David "was born at Blunderstone, in Suffolk" (*DC*, 2)[4]. The following passage[5] reveals why Dickens chose "Blunderstone" for his novel:

> Eight miles south of Yarmouth. Just west of the main

---

[3] John Forster (1893) *The Life of Charles Dickens*, p. 404.

[4] All the quotations are extracted from the texts in "Select Bibliography" below, and the abbreviated titles are shown in "Table of Abbreviations" above. The numbers following the abbreviated titles indicate the page numbers from which the quotations are extracted. The speaker of the quotation is sometimes inserted between the abbreviated title and the page number.

[5] This is quoted from the footnote to the letter to his wife, dated on 9 January 1849 (See *Let. V*, p. 471).

road, three and a half miles north-west of Lowestoft, lies Blundeston; it was clearly on this walk that CD saw its name on a sign-post "and took it" for *Copperfield* (*To* Mrs. Watson, 27 Aug 53)—"for the sound of its name" (*To* de Cerjat, 29 Dec 49).

Young David was taken to Yarmouth, Norfolk by his beloved nurse, Clara Peggotty. Yarmouth is her own country, where David met her brother Daniel Peggotty, Ham Peggotty, Em'ly, and Mrs. Gummidge, and spent few happy days with them. Except Em'ly they all employed broad East Anglia dialect.

To compensate the lack of the knowledge of East Anglia provincialisms, Dickens made good use of Edward Moor's *Suffolk Words and Phrases* (1823)[6]. On 7 August 1849, Dickens received a letter from the Rev. George Frederick Hill, in which we can find Hill's suggestion of Dickens's misuse of *bo'* for *bor* and of *Yarmouth flats* for *Yarmouth sands*.[7] The following is Dickens's reply for Hill's letter:

> I am extremely obliged to you for your kind letter, which has been forwarded to me here, this morning, and which I hasten to acknowledge the receipt of, and to thank you for.
> The information you give me as to the provincialisms, I have no doubt I shall find useful. The term "flats", is

---

[6] K. J. Fielding (1949) "*David Copperfield* and Dialect," *The Times Literary Supplement*. 30 April 1949, p. 288.

[7] Hill's letter says, "one who is universally & deservedly allowed to be the most faithful describer of every day life & every day people in this or perhaps in any age, to point out two small errors in your last very beautiful work", being "a Norfolk man and well acquainted with the vernacular of that County". "Once or twice ... you made 'Ham' to say 'Bo' when it should be Bor & again you talk about 'Yarmouth flats', a term I believe applied to some parts of the English Coast, but not used with us here. The correct expression is 'Sands'... The other Norfolk provincialisms are surprisingly correct." (*Let. V*, p. 590fn)

not used, I think, as any part of the local vernacular, but to explain to those who do not belong to that part of England, a general aspect of country which would hardly be understood if described by any other term. What we call "sands", here, for example, or in Kent, or Sussex, is something very unlike the great wild level at Yarmouth. (*Let. V*, p. 590)

The following letter gives us another important piece of information that Dickens must have received a list of East Anglia dialect words and phrases from Mrs. Milner Gibson, who came of a Suffolk family:

Many thanks for your list of words, which is particularly well-timed, and will be extremely useful to me. I have laughed over the letter (I think it is the finest I ever read) until my eyes are dim. (*Let. VI*, p. 11)

In *David Copperfield* Dickens set its scene in East Anglia: Yarmouth, south-east Norfolk and Blundeston, north Suffolk, which was changed into Blunderstone in the novel. Besides Mr. Peggotty's family in Yarmouth, Mr. Barkis, a carrier, speaks East Anglia dialect.

1.3 *Hard Times*

In *Hard Times* Dickens set its main scene in Coketown, a fictitious name of an industrial town situated in Lancashire,[8] and created Stephen Blackpool, a power-loom operative at Mr. Bounderby's mill and Rachael, as principal contributors to Lancashire dialect which he attempted to describe. Of all his works dealing with regional dialects, it may, however, be

---

[8] Not a few studies have been carried out whether Coketown is Manchester or Preston. See M. Simpson (1997) *The Companion to* Hard Times, pp. 77-9.

CHAPTER I   PROVENANCE AND SOURCE   13

Hard Times that has been subject to the greatest criticism both by literary scholars and philologists.[9]

According to Edgar Johnson[10] and Michael and Mollie Hardwick[11] (1973: s.v. "Manchester" and "Preston"), Dickens had paid a several short visits to Manchester[12] before his visit to Preston in 1854, all of which took place between 1838 and 1848. These facts make it possible to guess that he might have obtained some knowledge of the dialect around this area during his short visits, but neither in his letters nor writing records, can we find written evidence of his picking up any features of the dialect.

Norman Page describes in detail the main purpose of his visit to Preston in 1854 and its influence upon his rendering of the dialect through the mouths of Stephen Blackpool and others as follows:

> Dickens began to write *Hard Times* early in 1854, visiting Preston at the same period in search of material. A by-product of the Preston visit was a *Household Words* article 'On Strike', which contains evidence that his ears had been sensitive to the idiom and pronunciation, as well as to the content, of the Lancashire factory-workers' speech, for he reproduces in that article a speech by a Preston weaver which includes many of the forms which recur in the novel. Stephen's speech

---

[9] We shall discuss this matter in Chapter IV.

[10] *Charles Dickens: His Tragedy and Triumph*, Simon and Schuster: New York, 1952, 255ff., and Michael and Mollie Hardwick, eds. (1973) *The Charles Dickens Encyclopedia*, Osprey: London, s.v. "Manchester" and "Preston."

[11] *The Charles Dickens Encyclopedia*, Osprey: London, 1973, s.v. "Manchester" and "Preston."

[12] Dickens often visited Mrs. Burnett, his sister Fanny there, and in 1847 he performed Ben Jonson's *Every man in His Humour* with his fellow amateur players in Liverpool and Manchester.

was created, then, with vivid impressions of the dialect of the Preston area fresh in the novelist's mind, though his knowledge of it was certainly limited.[13]

On the 4th of September 1866, Dickens wrote the following letter to Charles Fechter:

> Of course you are free to show this note to Mr. Boucicault, and I suppose you will do so; let me throw out this suggestion to him and you. Might it not ease the way with the Lord Chamberlain's office, and still more with the audience, when there are Manchester champions in it, if instead of "Manchester" you used a fictitious name? When I did "Hard Times" I called the scene Coketown. Everybody knew what was meant, but every cotton-spinning town said it was the other cotton-spinning town. (*Let. XI*, 241-2)

Judging from the above discussion, Dickens set the main scene for *Hard Times* in Lancashire, whether Coketown is a fictitious name for Manchester or Preston.

Angus Easson first demonstrates that Dickens's major source for the dialect used in *Hard Times* is from *A View of the Lancashire Dialect*[14] by 'Tim Bobbin', the pseudonym of John Collier, first published in 1746. Dickens owned a copy of the 1818 edition. Patricia Ingham argues that though the conversation between Tummus and Meary "must have been unintelligible to Dickens, it is evident that the Glossary was invaluable."[15] Another source first introduced by N. Page is

---

[13] N. Page (1988) *Speech in the English Novel*, p. 67.

[14] A. Easson, (1976) "Dialect in Dickens's *Hard Times*," *Notes and Queries*, 23, p. 413.

[15] P. Ingham (1986) "Dialect as 'Realism': *Hard Times* and the Industrial Novel," p. 522.

CHAPTER I   PROVENANCE AND SOURCE   15

the Reverend William Gaskell's *Two Lectures on the Lancashire Dialect*[16], published in 1854 in the fifth edition of his wife's *Mary Barton*. P. Ingham can find no striking correspondences between Blackpool's speech and Mr. Gaskell's *Lectures*, and she regards them as "only of marginal use."[17]

1.4 *American Notes* and *Martin Chuzzlewit*
Steven Marcus describes Dickens's first trip[18] to America as "a six months' voyage into the English language."[19] Dickens treats some features of American English in *American Notes*, first published in 1842, *Martin Chuzzlewit*, first published in monthly instalments from January 1843 to July 1844, and his letters to Forster sent from America. It was not until his first visit to the United States that he perceived some of the differences between American and British English.[20] While staying there, he becomes interested in American English for its peculiarities in pronunciation, grammar, usage and vocabulary, and he often introduces many examples of these peculiar-

---

[16]   N. Page (1973, 1988) *Speech in the English Novel*, pp. 68-69.

[17]   P. Ingham (1986) "Dialect as 'Realism': *Hard Times* and the Industrial Novel," p. 523.

[18]   Dickens crossed the Atlantic to America twice. His first visit there is from January to June, 1842, and his second from November, 1867 to April, 1868. The main purpose of his first visit is to conduct his campaign for International Copyright, because there were a lot of acts of literary piracy of his works in America in those days. That of his second is for the public reading tour.

[19]   S. Marcus (1965) *Dickens from Pickwick to Dombey*. pp. 218-19

[20]   On 29th January 1842, Dickens writes to Forster about the difference between American and British English with his surprise: "... but for an odd phrase now and then—such as *Snap of cold weather*; a *tongue-y man* for a talkative fellow; *Possible?* as a solitary interrogation; and *Yes?* for indeed—I should have marked, so far, no difference whatever between the parties here and those I have left behind." (*Let. III*, 35-6)

ities in his letters to Forster. These examples help him to refresh his memory when he later writes *American Notes* and the American chapters of *Martin Chuzzlewit*.

In the following passage, L. K. Webb illustrates the method by which Dickens awakens his memory of American English when he later writes *American Notes* and *Martin Chuzzlewit*:

> When Dr Samuel Johnson, on Boswell's recommendation, made his visit to Scotland he wrote regularly to Mrs. Thrale, keeping her fully informed about his wanderings and excursions. It was from these letters that he collected his material for his *Journey to the Western Isles of Scotland*. Charles Dickens followed the same plan when he made his visit to America; he wrote at length to his friend John Forster. Later he refreshed his memory from these letters when he wrote *American Notes* for Chapman and Hall, and the novel *Martin Chuzzlewit* which followed.[21]

N. F. Blake observes that "Dickens is one of the first English writers to realize the potential of American speech, which no doubt came from his visits to America and his familiarity with American writings."[22]

Dickens's native American characters are General Cyrus Choke, militia officer, Hannibal Chollop, frontiersman who worships Eden, Colonel Diver, editor of *The New York Rowdy Journal*, Mrs. Hominy, intellectually pretentious woman, Captain Kedgick, landlord of the National Hotel in Watertoast, La Fayette Kettle, an inquisitive, bombastic American, Elijah Pogram, member of Congress, and Zephaniah Scadder, fraud-

---

[21] L. K. Webb (1983) *Charles Dickens*, p. 57.
[22] N. F. Blake (1981) *Non-standard Language in English Literature*, p. 159.

ulent land agent in *Martin Chuzzlewit*; and a forester who does not like overcrowding, a gaoler of The Tomb in New York, a bootmaker, subject of an extended vignette, a coachman, on the road to Columbus, and a gentleman in a straw hat, with considerable conversation in *American Notes*.

1.5 *Great Expectations*

Dickens described the main scene of *Great Expectations* through Pip's point of view at the very beginning of this novel: "Ours was the marsh country, down by the river, within, as the river wound, twenty miles of the sea" (*GE*, 4). David Paroissien notes that "This is an accurate description of the Hoo Peninsula, a triangular-shaped spur of land that forms the most northerly section of Kent."[23] We can determine without doubt that the main scene set by Dickens for *Great Expectations* is the villages, towns, or cities on the Hoo Peninsula and in its surroundings.

Dickens himself spent a happy childhood in Chatham from 1817 at the age of five to 1822 at the age of ten. When he was very young his father brought him on his back to Gad's Hill Place and then he made frequent visit to this house and its surroundings.[24] His "removal to Gad's Hill Place in August 1860 intensified his relationship with the whole lower Medway region."[25]

Dickens creates Joe Gargery, a blacksmith in Cooling village, his fierce wife Mrs. Joe Gargery as chief contributors

---

[23] D. Paroissien (2000) *The Companion to* Great Expectations, p. 27.
[24] This scene is described in *The Uncommercial Traveller*, pp. 61-62.
[25] D. Paroissien (2000) *The Companion to* Great Expectations, p. 27.

of Kentish dialect. However, Kent, "Garden of England," is so near to London, and the Thames and the Old Roman Road have provided easy access to the capital. Consequently the difference between London dialect and Kentish dialect had gradually become smaller from the beginning of early Modern English period.[26]

Table 1 The regional dialects in Dickens

	Scenes	Glossaries	Dialect speakers
NN	Bowes, north-west Yorkshire	—	John Browdie, and The guard.
AN MC	The United States of America and Canada.	—	Forester, Gaoler, Bootmaker, Coachman, and Straw Hat. (AN) Cyrus Choke, Hannibal Chollop, Colonel Diver, Mrs. Hominy, Captain Kedgick, La Fayette Kettle, Elijah Pogram, and Zephaniah Scadder. (MC)
DC	Yarmouth, south-east Norfolk, Blundeston, north Suffolk,	Moor, E. (1823) Suffolk Words and Phrases, R. Hunter: London.	Clara Peggotty, Daniel Peggotty, Ham Peggotty, Mrs. Gummidge, and Mr. Barkis.
HT	Manchester or Preston, Lancashire.	Collier, J. (1818) The Miscellaneous Works of Tim Bobbin, Esq.	Stephen Blackpool and Rachael.
GE	Rochester, Chatham, and Cooling, east Kent.	—	Joe Gargery and Mrs. Joe Gargery.

---

[26] See J. Franklyn (1953) *Cockney*, p. 34, and H. Hirooka (1965) *Dialects in English Literature*, pp. 69 and 73.

CHAPTER II

Spoken and Written

George Bernard Shaw once attempted to present a Cockney flower girl's speech in *Pygmalion* by using English alphabet and schwa[1], which he found impossible, and he explained thus:

> Here, with apologies, this desperate attempt to represent her dialect without phonetic alphabet must be abandoned as unintelligible outside London.[2]

N. Page agrees his remark and demonstrates that "the twenty-six letters of our alphabet, however ingeniously combined and supplemented by other graphological indications, can scarcely begin to represent the infinite variety and subtlety of speech."[3]

It is a truth universally acknowledged that it is almost impossible to represent the real human speech on the text. Besides Shaw, quite a few writers have made painstaking attempts to break this stronghold. Charles Dickens is of course one of them.

In this short chapter we shall examine Dickens's linguistic

---

[1] The reason why G. B. Shaw used schwas will be explained in the next section.

[2] G. B. Shaw (1916) *Pygmalion*, pp. 16-17.

[3] N. Page (1988) *Speech in the English Novel*, p. 10.

agony to represent regional varieties with phonetic spelling as veritably as possible in his literary texts.

2.1 Phonetic Spelling

English spelling system is notorious for the lack of correlation between spelling and real sound. Those whose mother tongue is English, according to G. L. Brook, "have been for so long accustomed to the varieties of English spelling that they take them for granted, but it is not uncommon to find even well-educated Englishmen who will admit cheerfully, or even with a touch of pride, that they cannot spell."[4] In Old English one letter represents each sound, at least each phoneme, but in the course of time sound changes[5] have continually occurred within the English language, which brings disagreements between spelling and real sound into Present-day English. In order to eliminate these disagreements, the spelling reform[6] has continually been called for by orthoepists since the sixteenth century[7]. Bernard Shaw is famous for enthusiastic spelling reformer, who devoted himself to the "lifelong battle for rational

---

[4] G. L. Brook (1958) *A History of the English Language*, André Deutsch: London, p. 100.

[5] The most influential and dramatic sound change is what we call the Great Vowel Shift, which took place in the transitional period from Middle English to Modern English.

[6] As for the spelling reform, see D. Crystal (1985) *The Cambridge Encyclopedia of the English Language*. Cambridge University Press: Cambridge, pp. 276-77. G. K. Chesterton mildly objected to this reform, referring the concern that the origin of words is not to be guessed through the reformed spellings. (*All Things Considered*. Darwen Finlayson: London, 1969, pp. 140-43.)

[7] According to D. Crystal, "The earliest reformers were the Greek scholar Sir John Cheke (1514-57) and the scholar and statesman Sir Thomas Smith (1513-77)." (*The Stories of English*. Allen Lane: London, 2004, p. 266.)

spelling."[8]

The central vowel [ə] is rendered in various spelling in Present-day Standard English. Bernard Show bitterly and ironically pointed out that "In the dialogue an e upside down indicates the indefinite vowel, sometimes called obscure or neutral, for which, though it is one of the commonest sounds in English speech, our wretched alphabet has no letter."[9]

Julian Franklyn, referring to the transcription of Cockney dialect, states that "IT GOES without saying that the moment the spoken word is dealt with in print, it becomes the written word; hence it is necessary to repeat and to emphasize that the spoken cockney word cannot be successfully rendered in writing, and that any system of phonetic spelling adopted must fall short of its intention."[10]

As well as the representation of Cockney speech, we have to estimate the real sound that Dickens intended to suggest from phonetic spellings or typographical devices which he rendered when he described regional dialects in his works. We shall take up two cases in which Dickens found difficulty in practicing phonetic spellings: one is American pronunciation of *prairie*, and the other Yorkshire dialect form of *nighbut*.

2.2 *Paraarer, parearer,* or *paroarer*?

While travelling through the United States, Dickens heard Americans pronounce *prairie* in three ways. He soon wrote to his friend John Forster of this variety:

---

[8] R. Chapman (1984) *The Treatment of Sounds in Language and Literature*, p. 56.

[9] G. B. Shaw (1916) *Pygmalion*, p.11.

[10] J. Franklyn (1953) *Cockney*, p. 241

Prairie is variously called (on the refinement principle I suppose) Para*a*rer; par*e*arer; and paro*a*rer[11]. (*Let. III*, 202)

During his stay in America, Dickens sent many letters to Forster, from which he later made his memory refreshed when he wrote *American Notes* and *Martin Chuzzlewit*. In the former he reproduced the pronunciations of *prairie*:

I MAY promise that the word Prairie is variously pronounced *paraaer*[12], *parearer*, and *paroarer*. The latter mode of pronunciation is perhaps the most in favour." (*AN*, 177)

As is mentioned in *American Notes*, in *Martin Chuzzlewit*, "Perearers" was his choice for Elijah Pogram:

"Verdant as the mountains of our country; bright and flowing as our mineral Licks; unspiled by withering conventionalities as air our broad and boundless *Perearers!*"[13] (533)

Judging from these extracts, Dickens intends to show that *prairie* is pronounced trisyllabically, which suggests anaptyxis[14], the insertion of a parasitic [ə] between *p* and *r* forming a cluster, takes place and that the main stress falls on the second syllable whose vowels he heard pronounced in three different ways. Artemisia Bear Bryson supports Dickens's portrayal of *prairie* and gives *pararie* as an example of the

---

[11] Italicized letters indicate Dickens's intention to represent each stress.

[12] This is misprinted or merely mistaken for *paraarer*. Please compare it with the example in his above letter to Forster.

[13] All the italics in quotations in this book are mine.

[14] See H. Kökeritz (1953) *Shakespeare's Ponunciation*, p. 292 and O. Jespersen (1909) *MEG*, Vol. 1, §9.78.

CHAPTER II SPOKEN AND WRITTEN   23

Texan accent[15]. Although he tries to reproduce the pronunciation for *prairie* precisely and faithfully, but I think such phonetic spellings are rather arbitrary and impressionistic.

2.3 *Nighbut, nighbout,* or *nighb't*?

"Textual Notes" to *Hard Times* by Fred Kaplan and Sylvère Monod[16] reveals Dickens's great difficulty in representing Stephen Blackpool's use of *nighbut*, which means "nearly."

> 'Not e'en so. I were one-and-twenty myseln; she were twenty *nighbut*.' (73)

On the original manuscript *nighb't* is chosen. On the first corrected proof the word is omitted and again *nighb't* is added. On the second corrected proof it is corrected to *nighbut*. On the article in *Household Words*[17] *nighbout* is employed. In the first edition in volume form[18] *nightbut* is used, but it is mere misprint, so in all the modern editions it is silently corrected to *nighbut*.

In word formation this adverb consists of the adverb *nigh* and the adverb *about*, according to *OED*[19] and *EDD*[20]. We could guess the reason why Dickens was confused in the choice of the form of this adverb. In January 1854 Dickens visited Preston in search of material for writing *Hard Times*. This short visit produced an article, "On Strikes" in *Household Words*[21].

---

[15] A. B. Bryson (1929) "Some Texas Dialect Words," p. 330.
[16] *Hard Times* (Norton Critical Edition). The third edition, 2001, p.251.
[17] No. 215, 6 May, 1854, p. 262.
[18] It was published by Bradbury & Evans in 1854, p. 66.
[19] See *nigh, adv.* 12. c.
[20] See *nigh, adv.* 6.
[21] No. 203, 11 February, 1854, pp. 553-559.

In this article, through his keen ear, Dickens successfully reproduced Lancashire factory workers' speech, in which we can easily recognise similar forms and pronunciations found in the speech of Blackpool in *Hard Times*. Dickens's knowledge of the dialect of the Preston area, however, is certainly limited as Norman Page[22] suggests. To supply the lack of his knowledge of this provincial dialect, he consulted Tim Bobbin's "Glossary" recorded in *The Miscellaneous Works of Tim Bobbin, Esq.* and read The Rev. William Gaskell's *Two Lectures on the Lancashire Dialect*. Unfortunately *nighbut*, *nighbout*, nor *nighb't* can be found in these works.

---

[22] N. Page (1988) *Speech in the English Novel*, p. 67.

CHAPTER III

Characterisation and Experiment

It is almost half a century since Randolph Quirk delivered his inaugural lecture of the Professor of the English Language at University of Durham on 26 May, 1959.[1] In this lecture he pointed out Dickens's application of innovative or experimental methods for representing the speech of his characters, which deviates from the standard norm. On Dickens's innovative or experimental use of language, Knud Sørensen wrote *Charles Dickens: Linguistic Innovator* in 1885, in which he concentrated mainly on neologisms in the vocabulary.

As well as linguists, literary critics have pointed out his innovative or experimental use of language. George H. Ford argued that "What we have lost is a sense of how shockingly revolutionary Dickens' prose seemed to his contemporaries,"[2] and Harry Stone also claimed that "It is only after reading Dickens's contemporaries that one is able to understand how fresh and impressive his experiments were."[3]

---

[1] R. Quirk (1959) *Charles Dickens and Appropriate Language*. The University of Durham: Durham.

[2] G. H. Ford (1955) *Dickens and his Readers*, Princeton University Press: New Jersey, p. 113.

[3] H. Stone (1959) "Dickens and Interior Monologue," *Philological Quarterly*, Vol. XXXVIII, No. 4, p. 65.

In this chapter we shall have a close look at Dickens's conventional use of dialect presentation through phonetic spellings and apostrophes, and his innovative or experimental use through capital letters, italics, hyphens, and diacritic marks.

3.1 Conventional use of phonetic spellings

One of the most conventional and prevailing methods for representing dialectal varieties of pronunciation is the use of phonetic spelling.[4] Young Boz took great pains to describe Yorkshire accent[5] in the speech of John Browdie[6] in *Nicholas Nickleby*. The following passage is one of the most typical examples of his local accent:

> 'Presently,' resumed John, 'he did *coom*. I *heerd* door shut *doonstairs*, and him a *warking*, *oop* in the *daark*. "Slow and *steddy*,' I says to myself, "*tak'* your time, sir—no hurry." He *cooms* to the door, turns the key—turns the key when there *warn't* nothing to *hoold* the lock—and *ca's oot* 'Hallo, there!'"—"Yes," thinks I, "you may do *thot agean*, and not *wakken* anybody, sir." "Hallo, there," he says, and then he stops. "Thou'd *betther* not aggravate me," says *schoolmeasther*, *efther* a little time. "I'll *brak'* every *boan* in your *boddy*, Smike," he says, *efther* another little time. Then all of a *soodden*, he sings *oot* for a *loight*, and when it *cooms*—ecod, such a *hoorly-boorly*! "*Wa'at's* the matter?" says I. "He's *gane*," says he,—stark mad *wi'* vengeance. "Have you *heerd* nought?" "*Ees*," says I,

---

[4] See N. Page (1988) *Speech in the English Novel*, p. 58, and R. Quirk (1959) "Charles Dickens and Appropriate Language," p. 14.

[5] "Accent" here means the mode of utterance peculiar to locality.

[6] G. L. Brook says that "One of the most sustained attempts to portray a regional dialect in the novels of Dickens is in the speech of the Yorkshireman John Browdie in *Nicholas Nickleby*." (*The Language of Dickens*, 1970, p. 122.)

CHAPTER III   CHARACTERISATION AND EXPERIMENT

"I *heerd* street-door shut, no time at *a'* ago. I *heerd* a person run *doon* there" (pointing *t'other wa'*—eh?) "Help!" he cries. "I'll help you," says I; and off we set—the wrong *wa'*! Ho! ho! ho!' (545)

Italicised words and phrases represent Browdie's broad Yorkshire accent by dint of various phonetic spellings[7]. In *Nicholas Nickleby*, the use of phonetic spellings and apostrophes is the only linguistic method for conveying the flavour of provincial dialect into the text, because young Boz did not obtain any dictionaries, glossaries, or books as the source of Yorkshire provincial words and phrases.

Let us chalk up some of the typical examples of John Browdie's Yorkshire accent. In his speech we have quite a few examples in which *t* is spelt with *th* and *tt* with *tth*. These spellings represent, according to G. L. Brook[8], "the replacement of an alveolar [t] by a dental consonant approaching [θ] in its place of formation." We have 14 words with this feature and the total number is 58. Examples are *efther* (508, 509, 543, 544$^{2\times 9}$), *garthers* (542), *(school-)measther* (157, etc. 26 times), *Misther* (542, 582, 823), *Monsther* (501), *pasthry* (541), *quarther* (545), *threat* (504), *thried* (501), *waither* (545, 552, 825); *betther* (504, 543, 545, 551, 586, 827), *butther* (108, 509), *latthers* (501, 509), and *matther* (157, 503, 504, 549, 823).

Diphthongs often become short vowels in his speech[10] as

---

[7] The substandard and dialectal pronunciation of John Browdie is well discussed by S. Gerson in his *Sound and Symbol*, 1967.
[8] G. L. Brook (1970) *The Language of Dickens*, p. 122.
[9] 544$^{2\times}$ means that *efther* occurs twice in p. 544.
[10] See S. Gerson (1967) *Sound and Symbol*, §15.1.2 and §19.2.1.

in *brak'* (545), *gratful* (544), *mak'* (542, 543), *mak* (549), *mak'st* (823), *shak* (506), *tak* (158, etc. 12 times), *tak*, (586), *takkin* "taking" (508), *takken* "taken" (544), *wakken* (502, 545); *brokken* (111, 157, 826), and *spok'n* (141, 142, 156, 274).

Dickens often applies *oi* for *i* to Browdie's speech to represent the change [ai] to [ɔi]as in *broid* (503²ˣ), *foind* (503, 509, 545, 827), *loit* (111, 504, 545), *loike* (157 etc 14 times), *noice* (826), *soight* (504), *soizable* (501), *sploiced* (509), *toight* (111), *troifling* (504),and *'soizes* (551³ˣ).

Some of the short vowels pronounced by John retains ME sound. Dickens employed the spelling *oo* to suggest his frequent use of [u] instead of [ʌ]. Examples are *anoother* (506, 582, 826), *boost* (509), *bootuns* (501), *coom* (501, etc. 31 times), *coomfortable* (552), *coot* (508²ˣ), *droonk* (823), *hoonger* (542), *hoongry* (541, 823), *loonching* (541), *loove* (157), *moonths* (501), *moothers* (824), *t'oother* (108, 542), *room* (823), *roon* (826), *roonaway* (551²ˣ), *snoog* (544), *soobjact* (551), *soodden* (545), *sooffer* (827), *soom* (544, 552²ˣ), *soomat* (552, 823²ˣ), *soom'at* (542, 544), *soom'ut* (550), *soop* (823), *sooper* (552), *oop* (502, 543²ˣ, 545²ˣ, 551, 823, 826), *yoong* (508, 509), and *yoongster* (157, 508, 826).

ME [u:] retains, spelt *oo*, instead of being diphthongized to [au], as in RP, according to G. L. Brook[11]. Instances are *aboot* (108, etc, 13 times), *doon* (508²ˣ, 545²ˣ, 550, 823²ˣ), *doonstairs* (545), *hoo* (157, 504, 506, 542, 544), *hoo'* (551), *looder* (826), *mooth* (504), *noo* (157, etc. 22 times), *oot*

---

[11] G. L. Brook (1970) *The Language of Dickens*, p. 123.

(509²ˣ, 545³ˣ, 552), *ootside* (508, 542, 586), *pooder* (823), *proodest* (542), and *toon* (823²ˣ).

3.2 Conventional use of apostrophes

In Stephen Blackpool's speech in *Hard Times*, we can find a lot of apostrophes, which Dickens intended to use in order to represent the speech habit of Lancashire people. The following extract is one of the most typical examples of this kind:

> 'I *ha'* paid her to keep *awa' fra'* me. These five year I *ha'* paid her. I *ha'* gotten decent fewtrils about me agen. I *ha'* lived hard and sad, but no ashamed and *fearfo' a'* the minnits *o'* my life.' (72)

One of the most striking features of Stephen Blackpool's Lancashire accent is the reduction of vowels and consonants.[12] It is regarded as one of the most characteristic points of Lancashire dialect. In this respect John Collier illustrated their peculiar way of speech as follows:

> In general we speak quick and short; and cut of a great many letters, and even words by apostrophes; and sometimes sound two, three, or more words as one.[13]

In Blackpool's speech, vowel reductions are to be found in the definite article and the preposition *to*. As for the consonant reductions, the loss of [d], [l], [n], [v], and [ð] frequently occur in Stephen's speech.

This reminds us of "On Strike" in which Dickens attempted to reproduce the dialectal speech of the Preston factory workers by using phonetic spellings and apostrophes. At that

---

[12] We shall discuss this respect in the next chapter.
[13] J. Collier (1818) *The Miscellaneous Works of Tim Bobbin, Esq.* p. 4.

time Dickens did not come by *The Miscellaneous Works of Tim Bobbin Esq.* or The Rev. Gaskell's *Two Lectures on Lancashire Dialect*, so his only method of representing the speech of Lancashire factory workers is phonetic spellings and apostrophes:

> The chairman was a Preston weaver, two or three and fifty years of age ... Now *look'ee heer* my friends. See what *t'* question is. *T'* question is, *sholl* these *heer* men be *heerd*. Then *'t cooms* to this, what *ha'* these men got *t'* tell us? Do they bring *mooney*? If they bring *mooney t'ords t'* expences *o'* this strike, they're welcome. For, Brass, my friends, is what we want, and what we must *ha'* (hear hear hear!). Do they *coom* to us *wi'* any suggestion for the conduct of this strike? If they do, they're welcome. Let, *'em* give us their advice and we will hearken to *'t*. But, if these men *coom heer*, to tell us what *t'* Labor Parliament is, or what Ernest Jones's opinions is, or *t'* bring in politics and differences *amoong* us when what we want is *'armony*, brotherly love, and con-cord; then I say *t'* you, decide for *yoursel'* carefully, whether these men *ote* to be *heerd* in this place. (Hear hear hear! and No no no!) Chairman sits down, earnestly regarding delegates, and holding both arms of his chair. Looks extremely sensible; his plain coarse working man's shirt collar easily turned down over his loose Belcher neckerchief.[14]

In the preceding passage, we can find the vowel reductions in the preposition *to* and *in*, the definite article *the*, the personal pronoun *hem*; and the consonant reductions in *with*, *harmony*, and *yourself* as well as such variant spellings as *amoong*, *coom(s)*, *mooney*, *heer*, *heerd*, *ote*, and *sholl*.

---

[14] C. Dickens (1854) "On strike" in *Household Words*, No. 203, 11 Feb. 1854, pp. 556-7.

3.3 Experimental use of capital letters

We can divide Dickens's use of capital letters representing some peculiarities of the American pronunciation into three types. First of all, the use of capital letters in *fesTIval* (*MC*, 531) indicates that the lightly-stressed or unstressed syllable receives more stress than it usually does under the influence of the level stress. We sometimes find this use of capital letters together with the use of a hyphen in *ac-Tive* (*MC*, 538) and *le-Vee* (*MC*, 538).

Secondly, the use of capital letters in *as-TONishin* (535) indicates added stress or the emphasis on the stressed syllable.

Lastly capital letters are sometimes used to represent the strong forms instead of the weak forms as in the indefinite article *A* and *An*, the preposition *Of* and *Toe*, "to" and the personal pronoun *My*. In the case of the indefinite article, Jespersen points out that "*a year* [ə 'jiə] (here Americans often say [ei], perhaps from Sc *ae.*)."[15] We shall show the examples in these cases below:

> "I am not surprised to hear you say so. It re-quires *An* elevation, and *A* preparation of the intellect. The mind of man must be prepared for Freedom, Mr Co." (*MC*, 519)
>
> He called this "planting the standard of civilization in the wilder gardens of *My* country." (*MC*, 521)
>
> "I have draw'd upon *A* man, and fired upon *A* man for less," said Chollop, frowning. "I have know'd strong men obleeged to make themselves uncommon skase for less. I have know'd men Lynched for less, and beaten into punkin'-sarse for less, by an enlightened people.

---

[15] *MEG*, Vol. I, 1909, § 9.215.

We are the intellect and virtue of the airth, the cream *Of* human natur', and the flower *Of* moral force. Our backs is easy ris. We must be cracked-up, or they rises, and we snarls. We shows our teeth, I tell you, fierce. You'd better crack us up, you had!" (*MC*, 523)

"Mr. Pogram! sir! A handful *Of* your fellow-citizens, sir, hearing *Of* your arrival at the National Hotel, and feeling the patriotic character *Of* your public services, wish, sir, to have the gratification *Of* beholding you, and mixing with you, sir; and unbending with you, sir, in those moments which—" (*MC*, 538)

"Which air so peculiarly the lot, sir, *Of* our great and happy country." (*MC*, 538)

"And therefore, sir," pursued the Doctor, "they request; as *A* mark *Of* their respect; the honour of your company at a little le-Vee, sir, in the ladies' ordinary, at eight o'clock." (*MC*, 538)

Mr. Pogram bowed to the Colonel individually, and then resumed: "Your approbation of *My* labours in the common cause goes *Toe My* heart. At all times and in all places; in the ladies' ordinary, *My* friends, and in the Battle Field"— (*MC*, 538)

"The name of Pogram will be proud *Toe* jine you. And may it, *My* friends, be written on *My* tomb, 'He was a member of the Congress of our common country, and was ac-Tive in his trust.'" (*MC*, 538)

"The Com-mittee, sir," said the shrill boy, "will wait upon you at five minutes afore eight. I take *My* leave, sir!" (*MC*, 538)

"It ain't that, sir," returned Pogram, "not at all. But I should wish you *Toe* accept a copy of *My* oration." (*MC*, 542)

"No, sir," retorted Pogram. "Not *A* dozen. That is more than I require. If you air content *Toe* run the hazard, sir, here is one for your Lord Chancellor," producing it, "and one for Your principal Secretary of

> State. I should wish them *Toe* see it, sir, as expressing what my opinions air. That they may not plead ignorance at a future time. But don't get intoe danger, sir, on my account!" (*MC*, 543)

It is very interesting and noticeable that Dickens made experimental use of capital letters only in the instalment No. XIII, published in January 1844.

3.4 Experimental use of italics

Dickens tries to represent the characteristic of the American pronunciation of *engine* by using three linguistic symbols, i.e. hyphens, diacritic marks, and italics. In all the cases these devices are attributed to the level stress. We have only one example of the use of italics together with a diacritic mark in "ĕn*gine*" (*AN*, 55).

Dickens sometimes employs italics in order to represent the unusual stressed syllable: "coin*ci*dence"[16] (*PP*, 463). In *coincidence*, its primary stress falls on the second syllable, but "coin*ci*dence" suggests that the stress falls on the third syllable.

Dickens sometimes applies italicised *h* to a word with an unaspirated *h* in order to aspirate the consonant. The following is one of the interesting examples of this kind:

> "Allow me the *h*onour, Sir?" said the gentleman with the whiskers, presenting his dexter hand, and aspirating the h. (*PP*, 641)[17]

---

[16] S. Gerson proclaimed that "Coin*ci*dence, pronounced [ai], I have heard from the comedian Arthur Askey who raised a laugh with it. It is the stress pattern of the verb *coincide* that is called to mind." (*Sound and Symbol*, 1967, "Appendix 3", p. 355.)

[17] The other examples in Dickens are: *h*onour (*NN*, 688; *MHC*, 80; *DS*, 532), *h*onors (*NN*, 183), *h*onourable (*MHC*, 95^{2x}; *BR*, 394; *MC*, 409).

Jespersen points out how authors find it difficult to reproduce the aspiration of unaspirated *h*:

> It is a curious consequence of the unphonetic character of the English spelling that it is extremely difficult to represent in writing the addition of [h] before a vowel spelt with a mute *h*, the authors use strange shifts to do so: "you do me Hhonour ... your hhonoured name" (Thackeray, *Newcomes* 11), "*h*nour" (Dickens, *Dombey* 344) ...[18]

3.5 Experimental use of hyphens

Dickens noticed the peculiarity of American pronunciation out of Boston and New York and described that "nasal drawl is universal" (*Let. III*, 196). In *Martin Chuzzlewit* he described the odd pronunciation[19] of a typical American Colonel Diver as follows:

> "The old ship will keep afloat a year or two longer yet, perhaps," said Martin with a smile, partly occasioned by what the gentleman said, and partly his manner of saying it, which was odd enough, for he emphasised all the small words and syllables in his discourse, and left the others to take care of themselves: as if he thought the large parts of his speech could be trusted alone, but the little ones required to be constantly looked after. (*MC*, 257)

Martin also observed the same kind of utterance in Major Pawkins's speech:

---

[18] *MEG*, 1909, Vol. I, §13.685.

[19] In this respect, G. L. Brook comments that "The greater care with which lightly-stressed words are pronounced in American speech is the subject of an amused comment of the kind that linguistic differences are apt to arouse." (*The Language of Dickens*, 1970, p. 134.)

CHAPTER III CHARACTERISATION AND EXPERIMENT

> Major Pawkins then reserved his fire, and looking upward, said, with a peculiar air of quiet weariness, like a man who had been up all night—an air which Martin had already observed both in the colonel and Mr. Jefferson Brick— (*MC*, 268)

In his letter, Dickens illustrates the peculiar pronunciation of "the women who have been bred in slave-states" as if they spoke "more or less like negroes" (*Let. III*, 196).

G. P. Krapp, American philologist, also comments on one characteristic feature of the American manner of speech compared with the British one:

> The typical native American speech is more level, the voice rising and falling but little. The American manner of speech because of its level stressing permits a fuller pronunciation of unstressed or secondarily stressed syllables than the kind of speech represented in the British pronunciation of *medicine* as ['mɛdɪsn], of *library* as ['laɪbrɪ], in which a heavy expiratory stress on the first syllable seems to exhaust a large share of the energy which might be devoted to the later syllables of the word.[20]

L. Pound agrees with Krapp in this respect and says, "The characteristic of New World utterance that he illustrated oftenest is the protraction of the initial syllable of trisyllabic words having penultimate accent, and sometimes of disyllabic words also."[21] Dickens did not fail to notice this peculiarity. He inserts a hyphen in the words with more than one syllable in order to represent this peculiarity. G. L. Brook makes mention on his use of hyphens:

---

[20] G. P. Krapp (1925) *The English Language in America*, Vol. II, p. 14.
[21] L. Pound (1947) "The American Dialect of Charles Dickens," p. 128.

> One general characteristic of pronunciation is indicated by the insertion of a hyphen in the spelling of many words of more than one syllable. The hyphen may indicate a pause, but it is more likely that it is a way of showing that the lightly-stressed syllables of the word receive more stress than usually do in British English.[22]

In addition to this, Brook makes another comment on this device:

> Words of two or more syllables are often printed with a hyphen after the first syllable. The hyphen may indicate a pause and it may also indicate that the word is pronounced with something approaching level stress.[23]

We can classify these hyphenated words into two groups: one is the words with the stress on the first syllable, and the other the words with the stress on the second syllable.

3.5.1 Words with the stress on the first syllable

Some of the disyllabic or trisyllabic words with the primary stress on the first syllable sometimes have a hyphen before the final syllable. These hyphens indicate that the unstressed final syllables have stress and that the sound of the vowel may change [i] to [i:] or [ai] on the final syllable. Examples are *sure-ly* (*MC*, 348, 503), *ĕn-gīne* (*MC*, 345), *en-gine* (*MC*, 531), *Ac-tive* (*MC*, 352), *ac-Tive* (*MC*, 538), *lĕ-vēe* (*MC*, 364), *le-Vee* (*MC*, 538), *na-tive* (*MC*, 520, 533, 536), *ene-mies* (*MC*, 532, 542), *prĕjŭ-dīce* (*MC*, 367), *preju-dice* (*MC*, 531, 533), *tongue-y* (*MC*, 352). With respect to this change, S. Gerson

---
[22] G. L. Brook (1970) *The Language of Dickens*, p. 135.
[23] G. L. Brook (1970) *The Language of Dickens*, p. 237.

CHAPTER III   CHARACTERISATION AND EXPERIMENT   37

points out thus:

> RP [i] in the above words does not carry the main stress. If [ai] is intended, it would involve in most cases a greater degree of stress on the syllable affected. As many of the "speakers" are American, Dickens is conveying the lesser degree of variation between stressed and unstressed syllables in American speech as compared with British English.[24]

We have *Eu-rope* (*MC*, 262, 290) as another example of this kind, but it has a different vowel quality. The sound of the vowel on the final syllable changes [ou] to [ə] on the final syllable.

3.5.2   Words with the stress on the second syllable

Some of the disyllabic or trisyllabic words with the primary stress on the first syllables often have a hyphen after the first syllable. As well as level stress and the protraction of the initial syllable, the sound change of the vowels on their first syllables are to be found in these words.

Under the influence of the level stress, the unstressed prefix *ex-* or *en-* has more stress than they usually do. These prefix have the change in their vowel sound. They become a strong form [e] or a long vowel [ɛ:] for [i]: *ex-alted* (*MC*, 533), *ex-cited* (*MC*, 371), *ex-citement* (*MC*, 371), *ex-clusiveness* (*MC*, 290), *ex-pect* (*MC*, 536), *ex-pression* (*MC*, 542), *En-tirely* (*MC*, 265). The unstressed prefix *com-* or *con-* has more stress than usual. The sound of their vowel becomes a strong form [ɔ] or a long vowel [ɔ:] for [ə]. Examples are *con-ceive* (*MC*, 523), *con-clude* (*MC*, 346), *con-cluded* (*MC*, 353),

---

[24] S. Gerson (1967) *Sound and Symbol in the Dialogue of the Works of Charles Dickens*. Appendix 2, 1 (c), p. 348.

con-sider (*MC*, 519, 533), *con-siderable* (*Let. III*, 89), *con-siderin* (*MC*, 259); *Com-mittee* (*MC*, 538), *com-pete* (*MC*, 531; *Let. III*, 90). The vowel sound in the initial unstressed syllable in *as-TONishing* (*MC*, 535) and *ac-quire* (*MC*, 536) becomes a strong form [æ] or a long vowel [a:] instead of [ə].

Influenced by the level stress, the vowel sound in the unstressed prefix *pre-* or *re-* becomes a long vowel [i:] instead of [i]. Examples are *pre-diction* (*MC*, 531); *re-ceive* (*MC*, 364), *re-quest* (*MC*, 539), *re-quire* (*MC*, 519), *re-quires* (*MC*, 519), *re-tard* (*MC*, 272). The vowel sound in the initial unstressed syllable in *e-mo-tion* (*MC*, 542) and *e-tarnal* (*MC*, 259, 345) also becomes a long vowel [i:] instead of [i].

Under the influence of the level stress, some of the disyllabic or trisyllabic words with the stress on the second syllable affect the change of their vowel sounds. They become diphthongs or long vowels. The vowel sound on the syllable *a-* becomes a diphthong [ei] or a long vowel [i:] instead of [ə]. Examples are *a-dopted* (*MC*, 358), *a-larming* (*MC*, 352), *a-live* (*MC*, 371), *a-mazing* (*MC*, 290). The vowel sound in the initial unstressed syllable in *di-rection* (*MC*, 519[2x]) becomes a diphthong [ai] or a long vowel [i:] for [i] or [ə]. The vowel sound in the initial unstressed syllable becomes a diphthong [ou] or a long vowel [ɔ:] for [ə] in *Co-lumbia* (*MC*, 346), *do-minion* (*MC*, 358[2x]), *po-session* (*MC*, 358), *Pro-fessor* (*MC*, 272, 537); for [ɔ:] in *o-ration* (*MC*, 531) and for [əu] in *lo-cation* (*MC*, 345, 362, 533), *lo-ca-tion* (*AN*, 63).

We have another interesting type of the hyphenated word. If we syllabify the word unite, we can describe its syllabicated form as *unit-ed*. Dickens, however, employed *U-nited* (*MC*,

345, 357, 368) in order to represent one of the features of the American pronunciation. S. Gerson illustrates that the function of this addition of a hyphen indicates "varying types of juncture, spacing between syllables."[25]

3.6 Experimental use of diacritic marks

Dickens uses three types of diacritic marks: slurs (ĕ, ŏ, ŭ), bars (ā, ē, ī) and an umlaut (ï). The slurs suggest the vowels on the stressed or unstressed syllables become glide vowels, the bars represent the vowels on the unstressed syllables become long vowels, and the umlaut indicates the vowel on the unstressed syllable becomes diphthongs. All the phenomena are attributed to the level stress discussed above. The examples are: *ĕngīne* (*Let. III*, 90), and *moŭntaïnoŭs* (*AN*, 151); with italics, *ĕngine* (*AN*, 55); and with hyphens, *ĕn-gīne* (*MC*, 345), *lĕ-vēe* (*MC*, 364), *prĕjŭ-dīce* (*MC*, 367), and *Gŏ-lāng* (*AN*, 140).

3.7 Dickens's linguistic experiments

Michael Slater points out on Dickens's use of punctuation thus:

> During the early 1840's Dickens was experimenting with a 'rhetorical' style of punctuation[26] based on speech-rhythms rather than on grammatical sense. This involves especially the lavish use of dashes, colons and semi-colons. It appears in *Christmas Carol* (1843), *The Chimes* (1844) and *The Cricket on the Hearth* (1845) but was considerably toned down in *The Battle of Life*

---

[25] S. Gerson (1967) *Sound and Symbol in the Dialogue of the Works of Charles Dickens.* Appendix 2, 3. p. 354.

[26] Kathleen Tillotson first referred to "rhetorical punctuation" in *Oliver Twist* in her "Introduction" to The Clarendon Dickens edition of *Oliver Twist*, pp. xxxi-xxxix.

(1846) and *The Haunted Man* (1848).[27]

The time of tone-down or termination of his experimental use of a rhetorical style of punctuation is paralleled with that of his experimental or innovative use of typographical devices. This fact also coincides with the literary criticism that Dickens's attitude toward writing his novels completely changed from *Dombey and Son* (1846-8), which is "the earliest of the fully-documented novels."[28]

3.8 Dickens's linguistic characterisation

In 1961 Randolph Quirk declared sympathetic ways to appreciate Dickens's use of language:

> We may come nearer to a sympathetic appreciation of Dickens's language if we consider it under four heads: his use of language for individualisation and for typification; his use of it structurally; and his use of it experimentally.[29]

The abundant use of phonetic spellings in John Browdie's speech and apostrophes in Stephen Blackpool's speech are important and essential methods for "linguistic typification." The former typifies Yorkshire accents and the latter Lancashire accents. Dickens experimentally applied capital letters, hyphens, or diacritic marks to the speech of American characters in *American Notes* and *Martin Chuzzlewit* for the purpose of typifying the American way of utterance.

---

[27] "A Note to the Text" to the Penguin Edition of *Christmas Books*, Vol. 1, pp. xxvii-xxviii.

[28] J. Butt & K. Tillotson (1957) *Dickens at Work*, p. 10.

[29] R. Quirk (1961) "Some Observations on the Language of Dickens," p. 20.

CHAPTER III   CHARACTERISATION AND EXPERIMENT   41

In this section we shall discuss Dickens's use of regional dialect for individualisation. Quirk asserts that particular locutions and systems of grammar are needed for a writer who works for instalment system of publication because this method provides the reader with a most immediate means of recall and identification.[30]

Ham Peggotty often addresses David as "Mas'r Davy bor'[31]" (88, 90, 121, 122, 266[32]), while Mr. Peggotty always uses "Mas'r Davy" without *bor'*. We can recognise Ham the moment "Mas'r Davy bor'" comes into our sight. The Rev. George Frederick Hill, curate of Rackheath, Norfolk, wrote from Norwich on 7 August 1849 to Dickens, saying:

> "one who is universally & deservedly allowed to be the most faithful describer of every day life & every day people in this or perhaps in any age, to point out two small errors in your last very beautiful work", being "a Norfolk man and well acquainted with the vernacular of that County". "Once or twice ... you made 'Ham' to say 'Bo' when it should be Bor & again you talk about 'Yarmouth flats', a term I believe applied to some parts of the English Coast, but not used with us here. The correct expression is 'Sands'... The other Norfolk provincialisms are surprisingly correct."[33]

Soon after he received this letter, he made immediate correction

---

[30] R. Quirk (1961) "Some Observations on the Language of Dickens," p. 20-21.

[31] Lexical study on East Anglia dialect words and phrases will be made in Chapter VI. G. L. Brook glosses *bor'* as "term of endearment to a child." (*The Language of Dickens*, 1970, p. 118.)

[32] "Mas'r Davy bor"

[33] See K. J. Fielding (1949) "*David Copperfield* and Dialect," p. 288, and *Let V*, p. 590fn.

for his misuse of *bo'* for *bor*. In the list of Errata issued with Nos. XIX and XX five instances of "bo'" were corrected to "bor'" (Chs. 7 and 10).[34]

"Lone and lorn[35]" is Mrs. Gummidge's favourite phrase. David observes:

> "I am a lone lorn creetur'‚ were Mrs. Gummidge's words, when that unpleasant occurrence took place, "and everythink goes contrairy with me" (*DC*, 33).

She uses this phrase so often that David applies this phrase to his "lone and lorn" circumstances: "a lone lorn child (as Mrs. Gummidge might have said)" (*DC*, 132). We have numerous examples of this phrase:

> "I am a *lone lorn* creetur'." (34^{2x}, 120, 125)
>
> It was a very cold day, with cutting blasts of wind. Mrs. Gummidge's peculiar corner of the fireside seemed to me to be the warmest and snuggest in the place, as her chair was certainly the easiest, but it didn't suit her that day at all. She was constantly complaining of the cold, and of its occasioning a visitation in her back which she called "the creeps." At last she shed tears on that subject, and said again that she was "a *lone lorn* creetur' and everythink went contrairy with her." (33)
>
> "I'm a *lone lorn* creetur' myself, and everythink that reminds me of creetur's that ain't *lone and lorn*, goes contrary with me." (125)
>
> "Nothink's nat'ral to me but to be *lone and lorn*." (383)
>
> "How could I expect to be wanted, being so *lone and lorn*, and so contrary!" (383)

---

[34] *Let V*, p. 590fn.
[35] The adjective *lorn* mean "forlorn."

CHAPTER III CHARACTERISATION AND EXPERIMENT

"my *lone lorn* Dan'l" (387)
"your *lone lorn* journeys." (391)
"I know you think that I am *lone and lorn*; but, deary love, 'tan't so no more!" (633)

Mr. Peggotty is a chief dialect speaker in *David Copperfield*. He also makes contribution to this linguistic characterisation. He has two favourite locutions, "kiender"[36] and "a mort of,"[37] both of which are genuine East Anglia provincialisms. We have seven instances of his use of *kiender*:

"I'm *kiender* muddle ..." (390)
Ham was just the same, "wearing away his life with *kiender* no care nohow for 't ..." (578)
"my niece was *kiender* daughter-like to me." (584)
"she kneeled down at my feet, and *kiender* said to me, as if it was her prayers, how it all come to be." (619)
"But, fear of not being forgiv ... turned her from it, *kiender* by force, upon the road ..." (622)
"Theer's been kiender a blessing fell upon us," (743)
"*kiender* worn; soft, sorrowful, blue eyes;" (743)

We have five examples of his use "a mort of":

"We have had *a mort of* talk, sir," (389)
"I've put the question to myself *a mort o'* times, and never found no answer." (578)
"Well, I've had *a mort of* con-sideration, I do tell you ..." (624)
"It's *a mort of* water ... fur to come across, and on'y

---

[36] The term is vulgar form of "kind of" and means "in a way," "as it were," or "to some extent." (*OED*, s.v. *kind*, *n*., 14. d.)

[37] This phrase is equal to a lot of in the meaning. (*OED*, s.v. *mort*, $n.^6$; *EDD*, s.v. *mort*, $sb.^1$.)

stay a matter of fower weeks." (742)

"She might have married well, *a mort of* times ..." (744)

In *David Copperfield* some of the East Anglia dialect words and phrases play a binary role for linguistic characterisation: one is for "individualisation" and the other for "typification." Ham's "Mas'r Davy bor'," Mrs. Gummidge's "lone and lorn," and Mr. Peggotty's "kiender" and "a mort of" play important roles to characterise their individual identity and to typify their social or regional identity at the same time.[38]

---

[38] In this respect, R. Quirk comments that the individualisation is usually made congruent with the typification. ("Some Observations on the Language of Dickens," p. 22.)

CHAPTER IV

Realism and Verisimilitude

Dickens's keen observation and accurate description of the daily life in London have sometimes been pointed out since the appearence of "A Dinner at Poplar Walk" in the *Monthly Magazine*, December 1833.[1] His keen observation and enthusiastic collection of the dialect materials play an essential part in making his representations of speech closer to the real life. This chapter will show how Dickens tried to make his representations of dialectal speech true to life, how he reflected on the application of standard speech to Oliver Twist when he wrote *Great Expectations*, and why some critics stigmatise

---

[1] In the December number for 1833 of what then was called the *Old Monthly Magazine*, his first published piece of writing had seen the light. He has described himself dropping this paper ("Mr. Minns and his Cousin," as he afterwards entitled it, but which appeared in the magazine as "A Dinner at Poplar Walk") stealthily one evening at twilight, with fear and trembling, into a dark letter-box in a dark office up a dark court in Fleetstreet; and he has told his agitation when it appeared in all the glory of print. "On which occasion I walked down to Westminster-hall, and turned into it for half an hour, because my eyes were so dimmed with joy and pride, that they could not bear the street, and were not fit to be seen there." He had purchased the magazine at a shop in the Strand; and exactly two years afterwards, in the younger member of a publishing firm who had called at his chambers in Furnival's-inn, to which he had moved soon after entering the gallery, with the proposal that originated *Pickwick*, he recognized the person he had bought that magazine from, and whom before or since he had never seen. (John Forster, *The Life of Charles Dickens*, 1893, p. 40.)

his rendering Lancashire dialect in *Hard Times*.

4.1 Dickens's natural gift and pursuit for dialect materials

John Forster first revealed Dickens's keen observation of the poorest life in Bayham Street, Camden Town, London as follows:

> That he took, from the very beginning of this Bayham Street life, his first impression of that struggling poverty which is nowhere more vividly shown than in the commoner streets of the ordinary London suburb, and which enriched his earliest writings with a freshness of original humour and quite unstudied pathos that gave them much of their sudden popularity, there cannot be a doubt. "I certainly understood it," he has often said to me, "quite as well then as I do now." But he was not conscious yet that he did so understand it, or of the influence it was exerting on his life even then. It seems almost too much to assert of a child, say at nine or ten years old, that his observation of everything was as close and good, or that he had as much intuitive understanding of the character and weaknesses of the grown-up people around him, as when the same keen and wonderful faculty had made him famous among men.[2]

Angus Wilson confirmed that Dickens's "greatest natural gift was his ear."[3] The gift enabled him to represent the speech of those whom he met or talked with when he visited Yorkshire, Lancashire, East Anglia, and the United States to collect dialectal materials for his works. In addition to his natural gift,

---

[2] John Forster (1893) *The Life of Charles Dickens*, p. 11.
[3] A. Wilson (1960) "Charles Dickens: A Haunting," *Critical Quarterly*, Vol. II, p. 104.

Dickens devoted himself to collecting provincial glossaries. On 15 December 1842 Dickens asked Thomas Cooke to show him a provincial glossary of Cornwall dialect:

> I am most unfeignedly and heartily obliged to you for your kind remembrance of me. I don't begin in Cornwall, though it is possible I may come there, in course of time. If you can get the dialect book without inconvenience, I shall be very glad to see it. (*Let. III*, 394)

In the following letter, he asked his close friend Mark Lemon for slang terms used by tumblers and circuspeople in order to collect the verbal materials for Sleary's circus scene in *Hard Times*:

> Will you note down and send me any slang terms among tumblers and Circuspeople, that you can call to mind? I have noted down some—I want them in my new story—but it is very probable that you will recall several which I have not got. (*Let. VII*, 279)

It is so much regrettable that neither Thomas Cooke's provincial glossary of Cornwall dialect nor Mark Lemon's notes for slang terms among tumblers and circuspeople remains, because he "burnt, in the field at Gad's Hill, the accumulated letters and papers of twenty years" (*Let. IX*, 304).

In the opening scene of *Pygmalion*, Shaw attempts eagerly to represent Eliza's speech without phonetic alphabet, but he declares that "Here, with apologies, this desperate attempt to represent her dialect without phonetic alphabet must be abandoned as unintelligible outside London" (16-7).

After Emily's death, Charlotte Brontë wrote the following letter to the publisher with respect to the modification of Emily's description of Joseph's use of Haworth dialect in *Wuthering Heights*: "It seems to me advisable to modify the orthography of the old servant Joseph's speeches; for though as it stands it exactly renders the Yorkshire dialect to a Yorkshire ear, yet I am sure Southerns must find it unintelligible; and thus one of the most graphic characters in the book is lost on them."[4]

It is widely known that Dickens was quite familiar with slang and colloquial expressions in those days. He was sometimes praised for his knowledge of them, with which Richard Ford claims that "Boz is regius professor of slang, that expression of the mother-wit, the low humour or the lower classes, their Sanscrit, their hitherto unknown tongue, which, in the present phasis of society and politics, seems likely to become the idiom of England."[5] With respect to Dickens's verbal depiction of the lowest classes in England, a reviewer of *Court Magazine* described thus:

> ... while 'Boz' brings before you with a graphic pen, the express image of the poorest and most ignorant orders, he never descends into vulgarity. The ordinary conversations of the loose and ribald multitude are faithfully reported, but by an adroit process of moral alchemy, all their offensive coarseness is imperceptibly extracted.[6]

Dickens, himself, demonstrated clearly his attitude toward

---

[4] K. M. Petyt (1976) "The Dialect Speech in *Wuthering Heights*," p. 501.

[5] From an unsigned review, *Quarterly Review*, January 1839, lxiv, pp. 83-102, in *Dickens: The Critical Heritage*, edited by P. Collins, 1971, p. 83.

[6] From an unsigned article, 'SomeThoughts on Arch-Waggery, and in especial, on the Genius of "Boz"', *Court Magazine*, April 1837, x, pp. 184-7, in *Dickens: The Critical Heritage*, edited by P. Collins, 1971, p. 35.

the reproduction of the underworld speech in "The Author's Preface to the Third Edition" of *Oliver Twist*, "I saw no reason, when I wrote this book, why the very dregs of life should not serve the purpose of a moral at least as well as its froth and cream, so long as their speech did not offend the ear."[7]

4.2 Heroic speech and dialect suppression

Critics of Dickens sometimes stigmatise Dickens's application of Standard English to the speech of Oliver Twist, although he was born and bred in a workhouse and received no proper education at all. In this respect Brook argues that "Squeers's constant use of vulgarisms helps to emphasize his unfitness to be a schoolmaster, while the failure of Oliver Twist and Lizzie Hexam to pick up even the smallest vulgarisms from the low-life characters with whom they come into contact reflects the author's belief that they are unsullied by their environment."[8] This kind of artificial speech was called "heroic speech"[9] by Norman Page or "dialect suppression"[10] by G. N. Leech and M. Short. If you have a look at the speech of Lizzie Hexam in *Our Mutual Friend*, you may easily understand that this kind of speech is not only restricted to a hero, but also a heroine. In this respect Leech and Short explains thus:

> Illiterate Lizzie Hexam, in *Our Mutual Friend*, speaks almost entirely in standard English, in contrast to the non-standard speech of her equally illiterate father. But

---

[7] "The Preface" to the Clarendon Edition of *Oliver Twist*, p. lxi.

[8] G. L. Brook (1970) *The Language of Dickens*, p. 99)

[9] N. Page (1969) "'A Language Fit for Heroes': Speech in *Oliver Twist* and *Our Mutual Friend*," *The Dickensian*, Vol. 65, Part 2, p. 100.

[10] G. N. Leech and M. Short (1981) *Style in Fiction*, p.170.

then Lizzie is destined to be the novel's heroine, and it could scarcely be allowed for a nineteenth-century heroine to speak dialect.[11]

Dickens, however, re-examined himself on the unnatural and far-fetched representations of Oliver's speech by the time when he wrote *Great Expectations*. His linguistic penance is to be found in Pip's following letter to Joe:

> mI deEr JO i opE U r krWitE wEll i opE i shAl soN B haBelL 4 2 teeDge U JO aN theN wE shOrl b sO glOdd aN wEn i M preNgtD 2 u JO woT larX an blEvE ME inF xn PiP.[12] (*GE*, 46)

This was written on a slate with his own hand when he was sitting side by side with Joe at the fireside one winter evening. *H*-droppings in *hope* and an *h*-adding in *able* clearly suggests that Pip belongs to the lower-class as well as Joe does.[13] The following quotations include Joe's *h*-droppings:

> "If you can cough any trifle on it up, Pip, I'd recommend you to do it,' said Joe, all aghast. 'Manners is manners, but still your *elth*'s your *elth*." (*GE*, 12)
>
> "I never was so much surprised in all my life—couldn't credit my own *ed*—to tell you the truth, hardly believed it *were* my own *ed*." (*GE*, 48)
>
> "The king upon his throne, with his crown upon his *ed*, can't sit and write his acts of Parliament in print,

---

[11] G. N. Leech and M. Short (1981) *Style in Fiction*, p.170.

[12] My dear Joe, I hope you're quite well. I hope I shall soon be able for to teach you, Joe, and then we shall be so glad. And when I'm apprenticed to you, Joe, what larks! And believe me. In affection, Pip.

[13] As for this, Linda Mugglestone claims that "The approximate version of *hope* and *able* which Dickens here conferred upon Pip unambiguously indicate the intended social affinities (and social meanings) in this context." (*Talking Proper*, 2003, p. 123)

CHAPTER IV   REALISM AND VERISIMILITUDE

> without having begun, when he were a unpromoted Prince, with the alphabet—" (*GE*, 72)
>
> "Well, Pip, you know ... you yourself see me put 'em in my *'at*, and therefore you know as they are here." (*GE*, 101)
>
> "Still more, when his mourning *'at* is unfortunately made so small as that the weight of the black feathers brings it off, try to keep it on how you may.' (*GE*, 221)
>
> "Thankee, Sir ... since you are so kind as make chice of coffee, I will not run contrairy to your own opinions. But don't you never find it a little *'eating*?" (*GE*, 221)
>
> "... when there come up in his shay-cart, Pumblechook. Which that same identical ... do comb my *'air* the wrong way sometimes, awful, by giving out up and down town as it were him which ever had your infant companionation and were looked upon as a playfellow by yourself." (*GE*, 223)
>
> "Old Orlick he's been a bustin' open a dwelling-*ouse*." (*GE*, 462)
>
> "a Englishman's *ouse* is his Castle, and castles must not be busted 'cept when done in war time." (*GE*, 462)
>
> "... 'Where is the good as you are a-doing? I grant you I see the *'arm*,' says the man, 'but I don't see the good. I call upon you, sir, therefore, to pint out the good.'" (*GE*, 465)

There are three examples of Joe's *h*-addings:

> The forge was shut up for the day, and Joe inscribed in chalk upon the door (as it was his custom to do on the very rare occasions when he was not at work) the monosyllable *HOUT*, accompanied by a sketch of an arrow supposed to be flying in the direction he had taken. (*GE*, 99)
>
> "Which I meantersay, Pip," Joe now observed in a manner that was at once expressive of forcible argumentation, strict confidence, and great politeness, "as

I *hup* and married your sister, and I were at the time what you might call (if you was anyways inclined) a single man." (*GE*, 100)

"... and you may *haim* at what you like ..." (*GE*, 111)

In the first extract, Joe's inscriotion of "HOUT" in chalk on the forge door was foregrounded by using small capital letters.

4.3 Linguistic stigmatisation in *Hard Times*

Of all Dickens's works treating regional dialects, it may, however, be *Hard Times* that has been subject to the greatest criticism both by literary scholars and philologists. Robert Langton claims that "one of the least successful attempts in this or any of the books of Charles Dickens, is his rendering of the Lancashire dialect; the utterances put into the mouths of Stephen Blackpool, and others, in *Hard Times*, are very far from correct."[14] L. K. Webb also strictly comments that "his ear for dialect was poor; what he imagined to be the speech of Lancashire is the speech of nowhere, grating continually on the reader's inner ear."[15] Humphry House suggests that the cause of these caustic remarks is that "Dickens was writing of People and things quite outside the range of his own experience."[16] G L. Brook, philologist, also founder of the Lancashire Dialect Society points out that "Stephen Blackpool and Rachael, in *Hard Times*, speak with a strongly-marked regional dialect. Many of the features of this dialect can be paralleled in north-country speech today."[17] He, however,

---

[14] R. Langton (1912) *Childhood and Youth of Charles Dickens*, p. 208.
[15] L. K. Webb (1983) *Charles Dickens*, p. 83.
[16] H. House (1942) *The Dickens World*, pp. 203-04.
[17] G. L. Brook (1970) *The Language of Dickens*, p. 125.

avoids identifying the dialect with the Lancashire dialect, and argues that some of the linguistic features of the dialect "seem to be of doubtful authenticity."[18]

We have already discussed the provenance and the source of the dialect used in *Hard Times* in Chapter I, so the objective of this section is to examine the accuracy and the consistency in Dickens's rendering the dialectal pronunciations applied to Stephen Blackpool considering the facts and illustrations offered by the dictionaries, letters and references and to discuss whether the dialect intended by Dickens can be identified with the dialect employed in Lancashire in the mid-nineteenth century. First of all we shall deal with the reduction of vowels and consonants.

4.3.1 Reduction of vowels and consonants

One of the most striking features of Stephen Blackpool's regional accents is the reduction of vowels and consonants. It is regarded as the most characteristic aspects of Lancashire dialect. John Collier illustrates that "In general we speak quick and short; and cut of a great many letters, and even words by apostrophes; and sometimes sound two, three, or more words as one."[19]

The reduction of the definite article to *th'* is constantly found in Stephen's speech. Brook suggests that "in some northern dialects it is reduced to *th'* before vowels and to *t'* before consonants."[20] In this novel we can find thirty-two examples

---

[18] G. L. Brook (1970) *The Language of Dickens*, p. 125.
[19] J. Collier (1818) *The Miscellaneous Works of Tim Bobbin, Esq.*, p. 4.
[20] G. L. Brook (1970) *The Language of Dickens*, p. 127.

(71 etc.) of this reduced form before consonants and only one before a vowel (159). *EDG* (§312) informs us that the reduction exists in m. and se. Lan.[21], wm. Stf. In the conversation between Tummus and Meary, we can find many examples of this form, but not listed at all in its glossary. *DSL* lists this form of the definite article in the glossary.

As well as the case above, we often find numerous examples of the reduction of the preposition *to* and the infinitive *to* to *t'*. The reduction of the infinitive *to* occurs sixteen times (*HT*, 65 etc.) and that of the preposition *to* appears thirteen times. Otto Jespersen demonstrates that "in the 18th c. this elision became rarer, and has now disappeared."[22] *OED* (s.v. *t'*[1]) stops recording examples of *t'* in 1746. Stanley Gerson concludes that "Dickens uses *t'* ... to indicate northern 'speech'."[23]

In Blackpool's speech the loss of *d* occurs in the final position, and less frequently in the medial position. The loss of final *d* occurs fifty times as *an'* (*HT*, 73 etc.), and once as *an* (*HT*, 159) and *stan* (*HT*, 148). The loss of medial *d* occurs in *unnerstan'in* (*HT*, 273[4x]) and *Gonnows* (*HT*, 71, 143), but the standard forms *understood* (*HT*, 74) and *understand* (*HT*, 161) are also found. Jespersen mentions that "*d* is very often dropped in *and*, thus regularly, but not exclusively, before consonants."[24] *OED* (s.v. *and, conj.*[1]) records the spelling *an* for *and* from the thirteenth to seventeenth century, and *an'* as

---

[21] The abbreviations of regions, counties, and directions used in the book are in accordance with those in *EDD* and *EDG*, and they are shown in "Abbreviations" above.

[22] *MEG*, Vol. I, §9.82.

[23] S. Gerson (1967) *Sound and Symbol*, §7.17.4.

[24] *MEG*, Vol. I, §7.55.

CHAPTER IV   REALISM AND VERISIMILITUDE   55

a dialectal form in the eighteenth and nineteenth century and argues that "the final *d* has from early times been often dropped, as now universally in the dialects, and commonly in familiar speech." Gerson suggests that "it will be noticed that Dickens uses *an'* mainly (and only consistently) in representations of northern 'speech'."[25] He also informs us that [ən] is recorded from Lancashire by K. G. Schilling[26] and by Hargreaves[27]. According to *EDG* (§307), *an* is generally used in Sc., Irel. and Eng., and *stan* occurs in Inv., ne. Sc., Ayr, Lth., Edb., Kcb., Uls., n. Nhb., n. and m. Cum., n. Wm., ne. Yks, ne., em. and se. Lan., I.Ma., ne. Der., nw. Lin., e. Man, ne. Der., nw. Lin., e. Oxf., Dor., w. Som., and Dev. *MW* and *DSL* record only the form *an*.

The loss of medial *l* is found in the speech produced by Blackpool. Examples are *a'toogether* (*HT,* 75), *awmost* (*HT,* 79), *awmust* (*HT,* 274), *faw'en* (*HT,* 151), *fawt*[28] (*HT,* 149), *gowd* (*HT,* 74), *owd* (*HT,* 72), *towd* (*HT,* 150, 159, 162), and *sma'est* (*HT,* 143). *EDG* (§253) comments that "medial *l* has often disappeared, especially in the combinations *ld, lf, lh, lk, ls,* and *lt*." According to *EDG* (§253), the loss of medial *l* occurs in *almost* in n. Dur., sw. Yks, m. Lan., w. Chs., n. Der., Lei., n. Shr., nw. Oxf., m. Bck., Hmp., nw. and me. Wil., and w. Som.; *gold* in w. Frf., w. Per., w. Ayr, Lth., Edb., Peb., se. and w. Nhb., n. Dur., m. Cum., n. Wm., Yks, Lan., nw. Der., n. Lin., ne. and m. Shr., and e. Suf.; *hold* in Sc., Nhb.,

---

[25] S. Gerson (1967) *Sound and Symbol*, §24.7.
[26] K. G. Schilling (1906) *A Grammar of the Dialect of Oldham*, §127.
[27] A. Hargreaves (1904) *A Grammar of the Dialect of Adlington*, §62.
[28] *MEG* (§10.481) makes a historical sketch of this form.

Dur., Cum., Wm., Yks, Lan., w. Chs., Stf., Der., Not., Lin., Lei., n. Wor., e. Hrf., w. Nrf., e. and w. Suf., Ess., ne. Ken., w. Sur., and w. Sus.; *old* in wm. Sc., Nhb., Dur., n. Cum., n. Wm., Yks, Lan., Chs., Flt., Dnb., Stf., Der., Not., Lin., Lei., sw. Nhp., n. Wor., Shr., e. Hrf., Bdf., se. Hrt. Cmb., ne. and w. Nrf., e. and w. Suf., Ess., e. Ken., w. Sur., and w. Sus.; *told* in Or.I., Lan., Chs., Flt., Dnb., Stf., Der., Not., nw. Lin., Lei., w. Wor., m. and se. Shr., n. Bck., ne. Nrf., e. and w. Suf., Ess., and Sus.; and *fault* in Sc., Ant., Nhb., w. Dur., n. and m. Cum., Wm., Yks, Lan., w. Chs., n. and wm. Stf., n. and nw. Der., w. Lin., Lei., w. War., n. Wor., m. Shr., nw. Oxf., ne. Nrf., e. Suf., Sus., Wil., and e. Som. *MW* and *DSL* list *owd, howd, towd, fawt,* and *gowd* and *fawn* are recorded only in *MW*.

EDG (§255) suggests that "final *l* has often disappeared after a guttural vowel, especially in Sc., Irel., north country, and north Midland dialects." We have a lot of examples of the disappearance of final *l* in Stephen's speech: *aw* (*HT,* 66 etc. 30 times), *faw* (*HT,* 73), *wa'* (*HT,* 143), *dreadfo'* (*HT,* 87), *faithfo'* (*HT,* 148), *fearfo'* (*HT,* 72, 88[2x], 147, 157), and *wishfo'* (*HT,* 88). *MW* records *faw, fo, fearfo,* and *DSL* lists *feerfo*. According to *EDG* (§255), the disappearance of final *l* is to be found in *all* in Sc., Ant., Nhb., Dur., Cum., Wm., Yks, Lan., Chs., n. Stf., and Der.; *fall* in Sc., Nhb., w. Dur., n. and m. Cum., Wm., nw. Yks, Lan., w. Chs., n. Stf., ne. and nw. Der., and ne. Shr.; *full* in Sh.I., Or.I., Sc., Wm., and se. Lan.; and *wall* in Sc., Ant., me. and se. Nhb., w. Dur., n. and m. Cum., Wm., ne., nw. Yks, n., nw., sm., se., sw., ms. and w. Lan., w. Chs., n. Stf., n. and ne. and nw. Der., and nw. Shr.

CHAPTER IV REALISM AND VERISIMILITUDE

Jespersen points out that "*i'* was especially frequent in the 16th and 17th century before *th'* (the)" and that "at the present day *i'th'* survives only as a poetic archaism (apart from Scotch and some Northern dialects)."[29] This combination is to be recognised in Stephen's speech: "*i'th'* papers" (*HT*, 73), and "*i'th'* road" (*HT*, 142). With respect to the loss of the final *n*, *EDG* (§271) suggests that the final *n* disappears in the preposition *in* in Sc., north countries, n. and w. Midl., w. Nrf., and w. Suf. Neither *MW* nor *DSL* lists *i'*.

The spelling with *ha'* and *o'* indicates the disappearance of [v] in *have* and the preposition *of*. *OED* (s.v. *o', prep.*[1]) says that "the contracted form is usual in the representation of dialectal or vulgar speech." Jespersen comments that "the preposition *of* often became *o'*; the writing *o* is found occasionally as early as 1300 ... but it does not become frequent till the 16th c."; and that "*have* was frequently *ha'* or *a*; in the infinitive this may be from ME *han*, but it is also found in the indicative."[30] The loss of [v] preceding a word beginning with a vowel occurs as the auxiliary *ha'* (*HT*, 148), the verb *ha'* (*HT*, 73) and the preposition *o'* (*HT*, 37 etc. 9 times). The loss of [v] preceding a word beginning with a consonant occurs as the auxiliary *ha'* (*HT*, 64 etc. 71 times), the verb *ha'* (*HT*, 72 etc. 13 times) and the preposition *o'* (*HT*, 74 etc. 42 times). *MW* and *DSL* lists *ha*, and with regard to the preposition *of* the former records *o'* and the latter *o*. *EDD* (s.v. *of, prep.*) suggests that the dialectal form *o* is to be found in Sc., Wxf., Nhb., e. Dur., Cum., Wm., n., e., and m.

---

[29] *MEG*, Vol. I, §2.424.
[30] *MEG*, Vol. I, §2.534.

Yks, Lan., I.Ma., Der., Lin., War., w. Wor., Glo., Brks., w. Som., and Cor. According to *EDG* (§279), "*v* has disappeared over an extensive area in *have*."

In Blackpool's speech the loss of medial [ð] is seen in such forms as *wi'in* (*HT*, 272) and *wi'out* (*HT*, 88, 141, 151[3x], 159, 160, 272[2x]). *EDD* (s.v. *within, prep.*) gives *wi'in* only in Sur. dialect. *EDD* (s.v. *without, prep.* and *conj.*) says that *wi'out* is to be found in Brks. and Dev. Neither *MW* nor *DSL* gives *wi'in* or *wi'out* in their glossary.

Stephen uses *wi'* instead of *with*, which indicates the loss of final [ð], thirteen times before vowels (*HT*, 74 etc.) and thirty-nine times before consonants (*HT*, 72 etc.). According to *EDG* (§317), *with* has generally become [wi] in all dialects. [wi] was formerly used in the dialects before a following consonants and [wiþ], [wið] before a following vowels. But most dialects now have [wi] in both positions. *MW* does not list the form *wi'*. *EDG* ('Index,' s.v. *with*) suggests that *wi* is to be found in Sh.I., Or.I., Cai, Frf., w. Ayr, Edb., Uls., n. and me. Nhb., n. Cum., n., w. and w. Wm., Yks, Lan., I.Ma, Chs., n., w. and w. Stf., n. and nw. Der., Not., n., nw. and e. Lin., Lei., m. Nhp., e. War., n. Wor., Glo., n. Oxf., m. Brks., e. Hrt., w. Nrf., e. Suf., Hmp., w. and nw. Wil., Dor., w. Dev. and w. Cor.

In Stephen's speech we find the insertion of semi-vowel [j] before a vowel which has become initial as a result of loss of *h* in the case of *year* (*HT*, 71, 74) instead of to *hear*. *EDG* ('Index,' s.v. *hear*) points out that [jiə(r)] occurs in m. Yks, se. Lan., Glo., Dor., and e. Dev. This verbal form is listed only in *MW*.

CHAPTER IV REALISM AND VERISIMILITUDE 59

Table 2 Reduction of vowels and consonants

HT	MW	DSL	*EDG, EDD, OED*, etc
th'	—	th'	*EDG* (§312) informs us that the reduction exists in m. & se. Lan., wm. Stf. (*EDG*, §312)
t'	t'	t'	Northern 'speech' (Gerson, §7.17.4)
an, an'	an	an	*an*: Sc., Irel. & Eng. (*EDG*, §307)
stan	—	—	*stan*: Inv., ne. Sc., Ayr, Lth., Edb., Kcb., Uls., n. Nhb., n. & m. Cum., n. Wm., ne. Yks, ne., em. & se. Lan., I.Ma., ne. Der., nw. Lin., e. Man, ne. Der., nw. Lin., e. Oxf., Dor., w. Som., & Dev. (*EDG*, §307)
unnerstan'in	—	—	—
Gonnows	—	—	—
a'toogether	—	—	—
awmost, awmust	—	—	*almost*: n. Dur., sw. Yks., m. Lan., w. Chs., n. Der., Lei., n. Shr., nw. Oxf., m. Bck., Hmp., nw. & me. Wil., & w. Som. (*EDG*, §253)
faw'en	fawn	—	—
fawt	fawt	fawt	*fault*: Sc., Ant., Nhb., w. Dur., n. & m. Cum., Wm., Yks, Lan., w. Chs., n. & wm. Stf., n. & nw. Der., w. Lin., Lei., w. War., n. Wor., m. Shr., nw. Oxf., ne. Nrf., e. Suf., Sus., Wil., & e. Som. (*EDG*, §253)
gowd	gowd	—	*gold*: w. Frf., w. Per., w. Ayr, Lth., Edb., Peb., se. & w. Nhb., n. Dur., m. Cum., n. Wm., Yks, Lan., nw. Der., n. Lin., ne. & m. Shr., & e. Suf. (*EDG*, §253)
howd	howd	howd	*hold*: Sc., Nhb., Dur., Cum., Wm., Yks, Lan., w. Chs., Stf., Der., Not., Lin., Lei., n. Wor., e. Hrf., w. Nrf., e. & w. Suf., Ess., ne. Ken., w.

				Sur., & w. Sus. (*EDG*, §253)
owd	*owd*	*owd*		*old*: wm. Sc., Nhb., Dur., n. Cum., n. Wm., Yks., Lan., Chs., Flt., Dnb., Stf., Der., Not., Lin., Lei., sw. Nhp., n. Wor., Shr., e. Hrf., Bdf., se. Hrt. Cmb., ne. & w. Nrf., e. & w. Suf., Ess., e. Ken., w. Sur., & w. Sus. (*EDG*, §253)
towd	*towd*	*towd*		*told*: Or.I., Lan., Chs., Flt., Dnb., Stf., Der., Not., nw. Lin., Lei., w. Wor., m. & se. Shr., n. Bck., ne. Nrf., e. & w. Suf., Ess., & Sus. (*EDG*, §253)
sma'est	—	—		—
aw	—	—		*all*: Sc., Ant., Nhb., Dur., Cum., Wm., Yks., Lan., Chs., n. Stf., & Der. (*EDG*, §255)
dreadfo'	—	—		—
faw	*faw*	—		*fall*: Sc., Nhb., w. Dur., n. & m. Cum., Wm., nw. Yks., Lan., w. Chs., n. Stf., ne. & nw. Der., & ne. Shr. (*EDG*, §255)
faithfo'	—	—		—
fearfo'	*fearfo*	*feerfo*		—
fu'	*fo*	—		*full*: Sh.I., Or.I., Sc., Wm., & se. Lan. (*EDG*, §255)
wa'	—	—		*wall*: Sc., Ant., me. & se. Nhb., w. Dur., n. & m. Cum., Wm., ne., nw. Yks., n., nw., sm., se., sw., ms. & w. Lan., w. Chs., n. Stf., n. & ne. & nw. Der., & nw. Shr. (*EDG*, §255)
wishfo'	—	—		—
i'	—	—		*in*: Sc., north countries, n. & w. Midl., w. Nrf., & w. Suf. (*EDG*, §271)
ha'	*ha*	*ha*		*ha*: an extensive area. (*EDG*, §279)

CHAPTER IV REALISM AND VERISIMILITUDE   61

o'	o'	o	o: Sc., Wxf., Nhb., e. Dur., Cum., Wm., n., e., & m. Yks, Lan., I.Ma., Der., Lin., War., w. Wor., Glo., Brks., w. Som., & Cor. (*EDD*, s.v. *of*, *prep.*)
wi'in	—	—	wi'in: Sur. (*EDD*, s.v. *within, prep.*)
wi'out	—	—	wi'out: Brks. & Dev. (*EDD*, s.v. *without, prep. & conj.*)
wi'	—	wi'	wi: Sh.I., Or.I., Cai, Frf., w. Ayr, Edb., Uls., n. & me. Nhb., n. Cum., n., w. & w. Wm., Yks, Lan., I.Ma, Chs., n., w. & w. Stf., n. & nw. Der., Not., n., nw. & e. Lin., Lei., m. Nhp., e. War., n. Wor., Glo., n. Oxf., m. Brks., e. Hrt., w. Nrf., e. Suf., Hmp., w. & nw. Wil., Dor., w. Dev. & w. Cor. (*EDG*, 'Index,' s.v. *with*)
year	year	—	[jiə(r)]: m. Yks, se. Lan., Glo., Dor., & e. Dev. (*EDG*, 'Index,' s.v. *hear*)

4.3.2 Short Vowels

The use of [u], spelt *oo*, instead of [ʌ] is frequently found in the speech of Blackpool. Examples are:

> *aboove* (*HT*, 273), *amoong* (*HT*, 148^{4x}), *anoother* (*HT*, 151), *coom, pr.* (*HT*, 142, 146), *coom, pp.* (*HT*, 71 etc. 19 times), *cooms* (*HT*, 72, 88), coompany (*HT*, 155), *coop* (*HT*, 155), *coover* (*HT*, 274), *discoosed* (*HT*, 143), *doon*[31] (*HT*, 148), *droonken* (*HT*, 148), *oother* (*HT*, 273), *soom,* 'some' (*HT*, 142, 273), *soom,* 'sum' (*HT*, 151), *soombody* (*HT*, 274), *tooches* (*HT*, 273), *toother* (*HT*, 151), *t'oother* (*HT*, 74), *yoong* (*HT*, 142, 273).

Alongside of these dialectal forms we sometimes encounter standard ones:

---

[31] Another dialectal form *dun* is to be found in p. 72.

above (*HT*, 73, 142, 151, 273), *among* (*HT*, 143²ˣ, 273), *another* (*HT*, 73, 74, 148³ˣ, 151²ˣ, 154, 159, 272, 273), *come, pr.* (*HT*, 66), *come, pp.* (*HT*, 67), *coming* (*HT*, 73, 84), *done* (*HT*, 65, 89, 154, 159, 160, 273²ˣ), *young* (*HT*, 65, 71 , 72, 154, 272).

EDG (§98) suggests that [ù] is to be heard in Nhb., Dur., Ant., n., ne., nw., em., se., sm. and w. Lan., I.Ma., Chs., Flt., Dnb., Stf., Der., Not., Lei., Nhp., War., Wor., Shr., Hrf., Glo., and Oxf. To represent the use of [u] for [ʌ], the spelling *u* instead of *ou* is sometimes employed in *MW* (*yunger*) and *DSL* (*yunger, yungster*). According to the 'Index' of *EDG*, [ù] in place of [ʌ] occurs in [əbùv] in w. Lan., w. Chs., n. and ne. Der., Lei., n. Wor., and se. Shr.; [əmùŋ] in sw. Yks, em. and w. Lan., I.Ma., w. Chs., n. Stf., n. Der., Lei., m. Nhp., War., and n. Shr.; [kùm] in n., m., sw. and w. Lan., I.Ma., w. Chs., Flt., em. Stf., e. Der., Not., Lei., m. Nhp., e., w. and w. War., ne. and se. Shr., and nw. Oxf.; [kùp] in Ant., sm., se., sw. and w. Lan., I.Ma., Dnb., nw. Der., Lei., m. and sw. Nhp., War., n. Wor., Shr., w. Oxf., and n. Bck.; [kùvə(r)] in sw. and w. Lan., nw. Der., and Lei.; [dùn] in m., sm., sw. and w. Lan., I.Ma., Chs., Flt., Dnb., n., em., wm. and w. Stf., n. Der., Not., Lei., ne. and sw. Nhp., War., n. and w. Wor., Shr., nw. Oxf., and n. Bck.; [drùŋkn] in nw., m., sw., ms and w. Lan., I.Ma., Chs., Flt., n., wm. and w. Stf., Der., Not., Lei., m. Nhp., e. War., w. Wor., n. and se. Shr., and nw. and w. Oxf.; [ùðə(r)] in sm. and w. Lan., w. Chs., Dnb., nw. Der., n. Lei., Nhp., n. and se. Shr., and n. and nw. Oxf.; [sùm] in Ant., m., se., sw. and w. Lan., I.Ma., Chs., Dnb., e. and wm. Stf., ne., nw., e. and w. Der., Lei., sw. Nhp., e. and w. War., Wor., n. and ne. Shr., w. and nw. Oxf., and n. Bck.; [tùtʃ] in Ant., sm. sw. Lan.,

I.Ma., w. Chs., nw. Der., Lei., and m. Nhp.; [jùŋ] in Ant., se., ms and w. Lan., I.Ma., w. Chs., Dnb., n. Lei., ne., m. and sw. Nhp., e. and w. War., n. and w. Wor., and n. and se. Shr. *EDD* (s.v. *company*, *sb*. and *v*.) suggests that [kùmpəni] is found in Sc., Yks, Chs., Lin., Shr., e.An., Sus., Dor., Som., and Dev. *EDD* (s.v. *sum*, *sb*.[1] and *v*.) records that [sùm] is used in Yks, Lan., Der., Not., Lei., Nhp., War., Glo., Brks., Hnt., e.An., Ken., Som., and Dev.

The change of *o* to *u* in *awlung* for *along* is found in pp. 272 and 273. Brook suggests that "this pronunciation is found in RP *among*, where it is generally thought to have been introduced from a regional dialect."[32] Joseph and Elizabeth Wright claim that "*o* became *u* before *ng* in the w. Midland dialects during the ME. Period, and a few words from these dialects have crept into standard NE. with the regular change of *u* to *a*, as *among*, *monger*, *mongrel* which were formerly often spelled with *u*."[33] *Awlung* is listed in both *MW* and *DSL*. We have one instance of the standard form *along* in Stephen's speech, "Not *along* of me." (*HT*, 71). As this standard form appears in the earlier issue of the weekly instalments, Dickens might not have had enough knowledge of this dialectal form when he wrote the sixth weekly number of this novel in *Household Words*, published on 6 May 1854. Another reason why Dickens employed this form is that this standard form is most strongly stressed in the sentence.

The use of *o* in *monny* and *onny* instead of *many* and *any*-

---

[32] G. L. Brook (1970) *The Language of Dickens*, p. 127.
[33] J. and E. M. Wright (1924) *An Elementary Historical New English Grammar*, §139.

is frequently found in Blackpool's speech. Examples are *monny* (*HT*, 141, 142[2x], 148, 151, 154), *onny* (*HT*, 141[2x], 148, 150, 154, 156, 160, 272), *onnything* (*HT*, 162), and *onnyways* (*HT*, 162). Brook remarks that "Stephen's *monny* is regularly from OE *monig* while his *onny*, also a common northern form, probably owes its stem-vowel to the analogy of *monny*."[34] *EDD* (s.v. *many*, *adj.* and *sb.*) illustrates that *monny* is found in Sc., w. Yks, Lan., Chs., and *EDG* ('Index,' s.v. *any*) suggests that [oni] occurs in Yks, sm., w. Lan. *Monny* and *onny* are both listed in *MW* and *DSL*. In addition to them, *DSL* lists *onnyway* and *onnythin*.

OED (s.v. *well*, *adv.*) comments that "an early lengthening of the vowel is indicated by the ME. *weel* (*wiel*, *wele*, etc.), which appears in northern and Scottish texts from the 14th cent., and is still the current form in Scottish, northern, and north midland dialects." Both *MW* and *DSL* refer to the pronunciation of this adverb. Examples are as follows:

> "I know *weel*" (*HT*, 142[3x], 152) / "yo know *weel*" (*HT*, 154) / "'tis as *weel* so ..." (*HT*, 159)

J. Wright demonstrates that "when *well* begins the sentence we use [wel], just as in literary English."[35] Dickens observes this rule with one exception:[36]

> "*Well*! She went bad ..." (71)
> "*Well*, missus, I ha' seen the lady ..." (154)
> "*Well well* said he ..." (162)

---

[34] G. L. Brook (1970) *The Language of Dickens*, p. 127.

[35] J. Wright (1892) *A Grammar of the Dialect of Windhill in the West Riding of Yorkshire*, §399.

[36] "they loves as *well* as gentlefok loves theirs ..." (272)

CHAPTER IV   REALISM AND VERISIMILITUDE   65

Table 3 Short vowels

HT	MW	DSL	*EDG, EDD, OED*, etc
aboove	—	—	[əbùv]: w. Lan., w. Chs., n. & ne. Der., Lei., n. Wor., & se. Shr. (*EDG*, 'Index,' s.v. *above*)
amoong	—	—	[əmùŋ]: sw. Yks, em. & w. Lan., I.Ma., w. Chs., n. Stf., n. Der., Lei., m. Nhp., War., & n. Shr. (*EDG*, 'Index,' s.v. *among*)
anoother	—	—	—
coom (*pr.*), *coom* (*pp.*), *cooms*	—	—	[kùm]: n., m., sw. & w. Lan., I.Ma., w. Chs., Flt., em. Stf., e. Der., Not., Lei., m. Nhp., e., w. & w. War., ne. & se. Shr., & nw. Oxf. (*EDG*, 'Index,' s.v. *come*)
coompany	—	—	[kùmpəni]: Sc., Yks, Chs., Lin., Shr., e.An., Sus., Dor., Som., & Dev. (*EDD*, s.v. *company, sb. & v.*)
coop	—	—	[kùp] in Ant., sm., se., sw. & w. Lan., I.Ma., Dnb., nw. Der., Lei., m. & sw. Nhp., War., n. Wor., Shr., w. Oxf., & n. Bck. (*EDG*, 'Index,' s.v. *cup*)
coover	—	—	[kùvə(r)]: sw. & w. Lan., nw. Der., & Lei. (*EDG*, 'Index,' s.v. *cover*)
discoosed	—	—	—
doon	—	—	[dùn]: m., sm., sw. & w. Lan., I.Ma., Chs., Flt., Dnb., n., em., wm. & w. Stf., n. Der., Not., Lei., ne. & sw. Nhp., War., n. & w. Wor., Shr., nw. Oxf., & n. Bck. (*EDG*, 'Index,' s.v. *done*)
droonken	—	—	[drùŋkn]: nw., m., sw., ms & w. Lan., I.Ma., Chs., Flt., n., wm. & w. Stf., Der., Not., Lei., m. Nhp., e. War., w. Wor., n. & se. Shr., & nw. & w. Oxf. (*EDG*, 'Index,' s.v. *drunken*)
oother	—	—	[ùðə(r)]: sm. & w. Lan., w. Chs., Dnb., nw.

				Der., n. Lei., Nhp., n. & se. Shr., & n. & nw. Oxf. (*EDG*, 'Index,' s.v. *other*)
soom (= 'some')	—	—		[sùm]: Ant., m., se., sw. & w. Lan., I.Ma., Chs., Dnb., e. & wm. Stf., ne., nw., e. & w. Der., Lei., sw. Nhp., e. & w. War., Wor., n. & ne. Shr., w. & nw. Oxf., & n. Bck. (*EDG*, 'Index,' s.v. *some*)
soom (= 'sum')	—	—		[sùm]: Yks, Lan., Der., Not., Lei., Nhp., War., Glo., Brks., Hnt., e.An., Ken., Som., & Dev. (*EDD*, s.v. *sum, sb.*[1] *& v.*)
soombody	—	—	—	
tooches	—			[tùtʃ]: Ant., sm. sw. Lan., I.Ma., w. Chs., nw. Der., Lei., & m. Nhp. (*EDG*, 'Index,' s.v. *touch*)
toother	—	—	—	
t'oother	—	—	—	
yoong	*yunger*	*yunger*		[jùŋ]: Ant., se., ms & w. Lan., I.Ma., w. Chs., Dnb., n. Lei., ne., m. & sw. Nhp., e. & w. War., n. & w. Wor., & n. & se. Shr. (*EDG*, 'Index,' s.v. *young*)
awlung	*awlung*	*awlung*		*awlung*: s. Stf., ne. Der., e. Hrf., & nw. Dev. (*EDG*, §32)
monny	*monny*	*monny*		*monny*: Sc., w. Yks, Lan., Chs. (*EDD*, s.v. *many, adj. & sb.*)
onny	*onny*	*onny*		[oni]: Yks, sm., w. Lan. (*EDG*, 'Index,' s.v. *any*)
onnything	—	*onnythin*	—	
onnyways	—	*onny way*	—	
weel	*weel*	*weel*		*weel*: Scottish, northern, & north midl& dialects. (*OED*, s.v. *well, adv.*)

4.3.3 Long vowels

Dickens uses the spelling with *owt* for either *aught* or *ought* to indicates the diphthong [au] for the RP long vowel [ɔ:]. We have eight instances of *nowt* (*HT*, 71^{2x}, 146, 147, 148^{2x}, 151, 159) and five instances of *thowt* (*HT*, 89, 142, 156, 273, 274). *EDG* (§127) suggests that [au] in *naught* is found in w. Nhb., n. Dur., Wm., nw. Yks, and nw., and w. Lan.; and that [au] in *nought* in sw. and w. Nhb., n. Dur., n. Cum., Wm., nw. Yks, em., se. and w. Lan., w. Stf., Glo., w. Oxf., Sus., and e. Dev. *EDG* (§166) illustrates that [au] in *thought* is heard in sw. Nhb., n. Dur., Wm., and em., se. and w. Lan. *Nowt* for *naught* is recorded in both *MW* and *DSL*, and *thowt* in *MW* only.

The spelling with *o* for *ou* in the second person pronoun in both nominative and accusative cases indicates the dialectal short vowel [ɔ] for the RP long vowel [u:]. Blackpool employs *yo* (*HT*, 68 etc.) twenty-one times in the nominative, *yo* (*HT*, 71 etc.) twenty-two times in the accusative, and *yo'* (*HT*, 74) once in the accusative. According to *EDG* ('Index,' s.v. *you*), the dialectal pronunciation [jɔ] is used in w. Yks, w. Lan., w. Chs., nw. Der., and w. Stf. This second person pronoun is surely recorded in both *MW* and *DSL*.

Table 4 Long vowels

HT	MW	DSL	EDG, EDD, OED, etc
nowt	*nowt*	*nowt*	[au] in *naught*: w. Nhb., n. Dur., Wm., nw. Yks, & nw., & w. Lan. (*EDG*, §127); [au] in *nought*: sw. & w. Nhb., n. Dur., n. Cum., Wm., nw. Yks, em., se. & w. Lan., w. Stf., Glo., w. Oxf., Sus., & e. Dev. (*EDG*, §127)
thowt	*thowt*	—	[au] in *thought*: sw. Nhb., n. Dur., Wm., & em., se. & w. Lan. (*EDG*, §166)

| yo, yo' | yo | yo | [jɔ]: w. Yks, w. Lan., w. Chs., nw. Der., & w. Stf. (*EDG*, 'Index,' s.v. *you*) |

4.3.4 Diphthongs

Blackpool utters [iə] or [i:r] instead of the RP diphthong [ɛə] in such words as *theer* (*HT*, 141, 154), *wheer* (*HT*, 149, 150, 154), *elsewheer* (*HT*, 152), *wheerever* (*HT*, 143). *EDG* ('Index,' s.v. *there*) shows that [iə] in *there* occurs in Dur., e., m. and w. Cum., Wm., ne., m., se., sw. and w. Yks, Lan., Chs., Flt., Dnb., Stf., Lin., Lei., m., sw. Nhp., War., Wor., Shr., Hrf., n., nw. and w. Oxf., Brks., Bck., Bdf., se. Hrt., w. Nrf., Ess., Dor., and w. Dev. *EDG* ('Index,' s.v. *where*) claims that [iə] in *where* is to be heard in n. Dur., ne., snw., e., m., se., sw. and w. Yks, Lan., Chs., Flt., Dnb., e., em. wm. and w. Stf., Der., Not., Lin., Rut., Lei., Nhp., War., n. Wor., Shr., e. Hrf., nw. Oxf., Brks., Bdf., se. Hrt., Hnt., e. Suf., Ess., e. and se. Ken., Dor., nw. Som., sw. and w. Dev., and Cor. *DSL* records both *thee-er* and *wheer*, but *MW* lists neither of them.

The spelling *heer* indicates the vowel lengthening [i:r] in place of the RP diphthong [iə]. Blackpool uses *heer* (*HT*, 142^{3x}, 143, 149, 151^{2x}, 273) eight times. *EDG* ('Index,' s.v. *here*) shows that the dialectal pronunciation [hi:r] is employed in Sh.I., Or.I., Cai, Inv., ne. and sn. Sc., w. Frf., e. Per., em., wm. and sm. Sc., Ant., and me. and sw. Nhb.

Table 5 Diphthongs

HT	MW	DSL	EDG, EDD, OED, etc
theer	—	thee-er	[iə] in *there*: Dur., e., m. & w. Cum., Wm., ne., m., se., sw. & w. Yks, Lan., Chs., Flt., Dnb., Stf., Lin., Lei., m., sw. Nhp., War., Wor., Shr., Hrf., n., nw. & w. Oxf., Brks., Bck., Bdf., se.

			Hrt., w. Nrf., Ess., Dor., & w. Dev. (*EDG*, 'Index,' s.v. *there*)
wheer	—	*wheer*	[iə] in *where*: n. Dur., ne., snw., e., m., se., sw. & w. Yks, Lan., Chs., Flt., Dnb., e., em. wm. & w. Stf., Der., Not., Lin., Rut., Lei., Nhp., War., n. Wor., Shr., e. Hrf., nw. Oxf., Brks., Bdf., se. Hrt., Hnt., e. Suf., Ess., e. & se. Ken., Dor., nw. Som., sw. & w. Dev., & Cor. (*EDG*, 'Index,' s.v. *where*)
elsewheer	—	—	—
wheerever	—	—	—
heer	—	—	[hi:r]: Sh.I., Or.I., Cai, Inv., ne. & sn. Sc., w. Frf., e. Per., em., wm. & sm. Sc., Ant., & me. & sw. Nhb. (*EDG*, 'Index,' s.v. *here*)

4.3.5 Consonants

Stephen employs the dialectal form *chilt* (*HT*, 74) instead of *child*. According to *EDG* (§302), OE. final *d* and medial *d* which has come to stand finally in the modern dialects have become *t* after *l*, *n*, *r* in monosyllables in Lan., Chs., n. Stf., and Der., as [tʃàilt] *child*, [fĩlt] *field*. This dialectal form is recorded in both *MW* and *DSL*.

Another dialectal form *brigg* in place of *bridge* is also employed by Blackpool (*HT,* 72). *OED* (s.v. *Bridge, n.*[1]) illustrates that "as in other OE. words in -*cg*, the northern dialect has retained hard [g] against the palatalized [dʒ] of the south." According to *EDG* ('Index,' s.v. *bridge*), *brig* is to be heard in Or.I., Bch., Abd., w. Frf., e. Per., n. Ayr, sm. Sc., Lth., Ant., me. and w. Nhb., Dur., n. and m. Cum., Wm., Yks, Lan., ne. Der., m. Not., Lin., Lei., m. Nhp., Bdf., Hnt., and e.An. This form is listed only in *MW*.

Table 6 Consonants

HT	MW	DSL	EDG, EDD, OED, etc
chilt	*chilt*	*chilt*	*chilt*: Lan., Chs., n. Stf., & Der. (*EDG*, §302)
brigg	*brigg*	—	*brig*: Or.I., Bch., Abd., w. Frf., e. Per., n. Ayr, sm. Sc., Lth., Ant., me. & w. Nhb., Dur., n. & m. Cum., Wm., Yks, Lan., ne. Der., m. Not., Lin., Lei., m. Nhp., Bdf., Hnt., & e.An. (*EDG*, 'Index,' s.v. *bridge*)

His accuracy of rendering the regional dialect is not so incomplete. Many of the dialectal pronunciations are to be found in *MW* and *DSL* and paralleled to the illustrations of the references, but "some of them seem to be of doubtful authenticity", as Brook has already mentioned. According to the discussion and the five tables above, the following phonetic descriptions are not to be assumed as Lancashire dialect: *anoother*, *discoosed*, *soombody*, *toother*, *t'oother*, *awlung*, *heer*, *Gonnows*, *a'toogether*, *faw'en*, *sma'est*, *wi'in*, and *wi'out*.

In the case of *weel* for *well*, Dickens strictly followed its dialectal usage except one example and used the standard form at the beginning of the sentence. We, however, find some inconsistencies of spellings representing dialectal pronunciations.

By using phonetic spellings Dickens aimed at the verisimilitude with respect to representing Lancashire dialect. Due to some examples that are not to be recognized as Lancashire dialect and a few inconsistencies of spellings, the dialect Dickens tried to describe so as to add some local colours to *Hard Times* has been subject to the most caustic criticism by both literary and linguistic scholars.

CHAPTER V

Stylistics and Sociolinguistics

David Copperfield is Dickens's semi-autobiographical novel related and developed by David as the first person "omniscient narrator."[1] In *Great Expectations* Pip also plays an important part as the first person omniscient narrator. Our chief concern in this chapter lies in stylistic analyses of Dickens's artistic creation of literary dialect through the viewpoint of David and Pip, and sociolinguistic approaches to his treatment of regional and class dialect, and British and American English.

5.1 Omniscient narrator as a dialect glossarist

K. J. Fielding[2] reveals that Dickens used Edward Moor's *Suffolk Words and Phrases* (1823) as his primary source of East Anglia dialect in *David Copperfield*. This provincial glossary enabled the author to introduce much more local words and phrases to *David Copperfield* than *Nicholas Nickleby*. Readers sometimes find it difficult to understand the meaning of the provincial words and phrases employed by Mr.

---

[1] It is otherwise called "implied author," or "supposed narrator," the former of which was popularised by W. C. Booth (1961) *The Rhetoric of Fiction*, p. 54, and the latter of which was employed by G. L. Brook (1970) *The Language of Dickens*, p. 118.

[2] "*David Copperfield* and Dialect," *The Times Literary Supplement*, 30 April 1949, p. 288.

Peggotty's family in Yarmouth. Dickens was so kind as to introduce a gloss into the text without the slightest hesitation through David's point of view as the omniscient narrator.[3] These glosses are sometimes inserted in parentheses or dashes. Examples are:

> "Like two young *mavishes*," Mr. Peggotty said. I knew this meant, in our local dialect, like two young thrushes, and received it as a compliment. (*DC*, 32)
>
> "Cheer up, old *Mawther*!" (Mr. Peggotty meant old girl.) (*DC*, 34)
>
> "I'll pound it, it's wot you do yourself, sir," said Mr. Peggotty, shaking his head, "and wot you do well—right well! I thankee, sir. I'm obleeged to you, sir, for your welcoming manner of me. I'm rough, sir, but I'm ready —least ways, I *hope* I'm ready, you unnerstand. My house ain't much for to see, sir, but it's hearty at your service if ever you should come along with Mas'r Davy to see it. I'm a reg'lar *Dodman*, I am," said Mr. Peggotty; by which he meant snail, and this was in allusion to his being slow to go, for he had attempted to go after every sentence, and had somehow or other come back again; "but I wish you both well, and I wish you happy!" (*DC*, 90)
>
> "Dan'l, my good man," said she, "you must eat and drink, and keep up your strength, for without it you'll do nowt. Try, that's a dear soul! An if I disturb you with my *clicketten*," she meant her chattering, "tell me so, Dan'l, and I won't." (*DC*, 391)
>
> "No, no, Dan'l," she returned, "I shan't be that. Doen't you mind me. I shall have enough to do to keep a *Beein* for you" (Mrs. Gummidge meant a home), "again you come back—to keep a *Beein* here for any that may hap to come back, Dan'l. In the fine time, I shall set outside the door as I used to do. If any should

---

[3] See G. L. Brook (1970) *The Language of Dickens*, p. 118.

> come nigh, they shall see the old widder woman true to 'em, a long way off." (*DC*, 391)
>
> "Unless my wits is gone a *bahd's neezing*"—by which Mr. Peggotty meant to say, bird's-nesting—"this morning, 'tis along of me as you a going to quit us." (*DC*, 619)
>
> "Betwixt you and me, Mas'r Davy—and you, ma'am—wen Mrs. Gummidge takes to *wimicking*,"—our old country word for crying,—"she's liable to be considered to be, by them as didn't know the old 'un, peevish-like. Now I *did* know the old 'un," said Mr. Peggotty, "and I know'd his merits, so I unnerstan' her; but 'tan't entirely so, you see, with others—nat'rally can't be!" (*DC*, 624)
>
> "Wheerby," said Mr. Peggotty, "my sister might—I doen't say she would, but might—find Missis Gummidge give her a leetle trouble now-and-again. Theerfur 'tan't my intentions to moor Missis Gummidge 'long with them, but to find a *Beein'* fur her wheer she can *fisherate* for herself." (A Beein' signifies, in that dialect, a home, and to fisherate is to provide.) (*DC*, 625)

The same device is also found in *Great Expectations* in which Pip plays the same role as David. The following extract occurs soon after Pip asks his sister, Mrs. Joe Gargery what Hulks is:

> "That's the way with this boy!" exclaimed my sister, pointing me out with her needle and thread, and shaking her head at me. "Answer him one question, and he'll ask you a dozen directly. Hulks are prison-ships, right 'cross th' *meshes*." We always used that name for marshes, in our country. (*GE*, 15)

In *Oliver Twist* Dickens depicts the London underworld and makes good use of thieves' cant and slang and underworld lingo, most of which readers are unable to understand. Dickens sometimes glosses the meaning of them into the text:

> 'You haven't opened the parcel and swallowed one or two as you come along, have you?' inquired Sikes, suspiciously. 'Don't put on an injured look at the question; you've done it many a time. *Jerk the tinkler.*'
> These words, in plain English, conveyed an injunction to ring the bell. It was answered by another Jew: younger than Fagin, but nearly as vile and repulsive in appearance. (*OT*, 94)

> Oliver was but too glad to make himself useful; too happy to have some faces, however bad, to look upon; and too desirous to conciliate those about him when he could honestly do so; to throw any objection in the way of this proposal. So he at once expressed his readiness; and, kneeling on the floor, while the Dodger sat upon the table so that he could take his foot in his laps, he applied himself to a process which Mr. Dawkins designated as *'japanning his trotter-cases.'* Which phrase, rendered into plain English, signifieth, cleaning his boots. (*OT*, 116)

Fagin's gangs sometimes explain the meaning of the underworld lingo to Oliver, when they notice him confused at it:

> 'Walking for sivin days!' said the young gentleman. 'Oh, I see. *Beak*'s order, eh? But,' he added, noticing Oliver's look of surprise, 'I suppose you don't know what a *beak* is, my flash com-pan-i-on.'
> Oliver mildly replied, that he had always heard a bird's mouth described by the term in question.
> 'My eyes, how green!' exclaimed the young gentleman. 'Why, a *beak*'s a madgst'rate; and when you walk by a *beak*'s order, it's not straight forerd, but always a-going up, and niver a-coming down agin. Was you never on the mill?' (*OT*, 47)

> 'And always put this in your pipe, Nolly,' said the Dodger, as the Jew was heard unlocking the door above,

CHAPTER V   STYLISTICS AND SOCIOLINGUISTICS   75

'if you don't take *fogels* and *tickers*—'
  'What's the good of talking in that way?' interposed Master Bates: 'he don't know what you mean.'
  'If you don't take pocket-handkechers and watches,' said the Dodger, reducing his conversation to the level of Oliver's capacity ... (*OT*, 118)

5.2 Visual effect and the point of view

In the following dialogue beween Mr. Peggotty and David, we can find Dickens's application of *drowndead* instead of *drownded* to the speech of Mr. Peggotty:

> After tea ... Mr. Peggotty was smoking his pipe. I felt it was time for conversation and confidence.
> "Mr. Peggotty!" says I.
> "Sir," says he.
> "Did you give your son the name of Ham, because you lived in a sort of ark?"
> Mr. Peggotty seemed to think it a deep idea, but answered: "No, sir. I never giv him no name."
> "Who gave him that name, then?" said I, putting question number two of the catechism to Mr. Peggotty.
> "Why, sir, his father giv it him," said Mr. Peggotty.
> "I thought you were his father!"
> "My brother Joe was *his* father," said Mr. Peggotty.
> "*Dead*, Mr. Peggotty?" I hinted, after a respectful pause.
> "*Drowndead*," said Mr. Peggotty.
> I was very much surprised that Mr. Peggotty was not Ham's father, and began to wonder whether I was mistaken about his relationship to anybody else there. I was so curious to know, that I made up my mind to have it out with Mr. Peggotty.
> "Little Em'ly," I said, glancing at her. "She is your daughter, isn't she, Mr. Peggotty?"
> "No, sir. My brother-in-law, Tom, was *her* father."
> I couldn't help it. "—*Dead*, Mr. Peggotty?" I hinted,

after another respectful silence.
"*Drowndead*," said Mr. Peggotty. (*DC*, 28)

A brief historical sketch of the adding of [d] after [aun] is made by Jespersen in his *Modern English Grammar*[4]:

> More frequent than the loss of [d] is the adding [d] after [n], especially after [u:], now [au]: ME *soun* OF *son* Mod *sound* ... In vulgar speech some of the early forms in -*nd* still survive, which have been discarded from Standard English: *gownd* for *gown*, *drownd* for *drown*.

The usual dialectal form *drownded* ending -*ded*, not -*dead* can be found in Moor's *Suffolk Words and Phrases*[5] and in the speech of Em'ly, which occurs in a few lines below:

> "That father was *drownded* in?" said Em'ly. "No. Not that one. I never see that boat." (*DC*, 29)

and in the following speech of Mr. Peggotty:

> "There was a certain person as had know'd our Em'ly, from the time when her father was *drownded* ..." (*DC*, 267)
>
> "I'm a going to seek my niece. I'm a going to seek my Em'ly. I'm a going, first, to stave in that theer boat, and sink it where I would have *drownded* him, as I'm a living soul, if I had had one thought of what was in him! As he sat afore me," he said, wildly, holding out his clenched right hand, "as he sat afore me, face to face, strike me down dead, but I'd have *drownded* him, and thought it right!—I'm a going to seek my niece." (*DC*, 387)

---

[4] *Modern English Grammar*, Vol., Ejnar Munksgaard: Copenhagen, 1909, §7.61.

[5] See *drownded*.

CHAPTER V STYLISTICS AND SOCIOLINGUISTICS   77

"When she was a child," he said, lifting up his head soon after we were left alone, "she used to talk to me a deal about the sea, and about them coasts where the sea got to be dark blue, and to lay a shining and a shining in the sun. I thowt, odd times, as her father being *drownded* made her think on it so much. I doen't know, now, you see, but maybe she believed—or hoped—he had drifted out to them parts, where the flowers is always a blowing, and the country bright." (*DC*, 498)

Then, why did Dickens employ -*dead* form only in the scene extracted above? This conversation between David and Mr. Peggotty is held on the first evening of David's stay at Mr. Peggotty's boat house. David becomes aware that he mistakes Mr. Peggotty's relationship to those who live there.

David's primary concern in this conversation is the relationship among the people in the boat house. He is so suddenly and unexpectedly informed of the death of Ham's father that this young and innocent omniscient narrator's mind is so upset and completely occupied by the image of death, therefore the image of death in his mind is reflected in and transferred to the verbal ending of *drowndead*.

David's second question about Em'ly's father in the sixth line from the bottom of the first long quotation makes it clearer that David's mind is completely ruled by the image of death. The dash followed by *Dead* indicates the absence of the cause of her father's death. For David, it does not matter whether her father died from drowning, burning or starving, but it is much more important for him to know whether her father was dead or not.

In all the instances above, which include *drownded*, David's mind is totally free from the image of death, so Dickens intended to use the usual dialectal form in each case. Both forms are phonetically quite similar, but visually and implicatively quite different from each other. The transcription of spoken words into written words sometimes falls short of its intention as Julian Franklyn has already mentioned[6], but the visual effect of the written word such as *drowndead* was considered so large and effective.

5.3 Regional dialect and class dialect

Pip lives in a small village near Rochester in Kent, which lies on the marsh between the mouth of the Thames and the Medway. Pip is brought up "by hand" (*GE*, 8) by his sister, and lives with her and her husband Joe Gargery, the blacksmith. Therefore he belongs to the working-class and he is supposed to share the substandard speech with Joe. However, from the beginning of this novel Dickens applies Standard English to Pip's speech. This application is strictly observed in the elision of the vowel of the definite article:

> "It's bad about here ... You've been lying out on *the meshes*, and they're dreadful aguish. Rheumatic, too." (*GE*, Pip, 19)
> "... Hulks are prison-ships, right 'cross *th' meshes*." We always used that name for marshes, in our country. (*GE*, Mrs. Gargery, 15)
> "I'm wrong in these clothes. I'm wrong out of the forge, the kitchen, or off *th' meshes*." (*GE*, Joe, 225)

The elision of the vowel sound of the definite article occurs in the speech of Mr. and Mrs. Joe Gargery, not in that of Pip,

---

[6] J. Franklyn (1953) *The Cockney: A Survey of London Life and Language*, p. 241.

CHAPTER V   STYLISTICS AND SOCIOLINGUISTICS   79

while Kentish provincialism *meshes* is found in the speech of Pip as well as in that of Mr. and Mrs. Gargery. *MEG* (§6.13) states, "this elided form was very frequent in early ModE, but now it is found in vulgar speech." Dickens allows Pip to use regional dialect but never to employ class dialect.

It was not until his first visit to Miss Havisham's Satis House that Pip was made to realise his social status by a beautiful young lady named Estella. She mercilessly threw Pip down into the lower-class by referring to his despicable verbal habit of "calling the knaves, Jacks" in playing-cards and to his "coarse hands and thick boots," both of which are vulgar appendages of a common labouring boy:

> "He *calls the knaves, Jacks*, this boy!" said Estella with disdain, before our game was out. "And what *coarse hands* he has. And what *thick boots!*" (*GE*, 61)

No dictionary refers to the connotation of social identity in "calling the knaves, Jacks". *SUE* (s.v. *Jack*, 11) suggests that the word in question was originally standard English and fell into colloquialism in the 19th century. According to *OED*, this noun underwent semantic generalisation.[7] *Century* (s.v. *Jack*[1], *n.*, 7) quotes this example with "said Estella with disdain, before our game was out," which *OED* excludes.

In Victorian England, thanks to the success of the Industrial Revolution, not a few people obtained some wealth. Next to wealth, they yearn for gentility and good education. The following is quoted from BBC's *The Story of English*, which

---

[7] *Cards*. Name for the knave of trumps in the game of all-fours; hence *gen.* any one of the knaves. (*OED*, s.v. *Jack, n*[1]., 5)

well explains the written standardisation in the 18th century and the spoken standardisation in the 19th century:

> Throughout the history of English there has been a contest between the forces of standardization and the forces of localization, at both the written and the spoken levels. The appearance of the first substantial English dictionaries in the eighteenth century was a move towards written standardization. It was Victorian England that realized the idea of "the Queen's English", a spoken standard to which the "lesser breeds" could aspire.[8]

There must have been many people among the readers of *Great Expectations* who was shocked to realize that "calling the knaves, Jacks" classified them into the lower and vulgar society. G. L. Brook proclaims that "if the author's works are widely read, his linguistic habits are likely to exert an important influence on others who use the language."[9] Pip's use of "Jacks" instead of "the Knaves" is considered as one of the best examples of Brook's remark. K. C. Phillipps suggests that "Refinement, or lack of it, was apt to be revealed when playing cards."[10]

In 1956, about a century after Dickens published *Great Expectations,* A. S. C. Ross defined *Jack*, in playing-cards as non-U and *knave* as U and informed us that it was his son who called his attention to this extract from *Great Expectations*.[11]

---

[8] R. McCrum, *et al.* (1986) *The Story of English*, p. 21

[9] G. L. Brook (1970) *The Language of Dickens*, p. 13.

[10] K. C. Phillipps (1984) *The Language and Class in Victorian England*, p. 59.

[11] A. S. C., Ross (1956) "U and Non-U." *Noblesse Oblige*, p. 30.

CHAPTER V   STYLISTICS AND SOCIOLINGUISTICS   81

Pip underwent a very rapid education into the social delicacies of language and its possibilities for social shame. Estella's disdainful ways of education into the sensibilities of status were much more effective than the haphazard teaching practices of "an evening school"[12] which Mr. Wopsle's great-aunt kept in the village:

> I took the opportunity of being alone in the courtyard, to look at *my coarse hands* and *my common boots*. My opinion of those accessories was not favourable. They had never troubled me before, but they troubled me now, as vulgar appendages. I determined to ask Joe why he had ever taught me to call those picture-cards, *Jacks, which ought to be called knaves*. I wished Joe had been rather more genteelly brought up, and then I should have been so too.(*GE*, 63)

In the following quotation Pip pondered over Estella's disdainful remarks again on his way back to the forge:

> I set off on the four-mile walk to our forge; pondering, as I went along, on all I had seen, and deeply revolving that I was a common labouring-boy; that *my hands were coarse*; that *my boots were thick*; that I had fallen into a despicable habit of *calling knaves Jacks*; that I was much more ignorant than I had considered myself last night, and generally that I was in a low-lived bad way. (*GE*, 66)

When Pip returned to the forge, his sister and Mr. Pumblechock was so curious as to know all about Miss Havisham's and asked a number of questions. Pip, however, felt too miserable and exhausted to explain himself at Miss Havisham's

---

[12] The description of the evening school occurs in pp. 44-45 and 73-75.

to his sister and Mr. Pumblechock because they were so rude to him. He told Joe that he told them lies. He told Joe all about Miss Havisham's Satis House thus:

> "I don't know what possessed me, Joe," I replied, letting his shirt sleeve go, and sitting down in the ashes at his feet, hanging my head; "but I wish you hadn't taught me to *call Knaves at cards, Jacks*; and I wish *my boots weren't so thick* nor *my hands so coarse.*"
> And then I told Joe that I felt very miserable, and that I hadn't been able to explain myself to Mrs. Joe and Pumblechook who were so rude to me, and that there had been a beautiful young lady at Miss Havisham's who was dreadfully proud, and that she had said I was common, and that I knew I was common, and that I wished I was not common, and that the lies had come of it somehow, though I didn't know how. (*GE*, 71)

Stylistically, we must notice that the sequence of the sentences has been reversed between the quoations (*GE*, 63, 66) and the quotation (*GE*, 71). In the quotations (*GE*, 63, 66), as you can see, the sequence is *hands*, *boots*, and *Jacks*, but in the quotation (*GE*, 71), the sequence is reversed, *Jacks*, *boots*, and *hands*. This can be considered as chiasmus in rhetoric, so as to suggest Pip's reverse psychology.

5.4 American English and British English

In the letter dated 15th April, 1842, Dickens himself says to Forster:

> I may as well hint that the prevailing grammar is also more than doubtful. (*Let. III*, 196)

G. L. Brook claims that ";in general Dickens's portrayal of

CHAPTER V   STYLISTICS AND SOCIOLINGUISTICS   83

American English, as in his portrayal of British regional dialects, regional features are heavily outnumbered by substandard features," and that "there are close parallels between the substandard speech of American and British characters."[13] Louise Pound also suggests, referring to the verbal and pronoun forms used by Dickens's American characters, that "most of these verbal and pronoun forms are used by Dickens's English speakers as well as by his Americans," and that they are "archaic in both English and American usage."[14] In this section we shall compare grammatical anomalies employed by Dickens's American characters with those by his low-life London characters and dialect speakers in Britain.

Dickens's native American characters are General Cyrus Choke, militia officer, Hannibal Chollop, frontiersman who worships Eden, Colonel Diver, editor of *The New York Rowdy Journal*, Mrs. Hominy, intellectually pretentious woman, Captain Kedgick, landlord of the National Hotel in Watertoast, La Fayette Kettle, an inquisitive, bombastic American, Elijah Pogram, member of Congress, and Zephaniah Scadder, fraudulent land agent in *Martin Chuzzlewit*; and a forester who does not like overcrowding, a gaoler of The Tomb in New York, a bootmaker, subject of an extended vignette, a coachman, on the road to Columbus, and a gentleman in a straw hat, with considerable conversation in *American Notes*.

As low-life London characters, we select some of the Cockneys in *Sketches by Boz*; Sam and Tony Weller in *Pickwick Papers*; and Fagin, Tom Chitling, Toby Crackit, The

---

[13] G. L. Brook (1970) *The Language of Dickens*, p. 136.
[14] L. Pound (1947) "American Dialect of Charles Dickens," P. 127.

Artful Dodger, and Bill Sikes, all of whom are thieves and housebreakers in *Oliver Twist*. As dialect speakers we pick up Ham Peggotty and Mr. Peggotty in *David Copperfield*, both of whom are speakers of East Anglia dialect; Stephen Blackpool in *Hard Times*, who speaks broad Lancashire dialect; and Joe Gargery and Abel Magwitch in *Great Expectations*, both of whom are users of Kentish dialect.

5.4.1 Morphology

There are two "special negative forms"[15] of the verb *to be* or *to have* in the speech of some American characters in Dickens. *An't* is used for *am not, isn't,* or *aren't* by some of the native American characters in *American Notes* and *Martin Chuzzlewit*. This form is often found in the speech of low-life London characters and dialect speakers in Dickens's other writings, but there is no instance of this form in the speech of Tony and Sam Weller:

(1) *an't* for "am not"
"No. I am a brown forester, I am. I *an't* a Johnny Cake." (*AN*, forester, 151)
"I *an't* a Johnny Cake, *I an't*. I am from the brown forests of the Mississippi, *I* am." (*AN*, forester, 151^{2x})
"I *an't* jealous" (*SB*, Emily, 273)
'Horrid dull, I'm blessed if I *an't*' (*OT*, Crackit, 262)
"I *an't* a scholar."(*DC*, Mr. Peggotty, 625)

(2) *an't* for "isn't"
"Well, it *an't* a very rowdy life, and *that's* a fact!" (*AN*, gaoler, 85)

---

[15] G. L. Brook (1970) *The Language of Dickens*, p. 242, § 81.

CHAPTER V   STYLISTICS AND SOCIOLINGUISTICS   85

"There *an't* no room at all, Sir." (*AN*, gentleman, 140)

I reckon that's Judge Jefferson, *an't* it? (*AN*, Straw Hat, 190)

No it *an't*. (*AN*, coachman, 190)

... it *an't* calculated to make you smart, overmuch. (*Let. III*, 89)

"My name *an't* Mary as it happens." (*SB*, young girl, 185)

'And Mr. Crackit is a heavy swell; *an't* he, Fagin?' (*OT*, Chitling, 263)

"It *an't* along o' you!" (*DC*, Mr. Peggotty, 34)

'But 't *an't* sommuch for that as I stands out.' (*HT*, Blackpool, 141)

(3)   *an't* for "aren't"

"No you *an't*. You're none o' my raising." (*AN*, forester, 151)

"You *an't* partickler, about this scoop in the heel, I suppose, then?" (*AN*, bootmaker, 250)

"P'raps ... them *an't* plants of Eden's raising. No!" (*MC*, Scadder, 361)

"Our citizens *an't* long of riling up, I tell you." (*MC*, Kedgick, 365)

"Why the deviou looking after that plate?" (*SB*, Fixem, 29)

'You may keep the books, if you're fond of reading. If you *a'n't*, sell 'em.'(*OT*, Sikes, 101)

There is no example of *an't* instead of "haven't" in the speech of American characters in Dickens, but Clara Peggotty (*DC*, 15) says, "Now let me hear some more about Crorkindills, for I *an't* heard half enough."

Another negative form of the verb *to be* or *to have* is *ain't*. It is used for *am not*, *isn't*, or even *hasn't* by some of the native American characters in *AN* and *MC*. We find many examples of this form in the speech of Tony and Sam Weller, and occasionally meet with this negative form in the speech of other low-life London characters and dialect speakers in Dickens. In the speech of Dickens's American characters we have no instance of *ain't* for "aren't", although we have many instances of it in the speech of the others:

(1) *ain't* for "am not"
"My! *ain't* I there?" (*MC*, Mrs. Hominy, 374)
"I *ain't* going to hurt him." (*SB*, Mr. Warden, 488)
"I *ain't* a goin' to get married." (*PP*, Sam Weller, 495)
'... he'll go away if I *ain't* there to my time.' (*OT*, Dodger, 299)
"I'm here o' nights ... she ain't heer, or I *ain't* theer." (*DC*, Mr. Peggotty, 384)
"I *ain't* a going ... to tell him nothink o' that natur, Pip." (*GE*, Gargery, 475)

(2) *ain't* for "isn't"
"If here *ain't* the Harrisburg mail at last." (*AN*, gentleman, 139)
"I tell you this—there *ain't* a ĕn-gīne with its biler bust." (*MC*, Kettle, 345)
"Well! it *ain't* all built." (*MC*, Scadder, 354)
"Let me see. No: that *ain't* built."(*MC*, Scadder, 354)
"There *ain't* a single one." (*MC*, Scadder, 354)
"P'raps that desk and stool *ain't* made from Eden lumber." (*MC*, Scadder, 357)
"P'raps no end of squatters *ain't* gone out there." (*MC*, Scadder, 357)
"P'raps there *ain't* no such lo-cation." (*MC*, Scadder, 357)

CHAPTER V STYLISTICS AND SOCIOLINGUISTICS

"He *ain't* like emigrants." (*MC*, Kedgick, 371)

"It *ain't* long, since I shot a man down with that." (*MC*, Chollop, 512)

"I should hope there *ain't* a swamp in all Americay." (*MC*, Chollop, 522)

"It *ain't* the thing I did expect."(*MC*, Kedgick, 537)

"It *ain't* quite that, sir, neither." (*MC*, Pogram, 542)

"Liberty *ain't* the window-tax, is it?" (*SB*, a red-faced man, 239)

"She *ain't* vithin hearin'." (*PP*, Tony Weller, 403)

'She *ain't* one to blab.' (*OT*, Sikes, 125)

"You see, the path *ain't* over light or cheerful arter dark." (*DC*, Mr. Peggotty, 383)

"I'm here o' nights ... she *ain't* heer, or I ain't theer." (*DC*, Mr. Peggotty, 384)

"And she *ain't* over partial to having scholars on the premises." (*GE*, Gargery, 50)

(3) *ain't* for "hasn't"

"A man *ain't* got no right to be a public man." (*MC*, Kedgick, 537)

"And if he *ain't* got enough out on 'em, Sammy, to make him free of the water company for life." (*PP*, Tony Weller, 405)

"My house *ain't* much for to see (*DC*, Mr. Peggotty, 90)

According to G. P. Krapp, this contracted form is not acceptable in careful cultivated speech and is very widely current in illiterate speech, in general colloquial speech, and perhaps in some communities it may be heard even on higher levels.[16] He also points out that this negative form was not so

---

[16] G. P. Krapp (1925) *The English Language in America, Vol. II.* p. 263.

reprehensible in colloquial style as it has become until the end of the eighteenth century when the critical judgement of grammarians was finally registered against it.[17]

G. L. Brook claims that in substandard English, "a number of strong verbs have weak forms of the preterite and past participle,"[18] but in the speech of American characters, Chollop and Captain Kedgick use *know'd* only as past participle in perfect tense:

> "I *have know'd* strong men obleeged to make themselves uncommon skase for less. I *have know'd* men Lynched for less, and beaten into punkin'-sarse for less, by an enlightened people." (*MC*, Chollop, 523)
>
> "Our fashionable people wouldn't have attended his le-Vee, if they *had know'd* it." (*MC*, Kedgick, 537)

The following examples of *know'd* as past participle in perfect tense are from the vulgar and dialectal speech in Dickens's other writings:

> I wish I'*d know'd* him, Sammy (*PP*, Tony Weller, 668)
> 'I might *have know'd*, as nobody but an infernal, rich, plundering, thundering, old Jew, could afford to throw away any drink but water; and not that, unless he done the River Company every quarter." (*OT*, Sikes, 76)
> 'If Mr. Bounderby *had* ever *know'd* me right—if he'*d* ever *know'd* me at aw—he would'n ha' took'n offence wi' me.' (*HT*, Blackpool, 273)

Two quotations in *OED* manifest that this past participle in perfect tense is regarded as substandard and that it was used

---

[17] G. P. Krapp (1925) *The English Language in America, Vol. II.* pp. 263-4.

[18] G. L. Brook (1970) *The Language of Dickens*, p. 241, § 77.

in the United States:

> *I have knowed* can be called substandard or 'incorrect.' (*OED*, s.v. *sub-standard*, a. 2.)
>
> One or two people I *have knowed* ... never said a superior word to me. (*OED*, s.v. *superior*, a. 7. b.)

The former quotation is from *An Outline of English Structure* (1951, p. 84) written by American structuralists, G. L. Trager and H. L. Smith, and the latter is from American novelist, O. Wister's *The Virginian* (1902, xviii).

Zephaniah Scadder uses both *rose* and *ris* instead of "raised" as past participle. G. L. Brook suggests that "the first of these forms is from the old preterite singular of the strong verb *rise* (OE *-rās*) while the second is from the old past participle of the strong verb (OE *-risen*)," and he considers these phenomena unusual because "the forms of the strong verbs are used instead of the weak; in substandard British speech the confusion is usually the other way round, with the result that we get *lay* for *lie* and *set* for *sit*."[19] Examples are:

> "It is a lot as should be *rose* in price. It is." (*MC*, Scadder, 357)
>
> "But you didn't ought to have your dander *ris* with *me*, Gen'ral." (*MC*, Scadder, 353)

We also find these forms in the speech of Mrs. Hominy and Hannibal Chollop:

> "Where was you *rose*?" (*MC*, Mrs. Hominy, 368)
>
> "Our backs is easy *ris*." (*MC*, Chollop, 523)

---

[19] G. L. Brook (1970) *The Language of Dickens*, p. 137.

OED and other references used for this book are all silent for these forms, and there is no example of them in other writings of Dickens so far as I know.

5.4.2 Syntax

In vulgar and dialectal speech the objective case of personal pronouns is sometimes used instead of the subjective case. Examples are:

> "... my husband and *me* lives in the front one." (*SB*, Mrs. Mackin, 192)
>
> "... *me* and my family ain't a goin' to be choked for nothin'." (*PP*, Sam Weller, 465)
>
> 'Toby and *me* were over the garden-wall the night afore last.' (*OT*, Sikes, 124)
>
> "*Them* belonging to the house would have stopped her." (*DC*, Mr. Peggotty, 623)
>
> ''Tis *them* as is put ower me, and ower aw the rest of us.' (*HT*, Blackpool, 150)
>
> "*Him* and *me* was soon busy." (*GE*, Magwitch, 348)

In *AN* and *MC*, however, we can extract only one instance of this kind. Scadder says, "*them* an't plants of Eden's raising" (*MC*, 357).

In substandard speech of low-life London characters and dialect speakers, *as* is often employed as a relative pronoun instead of "who (or whom)," "that," or "which." This relative pronoun is also found in the speech of American characters in Dickens. *OED* (s.v. *as*, *rel. pron.*, VI. 24. a.) illustrates that *as* used as an ordinary relative is "obsolete in standard English, but common dialect in England and the United States." Examples are:

CHAPTER V STYLISTICS AND SOCIOLINGUISTICS 91

(1) *as* for "who" or "that"

"... we didn't wish to sell the lots off right away to any loafer *as* might bid." (*MC*, Scadder, 353)

"... nobody *as* goes to Eden ever comes back a-live!" (*MC*, Kedgick, 371)

"He is a man *as* will come up'ards, right side up sir?" (*MC*, Chollop, 522)

"I'm the boots *as* b'longs to the house; the other man's my man, *as* goes errands and does odd jobs." (*SB*, top-boots, 408)

"... people *as* don't know the use on 'em." (*PP*, Sam Weller, 404)

"... a 'spectable old genelman *as* lives there." (*OT*, Dodger, 48)

"One as know'd his servant see 'em theer." (*DC*, Mr. Peggotty, 499)

'Look round town ... and see the numbers o' people *as* has been broughten into bein heer.' (*HT*, Blackpool, 149)

"Which? Him *as* sent the bank-notes, Pip?" (*GE*, Gargery, 464)

(2) *as* for "whom" or "that"

"I raise the dander of my feller-critturs, *as* I wish toe serve." (*MC*, Scadder, 353)

"... her oun' 'usband, *as* she's been married to twelve year come next Easter Monday." (*SB*, Mrs. Sulliwin, 70)

"Of all the ungratefullest, and worst-disposed boys *as* ever I see." (*OT*, Mr. Bumble, 23)

(3) *as* for "which" or "that"

"It is a lot *as* should be rose in price." (*MC*, Scadder, 357)

"... there ain't a swamp in all Americay, *as* don't whip *that* small island into mush and molasses." (*MC*, Chollop, 522)

"I can't con-ceive of any spotted Painter in the bush, *as* ever was so riddled through and through as you will be." (*MC*, Chollop, 523)

"I know ... them *as* hangs up in the linen-draper's shop." (*PP*, Sam Weller, 402)

'... the mill *as* takes up so little room.' (*OT*, Dodger, 47)

"... everything in her life *as* ever had been, or *as* ever could be, and everything *as* never had been, and *as* never could be, was a-crowding on her all at once." (*DC*, Mr. Peggotty, 621)

'I mun go th' way *as* lays afore me.' (*HT*, Blackpool, 142)

"I'm a old bird now, *as* has dared all manner of traps." (*GE*, Magwitch, 332)

We cannot find *as* for "whom" in the speech of dialect speakers of Dickens, and they frequently employ a contact clause instead.

We often find the form in *-ing* preceded by the prefix *a*(-) in substandard speech in Dickens. General Choke says, "Eden hadn't need to go *a begging*[20] yet, sir," (*MC*, 348). The prefix *a* is historically a weakened form of the Old English preposition *on* in unstressed position. Krapp mentions that in this construction the forms in *-ing* are "originally verbal nouns which have been assimilated in form and, to a considerable extent, in feeling, to present participles."[21] According to *OED* (*a, prep.*[1], 13. a.) "most of the southern dialects, and the vulgar speech

---

[20] *OED* (*go, v.* III. 32. e.) regards *to go a begging* as a set phrase, and G. P. Krapp observes that "a very frequent syntactical form of contemporary popular speech is that which puts an *a* before every present participle, especially after *go*, as in *to go a-fishing, ... daddy's gone a-hunting*, etc." (*The English Language in America, Vol. II.*, 1925, p. 268)

[21] G. P. Krapp (1925) *The English Language in America, Vol. II.* pp. 268.

CHAPTER V STYLISTICS AND SOCIOLINGUISTICS 93

both in England and America retain this construction." The following examples of this construction are from the speech of American characters in Dickens:

"You air *a going*?" (*MC*, Kedgick, 371)

"I am *a going* easy." (*MC*, Chollop, 522)

"They did ex-pect you was *a goin* to settle." (*MC*, Kedgick, 536)

"... the leading Journal of the United States, now in its twelfth thousand, and still *a printing* off:—Here's the New York Sewer." (*MC*, news-boy, 256)

As well as in the speech of his American characters, this construction is constantly found in the speech of British vulgar characters and dialect speakers:

"... (my) kittle's jist *a-biling*, and the cups and sarsers ready laid." (*SB*, Mrs. Walker, 53)

'... it's not straight forerd, but always *a going* up, and nivir *a coming* down agin.' (*OT*, Dodger, 47)

"... he's *a waitin'* in the drawing-room." (*PP*, Sam Weller, 214)

"He's *a going* out with the tide." (*DC*, Mr. Peggotty, 380)

'... the mills is awlus *a goin*.' (*HT*, Blackpool, 150)

"Arthur was *a dying* and *a dying* poor and with the horrors on him, and Compeyson's wife ... was *a having* pity on him when she could, and Compeyson was *a having* pity on nothing and nobody." (*GE*, Magwitch, 346)

Mark Tapley and Mrs Gamp, both of whom are British vulgar characters in *Martin Chuzzlewit*, are especially fond of this construction[22], as G. L. Brook points out.

---

[22] G. L. Brook (1970) *The Language of Dickens*, p. 248, § 103.

Ought is sometimes used with the periphrastic auxiliary *did*. *OED* (*ought*, *v*., A. IV. 8.) labels this use of *ought* as "dialectal," "colloquial," and "vulgar." Brook claims that "since *ought* is historically the past tense of the verb *owe*, there are objections to its use as an infinitive, which even hatred of the prescriptive grammarian has not completely overcome."[23] Scadder and Captain Kedgick, "like many an English schoolboy,"[24] employ this construction:

> "You speak a-larming well in public, but you *didn't ought* to go ahead so fast in private." (*MC*, Scadder, 352)
>
> "But you *didn't ought* to have your dander ris with me, Gen'ral." (*MC*, Scadder, 353)
>
> "You *didn't ought* to have received 'em." (*MC*, Kedgick, 536)

Otto Jespersen remarks that "*do* with *ought* (*to*) is given as an Americanism in Dickens,"[25] and he quotes Scadder's examples above.

This construction is to be found in the speech of dialect speakers, but not in the speech of low-life London characters. Ham and Mr. Peggotty always use its dialectal form *doen't ought* in the present tense:

> "Howsever they come, they *didn't ought* to come, and they come from the father of lies, and work round to the same." (*GE*, Gargery, 71)
>
> "Doen't, my dear! You *doen't ought* to cry so, pretty!" (*DC*, Ham Peggotty, 289)

---

[23] G. L. Brook (1970) *The Language of Dickens*, p. 137.
[24] G. L. Brook (1970) *The Language of Dickens*, p. 137.
[25] *MEG*, Vol. V, 1940, § 25.87.

"We have had a mort of talk ... of what we ought and *doen't ought* to do." (*DC*, Mr. Peggotty, 389)

When we discuss the use of adjectives as adverbs, the historical sketch of its development is needed. The Old English adverbial endings were *-e* and *-līce*. The both endings were formed by adding *-e* to the positive degree of adjectives. G. L. Brook historically illustrates the both cases of forming adverbs from adjectives:

> There were several different ways of forming adverbs in Old English. The most common was by the addition of the ending *-e* to an adjective, as in *wide* 'widely' beside *wid* 'wide'. If the adjective ended in *-e* there was usually no distinction in form between the adjective and the adverb, and when final *-e* disappeared in pronunciation in the fifteenth century many more adjectives and adverbs came to be alike in form. This is the origin of the construction, generally regarded as ungrammatical in present-day English, of the apparent use of an adjective in place of an adverb, as in the sentence *Come quick!*
> A more distinctive way of forming adverbs in Modern English is by the use of the suffix *-ly*. Old English had a common adjectival suffix *-līc* and an adverbial suffix formed from it in the usual way by the addition of *-e*, as in *sōþlīce* 'truly' beside *sōþlīc* 'true'. Both of these suffixes have given *-ly* in Modern English, as in the adjective *kindly* and the adverb *truly*. Although we have some adjectives in *-ly*, the suffix is felt to be characteristic of adverbs, and it is still a living suffix by means of which we can form new adverbs from adjectives.[26]

H. L. Mencken suggests that "the result of this movement toward identity in form was a confusion between the two classes

---

[26] G. L. Brook (1958) *A History of the English Language*, pp. 121-22.

of words from the time of Chaucer[27] down to the Eighteenth Century one finds innumerable instances of the use of the simple adjectives as adverbs."[28]

In Shakespeare's plays we sometimes find adverbs without -*ly* endings, which are generally called "flat adverbs." We shall take up these examples from E. A. Abbott[29]:

> Which the false man do's *easie*. (*TheTragedie of Macbeth*, II. iii. 750)
> 'Tis verie true, thou didst it *excellent*: (*The Taming of the Shrew*, Induction. i. 87)
> ... for he is *equall* rau'nous
> As he is subtile, (*All is True*, I. i. 193-94)

Throughout the nineteenth century, however, we can hardly find the comment on this use in such writings of British prescriptive grammarians as R. G. Latham's *The English Language* (1841) and *A Hand-Book of the English Language* (1851).

Apart from British English, it is generally acknowledged that flat adverbs are frequently and freely used in the present-day colloquial American English. Some instances of flat adverbs are to be found in Dickens's American writings. The following examples of flat adverbs are used by his American characters or used to represent one of the features of American English by Dickens himself in a letter to Forster. As well as in the speech of his American characters, we can constantly find flat adverbs

---

[27] The following example is from *The General Prologue* to *The Canterbury Tales* (c1386): Ful *loude* he soong "Com hider, love, to me!" (l. 672)

[28] H. L. Mencken (1962) *The American Language*. p. 465.

[29] E. A. Abbott (1869, 1870², rpt. 1929) *A Shakespearian Grammar*. § 1.

in the speech of low-life British characters and dialect speakers in the other novels of Dickens:

(1) *alarming*

"You speak *a-larming* well in public, but you didn't ought to go ahead so fast in private." (*MC*, Scadder, 352)

(2) *awful*

"It is an *awful* lovely place, sure-ly." (*MC*, Kettle, 348)
"I tell you beforehand I am *awful* dull, most *awful* dull[30]." (*GE*, Gargery, 49)

(3) *complete*

... it does use you up *com-plete*. (*Let. III*, 90)

(4) *considerable*

"... it was used up *considerable*." (*MC*, Kettle, 344)
"Do they never walk in the yard?"
"*Considerable* seldom." (*AN*, gaoler, 84)
... you may have a pretty *con-siderable* damned good sort of a feeble notion that it don't fit nohow. (*Let. III*, 89)
... it ... makes you quake *considerable*. (*Let. III*, 90)

(5) *dreadful*

"That's *dreadful* true." (*MC*, Kettle, 343)
"That ... is *dreadful* true." (*MC*, Kettle, 344)
"If here ain't the Harrisburg mail at last, and *dreadful* bright and smart to look at too." (*AN*, gentleman, 139)
"Mr. Harris who was *dreadful* timid." (*MC*, Gamp, 748)
"... he not only blow'd her up *dreadful*, and swore he'd never see her again." (*SB*, Ikey, 451)

---

[30] Tanaka points out that it is interesting and noticeable that Joe always uses *awful* together with *dull*. ("Regional and Occupational Dialect of Joe Gargery," 1972, p. 177.)

(6) *easy*

"Our backs is *easy* ris." (*MC*, Chollop, 523)

"... that argument's very *easy* upset." (*SB*, undertaker, 682)

"... ven you grow as old as your father, you von't get into your veskit as *easy* as you do now, my boy." (*PP*, Tony Weller, 845)

'You'd like to be able to make pocket-handkerchiefs as *easy* as Charley Bates, won't you, my dear?' (*OT*, Fagin, 54)

(7) *frightful*

"It is an awful lovely place, sure-ly. And *frightful* wholesome, likewise!" (*MC*, Kettle, 348)

"... they blowed up quite *frightful*." (*SB*, Bung, 29)

(8) *moderate*

"One *moderate* big 'un could convey a dozen of champagne, perhaps." (*MC*, Diver, 259)

(9) *'special*

... you don't feel *'special* bright. (*Let. III*, 89)

(10) *uncommon*

"You're lookin most *uncommon* bright, sir." (*MC*, captain of *The Screw*, 259)

"I have know'd strong men obleeged to make themselves *uncommon* skase for less." (*MC*, Chollop, 523)

"She looks *uncommon* well this morning." (*SB*, Percy Noakes, 391)

"... you look so *uncommon* cheerful, and seem altogether so lively." (*PP*, Sam Weller, 601)

'She's *uncommon* strong in the arms.' (*OT*, Sikes, 104)

"It's *oncommon* kind." (*DC*, Ham Peggotty, 378)

"I'm *oncommon* fond of reading." (*GE*, Gargery, 47)

CHAPTER V   STYLISTICS AND SOCIOLINGUISTICS   99

Table 7 Flat adverbs

	American English			London English			English Dialects		
	AN	MC	Let.	SB	PP	OT	DC	HT	GE
alarming	−	+	−	−	−	−	−	−	−
awful	−	+	−	−	−	−	−	−	+
complete	−	−	+	−	−	−	−	−	−
considerable	+	+	+	−	−	−	−	−	−
dreadful	+	+	−	+	−	−	−	−	−
easy	−	+	−	+	+	+	−	−	−
frightful	−	+	−	+	−	−	−	−	−
moderate	−	+	−	−	−	−	−	−	−
'special	−	−	+	−	−	−	−	−	−
uncommon	−	+	−	+	+	+	+	−	+

As is shown in the table above, the adverbial use of *alarming, complete, considerable, moderate* and *'special* cannot be found in the speech of low-life London characters or dialect speakers dealt with in this section, but that of *uncommon* is to be extracted in all the speech except in Lancashire dialect speech in *Hard Times*. It may safely be said that the use of adjectives as adverbs is one of the salient features of American English.

Grammatical features of American English described by Dickens are not so different from substandard and dialectal British English as phonological and lexical ones. Grammatical anomalies in the speech of his American characters are closely parallel with that of both British low-life characters and dialect speakers as Brook has already mentioned.

On the other hand, judging from the present survey, the use of *ris* and *rose* instead of "raised" as past particple, of *ought* with periphrastic *didn't*, and of *alarming, complete, considerable, moderate* and *'special* as flat adverbs represent salient features of American English clearly. All of them are deeply connected with earlier stage of the English language. This phenomenon has a good deal in common with the fact that archaic or obsolete English remains in substandard and dialectal speech in Britain. As the titles of their books imply, G. P. Krapp considers American English as one of the dialects of the English language, and H. L. Mencken, on the contrary, regards it as one indigenous and independent language. All things considered, the grammatical anomalies of American English Dickens describes combine many features of both substandard and dialectal British English. In this respect Krapp's view on the English language in America is luculent and persuasive.

CHAPTER VI

Provincialisms and Americanisms

Dickens introduced a lot of English provincialisms and Americanisms to the reader through his works. He obtained the knowledge of them through his visit to the places where the dialects are spoken, the provincial glossaries, and the letters from the correspondents.[1] Some of the preceding studies have already referred to some of the English provincialisms and Americanisms, but not all of them. In this chapter we shall examine all the provincialisms and Americanisms consulting *EDD*, *OED*, and provincial dictionaries and glossaries.

6.1 Yorkshire provincialisms in *Nicholas Nickleby*
In contrast to *David Copperfield* and *Hard Times*, Dickens did not possess any glossarial references for Yorkshire provincialisms when he wrote *Nicholas Nickleby*. Consequently we seldom encounter Yorkshire words and phrases while his keen ear for the dialect helped him to reproduce Yorkshire accents in the mouth of John Browdie. N. Page asserts that Browdie's speech "contains few dialect words or expressions,"[2] but we can find a few Yorkshire provincialisms in the speech of

---

[1] We have already discussed this point in detail in Chapter I.
[2] N. Page (1988) *Speech in the English Novel*, p. 64.

Browdie and the guard on the stage-coach. Let us start with *afeard*.

John Browdie employs *afeard* twice in the negative sentence: 'Dean't be *afeard*, mun,' (158) and 'Dang it, thee bean't *afeard* o' schoolmeasther's takkin cold, I hope?' (508). The variant spelling *afeared* is found in 'Dinnot be *afeared* on it.' (826). *OED* (s.v. *afeard, ppl. a.*) gives us some information that it is "used more than 30 times by Shakespeare, but rare in literature after 1700, having been supplanted by *afraid*," and that "it survives everywhere in the popular speech, either as *afeard*, or *'feard*; and has again been used in poetry by W. Morris." *EDD* (s.v. *afeard, adj.*) suggests that it is found throughout Sc.[3], Irel. and Eng.

Afore, whose place is now taken by *before*, is used by Browdie in three ways: one is used as a conjunction[4], 'But if thee keep'st a good hart, thee'lt be at whoam *afore* they know thee'st gotten off.' (509); another as an adverb, 'she coom a deal closer and squeedged a deal harder than she'd deane afore.' (543); and the other as a preposition, 'Yorkshire schools have been shown up at 'Soizes *afore* noo,' (551). *EDD* (s.v. *afore*) shows that the word is generally used in various dialects of Sc., Ir., and Eng. *OED* (s.v. *afore, adv., prep.,* and *conj.*) comments that *afore* is "common in the dialects generally as well as, in 'vulgar' London speech, and in nautical language".

---

[3] The abbreviations of regions, counties, and directions used in the book are in accordance with those in *EDD* and *EDG*, and they are shown in "Abbreviations" above.

[4] *OED* (s.v. *afore*, C. *conj.*) suggests that the use of *afore* as a conjunction is "elliptical use of the prep. of time, as *afore the time that* he came, *afore that* he came, *afore* he came."

CHAPTER VI PROVINCIALISMS AND AMERICANISMS

In other writings of Dickens, *afore* is often to be heard in the speech of such dialect speakers as Mr. Peggotty (266, etc. 33 times) and Ham Peggotty (387, 390, 397, 631) in *David Copperfield*, both of whom employ East Anglia dialect, Stephen Blackpool (141,142,143, 151, 162) in *Hard Times*, who speaks broad Lancashire dialect, and Joe Gargery (47, 72, 461, 465) in *Great Expectations*, who lives near Rochester in Kent, and in the speech of such low-life London characters as Tony Weller (327, etc. 10 times) in *Pickwick Papers*, and Bill Sikes (77, etc. 5 times) in *Oliver Twist*.

To gang, according to *EDD* (s.v. *gang*, v.), signifies "to go" or "to walk, travel on foot" and is used in Sc. Ire. Nhb. Dur. Cum. Wm. Yks. Lan. Der. Lin. and e.An. *OED* (s.v. *gang*, v.[1]) labels this verb as *Obs*. exc. *Sc* and *dial*, and illustrates that "In Sc. *gang* is now used chiefly in the inf. and pres. tense, while *go* furnishes the pa. tense (*gaed*) and the pa. pple." Dickens's application of *to gang* is paralleled to *OED*'s information. Browdie uses the verb in the infinitive: 'let 'un *gang* on, let 'un *gang* on.' (108); 'Do ye *gang* whoam wi' me?' (111) and 'But I think they'll a' *gang* daft,' (825): in the present tense: 'As we *gang* awa' fra' Lunnun tomorrow neeght...' (582); 'But I think they'll a' *gang* daft,' (825); 'there's no *ganging* oot to neeght, noo,' (552): and in the imperative: '*Gang* awa' to Lunnun afoot!' (157); and '... *gang* to the Sarah's Head, mun.' (502). It is also used in the Preface to the 1848 edition: 'But I'm dom'd if ar can *gang* to bed ...' (xliv) and in the speech of the guard: 'Dang 'em, they'll *gang* whoam fast eneaf!' (The guard, 53).

The conjunction *gin* corresponds to *if* and is employed in

Sc. Nhb. Dur. Cum. Yks. Lan., according to *EDD* (s.v. *gin, prep.* and *conj.*). There is one example of *gin* in Browdie's speech: 'Ye'd never coom near it '*gin* you thried for twolve moonths.' (501). *OED* (s.v. *gin, conj.*) labels this conjunction as *Sc.* and *dial.*

The adjective *daft* is used by Browdie once: 'But I think they'll a' *gang* daft,' (825). *EDD* (s.v. *daft, adj.*) suggests that the word signifies "silly, stupid, foolish" and is "in *gen.* dial. and colloq. use in Sc. Irel. and Eng." This adjective is now chiefly used in Scotland and northern counties, according to *OED* (s.v. *deft, a.*).

The phrase *I reckon*[5], whose meaning is "to think, suppose," is used parenthetically or finally in Browdie's speech:

> 'Monsther!—Ye're aboot right theer, *I reckon*, Mrs. Browdie,' (501)
> 'She wean't be a bride in a hurry, *I reckon*.' (546).

According to *OED* (s.v. *reckon, v.* 6.b.), this phrase is "formerly in literary Eng. use; still common in Eng. dialects, and current in the southern States of America in place of the northern *I guess*."[6]

Table 8 Yorkshire provincialisms in *Nicholas Nickleby*

	OED	EDD
afeard	Everywhere in the popular speech.	Throughout Sc. Irel. and Eng.
afore	Arch. and *dial.*	In var. dial. of Sc. Ir. and Eng.

---

[5] *EDD* (s.v. *reckon, v.* 2.) labels this verb as "Var. dial. and colloq. uses in Sc. Eng. And Amer."

[6] For the use of "I guess" and "I reckon", see §6.5.1, pp. 136-38.

gan	*Obs.* exc. *Sc* and *dial.*	Sc. Ire. Nhb. Dur. Cum. Wm. Yks. Lan. Der. Lin. and e.An.
gin	*Sc.* and *dial.*	Sc. Nhb. Dur. Cum. Yks. Lan.
daft	Now chiefly *Sc.* and *north.*	In *gen.* dial. and colloq. use in Sc. Irel. and Eng.
I reckon	Still common in Eng. dialects.	Var. dial. and colloq. uses in Sc. Eng. and Amer.

6.2 Lancashire provincialisms in *Hard Times*

We have already seen in Introduction, Dickens's major source for the dialect vocabulary[7] used in *Hard Times* is from *A View of the Lancashire Dialect*[8] by 'Tim Bobbin', the pseudonym of John Collier, first published in 1746. Dickens owned a copy of the 1818 edition[9]. P. Ingham argues that though the conversation between Tummus and Meary "must have been unintelligible to Dickens, it is evident that the Glossary was invaluable"[10]. Another source introduced by N. Page[11] is the Reverent William Gaskell's *Two Lectures on the Lancashire*

---

[7] See A. Easson "Dialect in Dickens's *Hard Times*," *Notes and Queries*, 23, pp. 412-413, and P. Ingham (1986) "Dialect as 'Realism': *Hard Times* and the Industrial Novel," *The Review of English Studies*, 37, pp. 518-27.

[8] G. L. Brook illustrates this book thus: "The first edition of *A View of the Lancashire Dialect* was short but the author later added several episodes. The book belongs to the literature of low life and roguery. The two characters are Tummus and Meary, but Meary is clearly subordinate, as may be seen by her comparative taciturnity: she has 44 lines to Tummus's 320. The book was remarkably popular and had a good deal of influence on later Lancashire dialect authors; more than sixty editions have been published." (*English Dialect*, 1978, p. 193)

[9] J. H. Stonehouse (1935) *Reprints of the Catalogues of the Libraries of Charles Dickens and W. M. Thackeray etc.*, p. 111.

[10] P. Ingham (1986) "Dialect as 'Realism': *Hard Times* and the Industrial Novel," p. 522.

[11] N. Page (1988) *Speech in the English Novel*, pp. 68-68.

Dialect, published in 1854 in the fifth edition of his wife's *Mary Barton*. She can find no striking correspondences between Blackpool's speech and Mr. Gaskell's *Lectures*, and she regards them as "only of marginal use."[12]

The word *afore*, whose place is now taken by *before*, is used by Stephen Blackpool, Sleary, and the chairman of a labour meeting. It is used as an adverb (143), as a preposition (141, 142, Sleary 292), and as a conjunction (150-1, 162, chairman 142, Sleary 280, Sleary 292). The *EDG* ("Index", s.v. *afore*) gives [əfoə(r)] and [əfuə(r)] as the pronunciation for s.Lan. *MW* gives a variant form, *ofore*, but *DSL* is silent, while *GLD* lists *afore* as an adverb, a preposition and a conjunction.

Dickens puts two dialectal forms, *ahind* (65) and *ahint* (149, 274), as a preposition instead of *behind* into the mouth of Blackpool. *Ahind* is, according to *EDD*, heard in Sc., n.Ir., and all the counties to Chs. and Lin., and *ahint* is, according to the *EDG* ("Index", s.v. *ahind*), found in Abd., Per., Ayr., Lth., Edb., Peb., Nhb., n.Dur., n.Cum., and Wm., while these forms are recognised in neither *MW*, *DSL* nor *GLD*.

The chairman of a labour meeting speaks aloud to his fellow workmen, "You know him *awlung o'* his misfort'ns, and his good name." (141). Blackpool says, "Thou know'st ... how she died, young and misshapen, *awlung o'* sickly air as had'n no need to be, an' *awlung o'* working people's miserable homes." (272-3). As well as the dialectal form, a standard one is to be recognised in his speech: "Well! She went bad—soon.

---

[12] Ingham (1986) "Dialect as 'Realism': *Hard Times* and the Industrial Novel," p. 522.

Not *along of* me." (71). *Awlung o'*, which is a dialectal form of *along of*, denotes "owing to, on account of." *OED* (s.v. *along, a.*[1]) illustrates that this phrase is "common in London, and southern dialects generally," while *EDD* (s.v. *along of, on, with*) points out that it is also found in all northern counties. The phrase is to be found in the speech of Mr. Peggotty[13] and Mrs. Gummidge (*DC*, 34) in *David Copperfield*, and of Miss Price, a daughter of a Yorkshire miller (*NN*, 110) and Browdie (*NN*, 545) in *Nicholas Nickleby*.

The Rev. William Gaskell tells us an interesting story about *dree*:

> Lancashire people talk of "dree rain," which often puzzles those who fancy it is a corruption of "dry." And they say it rains "dreely," meaning that it is continuous and enduring.[14]

Stephen uses the adjective together with *long* twice: "I were married on Eas'r Monday nineteen year *sin*, long and *dree*." (71), and "I ha' been—dreadful, and *dree*, and long, my dear—but 'tis ower now." (272). This word pair is to be found in one of the quotations in *OED* (s.v. *dree, a.*, 3), which is from Fergusson's *Leith Races Poems*, a1774: "There's *lang* and *dreech* contestin." *EDD* (s.v. *dree, adj.*) illustrates that the adjective is heard in Sc., Ir., Nhb., Lakel., Yks., Lan., Chs., Der., Not., Lin., Lei., and War.

The conjunction *ere*, which always appears with the addition of *ever*, is found six times in Stephen's speech (72, 143, 148,

---

[13] *Along of* appears in pp. 384, 618, 619 and 622, while *along o'* twice in p. 34.

[14] W. Gaskell (1850) *Two Lectures on the Lancashire Dialect*, p. 22.

150, 155, 159). This phrase functions as a conjunction and it has the same meaning as *before*. *EDD* ("Supplement", s.v. *ere, adv.*) records that s.Lan. is the only place where *ere ever* is to be heard.

Stephen shows his respect to "great fok" who can be set free from their unfortunate marriages, and says, "*fair faw* 'em a'! I wishes 'em no hurt!" (73). He would like to marry Rachael, so he asks Mr. Bounderby how ordinary people like him can be set free from their dreadful wives. *Fair faw* (= *fair fall*) is used as the optative denoting "may good befall". *EDD* (s.v. *fair*, 15. *sb.* 2.a.) quotes the examples from Sc., Nhb., w.Yks., and Chs. *GLD* makes no reference to the phrase.

Fewtrils whose meaning is "little things, trifles" occurs in Blackpool's following speech: "These five year I ha' paid her. I ha' gotten decent *fewtrils* about me agen" (72). The noun is always used as a plural invariable noun. It is, according to *EDD* (s.v. *fewtrils, sb.*), found only in Lan.

The noun *fratch* stands for "a disagreement, a quarrel". Stephen has never had a quarrel since he was born, and says, "I ha' never had no *fratch* afore, sin ever I were born." (143). We cannot recognise *fratch* in *DSL*. *EDD* (s.v. *fratch*, 6. *sb.*) records some examples of Nhb., Cum., Wm., Yks., Lan., Lin., and Bdf.

OED (s.v. *fro, prep.* 1.) illustrates that ON *frá* corresponds to OE *fram,* and both *fro* and *fra* are equal to *from* in all senses. Dickens employs four types of spelling: *fro, fro', fra,* and *fra'*. The apostrophes attached to *fro* and *fra* suggest Dickens regards the forms as the omission of *m* from *fram* or *from*. Stephen uses *fro* seven times (141 twice, 143, 150 three

CHAPTER VI   PROVINCIALISMS AND AMERICANISMS   109

times, and 154); *fro'* four times (73, 159, and 272 twice); and both *fra* and *fra'* once respectively (72). Rachael uses *fro'* once (65). *Fro* and *fro'* are heard in Yks., Lan., Chs., Der., and Lin., according to *EDD* (s.v. *fro*, I. 14.). *Fra* and *fra'* are both used in Sc., Nhb., Dur., Wm., Yks., Lan., and Lin., according to *EDD* (s.v. *fro*, I. 3.). In *Nicholas Nickleby*, John Browdie twice uses *fra'* (582, 827), whom Dickens intends to create as a Yorkshire dialect speaker. When he wrote manuscript, he adopted *fra* instead of *fro* and *fro'* except the examples in pp. 65 and 154. The instance in p. 159, is added to the corrected proof.[15]

Haply is an adverb with the meaning of "perhaps". It occurs in the speech of Rachael (84) and Stephen (73, 143, 147, 154). *EDD* (s.v. *haply, adv.*) regards it to be obsolete and compiles its records from Chs. and Der. Neither *DSL* nor *GLD* is silent about the adverb. *MW* gives *happly*, not *haply*. At the stage of manuscript, Dickens adopted *happly*[16] to the instances in pp. 73 and 84 instead of *haply*, which provides conclusive evidence that Dickens's major source for the dialect is *MW*, because the spelling, *happly* is only found in *MW*.

In the speech of Slackbridge, we find the predicative use of an adjective *hetter*, whose meaning is "keen" or "eager". This is well applied for representing the aggressive character of Slackbridge who is a demagogic agitator of the United

---

[15] These corrections and additions are suggested in "Textual Notes" to *Hard Times* (A Norton Critical Edition), edited by F. Kaplan and S. Monod, 2002, pp. 252, 258, 259, and 260.

[16] The corrections are introduced in "Textual Notes" to *Hard Times* (A Norton Critical Edition), edited by F. Kaplan and S. Monod, 2002, pp. 252 and 253.

Aggregate Tribunal, a trade union active in Coketown, and makes Stephen's refusal to become its member in public. Examples are "our friend Slackbridge, who may be a little over *hetter* in this business" (141); "Slackbridge, y'or over *hetter* in't; y'or a goen too fast!" (248). *EDD* (s.v. *hetter*, *adj*.) shows that it appears in Nhb., Yks., Lan., and Der.

Hey-go-mad is "a phrase expressive of boisterous excitement, and sometimes used as adjective," says *OED* (s.v. *hey*, 3. b.). *DSL* (s.v. *heigh-go-mad*) glosses it as "mad, shouting or galloping like mad. Stephen says to Mrs. Pegler, "Yo'r not fearfo' o' her. Yo was *hey-go-mad* about her, but an hour sin." (157). *EDD* (s.v. *heigh-go-mad*) tells us that the compound adjective is heard in Yks. and Lan. It is not to be found in *GLD*.

Hottering mad is almost the same meaning as *hey-go-mad*. Both *MW* and *DSL* gloss it as "very mad", but *GLD* is silent. This phrase is also, according to *EDD* (s.v. *hotter*, 5. 2.), recognised in Yks. and Lan. "Haply, but for her (=Rachael), I should ha' gone *hottering mad*." (73), exclaimed Stephen who is vexed at his dreadful drunken wife.

Mrs. Pegler asks Stephen whether Mr. Bounderby is healthy, and he returns, "He were ett'n and drinking—as large and as loud as a *Hummobee*." (78). *Hummobee* refers to a "hummer-bee", according to *EDD* (s.v. *hummer-bee*, *sb*.), and is used in Lan., Chs., and nw. Der. *MW* (s.v. *hummobee*) defines it as "the large ground bee."

Rachael applies *lad* familiarly and endearingly to Stephen as a vocative (65, 68). She calls him *poor lad* (159, 266). She frequently employs "the poor *lad*" referring to Stephen,

CHAPTER VI   PROVINCIALISMS AND AMERICANISMS

who is named as a thief in print, as a subjective (250, 251) and an objective (159, 252, 253). Her affection and sympathy towards Stephen are to be found in her use of "the poor dear *lad*" (256). When her indignation against the ill use of him marks the climax, she cries, "Stephen! The honestest *lad*, the truest lad, the best!" (250). Mr. Bounderby (71) and the chairman (142) also call him *lad*. Mr. Gradgrind (31) reckons him as "a very obtrusive *lad*" and Mrs. Pegler considers him as "a steady *lad*".

According to *OED* (s.v. *lass*, 1. a.), in the northern and north midland dialects, *lass* referring to a girl is the ordinary word; while in the southern counties it has little or no popular currency, so *EDD* (s.v. *lass, sb.* 1.) puts a question mark before Ken. and Som. Stephen applies this term to Rachael (65, 66) as she applies *lad* to him. He attributes epithets to it, and call her "dear *lass*" (66) and "beloved *lass*" (274). Mrs. Pegler applies "this good *lass*" (153) three times to Rachael when she is talking with Stephen.

Blackpool is perplexed with the increasing suspicion thrown on him by Tom Gradgrind who stole a large sum of money from his employer, Mr. Bounderby. The weaver has, however, left his work, and said with truth, "I'm more *leetsome*, Rachael, under 't, than I could'n ha' believed." (155). The adjective *leetsome* is a dialectal form for *lightsome*, meaning "light-heated, cheerful, merry". *EDD* (s.v. *lightsome, adj.*², 2.) suggests that the dialectal form occurs in Nhb., Dur., Cum., Wm., Yks., and Lan.

OED (s.v. *lief, adj.* 1.d.) introduces various constructions concerning *lief* and states that it is used "in various constructions with *have*...: *I had as lief as, I had liefer* (*than*), †*liefest*, with object a *n., inf.* phrase (with or without *to*), or subordinate clause". In Blackpool's speech, we recognise the constructions with two types of object: "I'd *liefer* you'd hearn the truth concernin myseln." (141); and "I'd *leefer* not coom to 't, sir." (147). Strange enough, Dickens applies two different spellings in the same number of *Household Words*, No. 220, Saturday, June 10, 1854. According to *EDD* (s.v. *liefer, adv.*), the former form is in general dialectal use in Sc., Ir. and Eng., while the latter appears in Sc., ne. Yks., Lan., Chs., and nw. Der.

Blackpool's innocent shyness appears when he makes his address in front of his fellow workers at a meeting of a trade union: "I never cud'n speak afore so monny, wi'out bein *moydert* and muddled." (141). The past participle has almost the same meaning as its fellow word, *muddled*. *Moydert* is a dialectal variation for *moidered* and this dialectal form, notes *EDD* (s.v. *moither*, 1. *v.*), occurs in Cum., w.Yks., Lan., Chs., and Der.

We have nine examples of *mun* in Blackpool's speech. *OED* (s.v. *mun, v.*) illustrates that "*mun* is an auxiliary verb, followed by infinitive without *to*" and that "in modern dialects equivalent to 'must'". *EDD* (s.v. *mun, v.*[1], 1.) defines that it is used in Sc. and Eng. down to Oxf. and Brks. Examples are:

> "I *mun* be ridden o' her." (73)
> "I *mun* be ridden o' this woman." (74)
> "I *mun* mak th' best on." (142)
> "I *mun* go th' way as lays afore me." (142)
> "I *mun* tak my leave o' aw heer." (142)
> "I *mun* do 't." (143)

"Anyways it *mun* be done. I *mun* turn my face fro Coketown." (154)
"I *mun* quit this part, and try another." (159)
"we *mun* bear and forbear." (273).

OED (s.v. *nigh, adv.*) suggests that the adverb *near* in all senses has taken the place of *nigh* except in archaic or dialectal use, and is used with dependent dative, or followed by *to*. The instances in *EDD* (s.v. *nigh*, 4. *adv.*) indicates that *nigh* is heard in Sc., Wxf., Nhb., n. & w.Yks., Lan., Der., Shr., Wor., s.Oxf., Nrf., Suf., Sus., n.Wil., w.Som., e.Dev., and Cor. The following examples are all from Blackpool's speech: "Not drawin *nigh* to fok, wi' kindness and patience an' cheery ways, that so draws *nigh* to one another in their monny troubles." (151); "Thou'rt not like to forget her now, and me so *nigh* her." (272). The adverb is not listed in either *MW*, *DSL*, or *GLD*.

Dickens puts *nighbut*, which means "nearly", into the mouth of Stephen (73), but he takes great pains to decide its spelling. *Nighb't* is recognised in the manuscript, but omitted from the first corrected proof. Then we find the addition of a corrected form, *nighbut* in the second corrected proof. To our surprise, when he publishes *Hard Times* in *Household Words*, he adopts *nigh-bout*. Finally, however, he adopts *nighbut* for the first edition in 1854.[17] On the other hand, Dickens makes no corrections for Stephen's use of *nigh 'bout* (161), which suggests that he considers *nigh 'bout* as two words, *nigh* and *about*. *OED* (s.v. *nigh*, IV. *adv.* 12. c.) gives us "nigh about"

---

[17] "Textual Notes" to *Hard Times* (A Norton Critical Edition), edited by F. Kaplan and S. Monod, 2002, p.251. See Chapter II, §2.3, pp. 23-4.

and "nighbut". *EDD* (s.v. *nigh*, 6.) gives us *nigh-abouts* and consider it as a compound word. *MW*, *DSL*, and *GLD* are all silent about these forms.

"I ha' *nobbut* work to live by." (143), said Blackpool. *GLD* (s.v. *nobbut*) regards *nobbut* as "a peculiar negative and emphatic form of the conjunction *but*". It signifies "only, merely, just". *EDD* (s.v. *nobbut*, 1. *adv.*) indicates that it is recognised in Sc., Ir., Nhb., Dur., Cum., Wm., Yks., Lan., Chs., Der., Lin., Lei., War., Glo., Bdf., Hnt., and e.An.

Sin is a contracted form of *sithen* and functions as an adverb and a conjunction with the same meaning as *since*. We can find two examples of *sin* as an adverb in the speech of Stephen: "I were married on Eas'r Monday nineteen year *sin*, long and dree." (71); and "Yo was hey-go-mad about her, but an hour *sin*." (157). Blackpool employs *sin* as a conjunction with the meaning "from or since that time that", which sometimes followed by *ever*: "I never had nowt to say, not fitten for a born lady to year, *sin* I were born mysen." (71); "wheerever can I go, I who ha' worked *sin* I were no heighth at aw, in Coketown heer?" (143); "I have written to him once before *sin* he went away." (251); "I ha' never had no fratch afore, *sin* ever I were born." (143); "yo ... never had'n no reason in us *sin* ever we were born." (150); and "when ha' we not heern, I am sure, *sin* ever we can call to mind, o' th' mischeevos strangers!" (150). He also uses the conjunction with the meaning "seeing or considering that": "I'd leefer not coom to 't, sir; but *sin* you put th' question ... I'll answer." (147). *OED* labels *sin* as "Now *Sc.* and *north. dial.*" and *EDD* states that it is in general dialectal use in Sc., Ir., and Eng.

CHAPTER VI PROVINCIALISMS AND AMERICANISMS

Stephen's use of *Strike o' day* (141) denoting "daybreak" is very controversial. *OED* (s.v. *strike, n.* 6.c.) labels this phrase as obsolete or spurious, and notes that if it is genuine, perhaps it refers to "the striking of the hour", but that it is possibly a mistake of Grose, followed by Dickens, for *shrike of day*. *OED* gives two examples for the phrase: one is from Francis Grose's *A Provincial Glossary* (1790), and the other from Blackpool's. In addition to *OED*'s quotations, *EDD* (s.v. *strike, sb.*[1], 1.1.) records one more extraction from F. E. Taylor's *The Folk Speech of South Lancashire* (1901). The phrase is not listed in either *MW*, *DSL*, or *GLD*.

Judging from the study above and Table 9 below, *fair faw, haply, nighbut, nigh 'bout* are not regarded as the dialectal vocabulary in Lancashire by *EDD* and *GLD*. Besides *DSL* and *GLD*, *MW* is silent about *nighbut* and *nigh 'bout*, which made Dickens so much confused when he decided its forms, because *MW* was major source for his rendering Lancashire dialect. Many of the terms, however, are to be regarded as Lancashire dialect from the evidence shown by the dictionaries and references.

We can find hundreds of words and phrases of Lancashire dialect in the Glossary of *MW*. The number of the vocabulary used in *Hard Times* is no more than twenty-six out of them. It is true that these terms play an important part to pour some local flavours into the text, but in the speeches of dialect speakers there coexist standard and dialectal vocabulary, which has sometimes caused caustic remarks by literary scholars and philologists on his rendering Lancashire dialect.

Table 9 Lancashire provincialisms in *Hard Times*

	MW	DSL	GLD	OED, EDD, EDG
afore (*adv.*, *prep.*, *conj.*)	*ofore*	—	*afore* (*adv.*, *prep.*, *conj.*)	General use in various dialects of Sc., Ir., and Eng. (*EDD*, s.v. *afore*)
ahind *ahint*	*behint,* *behunt,* *behund*	*behúnt,* *behúnd,* *behínt,* *be-índ*	—	Sc., n.Ir. and all the n.counties to Chs. and Lin. (*EDD*, s.v. *ahind*) Abd., Per., Ayr., Lth., Edb., Peb., Nhb., n.Dur., n.Cum., Wm. (*EDG*, "Index", s.v. *ahind*)
along of *awlung o'*	*awlung*	*awlúng*	*along,* *alung*	Common in London, and southern dialects generally. (*OED*, *along*, *a.*[1]) All n. counties. (*EDD*, *along of, on, with*)
dree	*dree*	*dree* "a dree road"	*dree*	Sc., Ir., Nhb., Lakel., Yks., Lan., Chs., Der., Not., Lin., Lei., War. (*EDD*, s.v. *dree, a.*)
ere ever	*ere ever*	—	—	s. Lan. (*EDD*, "Supplement", s.v. *ere, adv.*)
fair faw	*fair-faw*	*fair fo,* *fair fall*	—	Sc., Nhb., w.Yks., Chs. (*EDD*, s.v. *fair*, 15. *sb.* 2.a.)
fewtrils	*fewtrils*	*fewtrils*	*fewtrils*	Lan. (*EDD*, s.v. *fewtrils, sb.*)
fratch	*fratch*		*fratch*	Nhb., Cum., Wm., Yks., Lan., Lin., Bdf. (*EDD*, s.v. *fratch*, 6. *sb.*)
fro, fro' *fra, fra'*	*fro*	*fro*	—	Yks., Lan., Chs., Der., and Lin. (*EDD*, s.v. *fro, prep.* and *adv.*, I. 14.) Sc., Nhb., Dur., Wm., Yks., Lan., Lin. (*EDD*, s.v. *fro, prep.* and *adv.*, I. 3.)
haply	*happly*	—	—	Chs. and Der. (*EDD*, s.v.

CHAPTER VI PROVINCIALISMS AND AMERICANISMS

haply, adv.)

hetter	*hetter*	*hetter*	—	Nhb., Yks., Lan., Der. (*EDD*, s.v. *hetter, adj.*)
hey-go-mad	*hey-go-mad*	*heigh-go-mad*	—	Yks., Lan. (*EDD*, s.v. *heigh-go-mad*)
hotter	*hottering-mad*	*hotterin'-mad*	*hotterin'-mad*	Yks., Lan. (*EDD*, s.v. *hotter, v.* and *sb.*[1], 5.2.)
hummobee	*hummo-bee*	*hummo-bee*	*humma-bee*	Lan., Chs., nw. Der. (*EDD*, s.v. *hummer-bee, sb.*)
lad	*lad*	*lad*	—	Sc., Nhb., Dur., Yks., Lan. (*EDD*, s.v. *lad, sb.*[1])
lass	—	*lass*	—	Sc., Ir., Nhb., Dur., Yks., Lan., Chs., Lin., ?Ken., ?Som. (*EDD*, s.v. *lass, sb.* 1.)
leetsome	*leetsome*	*leetsum*	*leetsome*	Nhb., Dur., Cum., Wm., Yks., Lan. (*EDD*, s.v. *lightsome, adj.*[2], 2.)
liefer *leefer*	*leefer*	*leefer, liever*	—	*Liefer* is in general dialectal use in Sc., Ir. and Eng., while *leefer* appears in Sc., ne. Yks., Lan., Chs., and nw. Der. (*EDD*, s.v. *liefer, adv.*)
moydert	*moydert*	*moydert (ppl.)*	*moider, moither*	Cum., w.Yks., Lan., Chs., Der. (*EDD*, s.v. *moither*, 1. *v.*)
mun	*mun, munt*	*mun, munt*	*mun, munt*	Sc. and Eng. down to Oxf. and Brks. (*EDD*, s.v. *mun, v.*[1], 1.)
nigh	—	—	—	Sc., Wxf., Nhb., n. & w.Yks., Lan., Der., Shr., Wor., s.Oxf., Nrf., Suf., Sus., n.Wil., w.Som., e.Dev., Cor. (*EDD*, s.v. *nigh*, 4. *adv.*)
nighbut *nigh'bout*	—	—	—	s. Hmp. (*EDD*, s.v. *nigh*, 6. *Comb.* 1.)

118   Charles Dickens and Literary Dialect

nobbut	—	nobbut, nobbo	nobbut	Sc., Ir., Nhb., Dur., Cum., Wm., Yks., Lan., Chs., Der., Lin., Lei., War., Glo., Bdf., Hnt., e.An. (*EDD*, s.v. *nobbut*, 1. *adv.*)
sin, adv. *sin, conj.*[1] *sin, conj.*[2]	*sin*	*sinn*	*sin'*	General dialectal use in Sc., Ir., Eng. (*EDD*, s.v. *sin, adv, prep.,* and *conj.*)
Strike o' day	—	—	—	n.Cy, s.Lan. (*EDD*, s.v. *strike, sb.*[1], 1.1.)

6.3 East Anglia provincialisms in *David Copperfield*

Dickens's glossarial source for his rendering East Anglia provincialisms is Edward Moor's *Suffolk Words and Phrases* (1823) as is shown in the first chapter of this book. In this section we shall enumerate and discuss East Anglia words and phrases used in *David Copperfield*, making frequent reference to *Moor, Forby, OED,* and *EDD*. The main contributor to East Anglia provincialisms is undoubtedly Mr. Peggotty. Ham Peggotty, Clara Peggotty, and Mrs. Gummidge sometimes use them.

Mr. Peggotty used *afeerd* three times in the affirmative[18] and three times in the negative[19], in all the cases of which this adjective is spelt with *afeerd*, not *afeard* as in *Moor*. Dickens applied this form to Mr. Peggotty on the analogy of his frequent use of such spellings as *heer, heerd, theer* and *wheer*. *Moor*

---

[18] "You'll be a solitary woman heer, I'm *afeerd*!" (391) / "I was *afeerd* it was too late." (497) / "I'm *afeerd* I couldn't hardly bear as she should be told I done that." (631)

[19] "You ain't *afeerd* of Em'ly not being took good care on, *I* know." (378) / "... you han't no call to be *afeerd* of me ..." (390) / "Doen't be *afeerd*! It's Dan'l!" (500)

CHAPTER VI   PROVINCIALISMS AND AMERICANISMS   119

(s.v. *afeard*) shows that *afeard* is an "old and good word for *afraid*[20]" and "is still much used in Suffolk; as it is by Shakespeare, and other old writers." *OED* (s.v. *afeard, ppl. a.*) gives us more information that it is "used more than 30 times by Shakespeare, but rare in literature after 1700, having been supplanted by *afraid*," and that "it survives everywhere[21] in the popular speech, either as *afeard*, or *'feard*; and has again been used in poetry by W. Morris."

One of the most mysterious dialect words in Mr. Peggotty's speech is the verb to *arrize*: "I have thowt of it oftentimes, but I can't *arrize* myself of it, no matters." (578) There is no entry or explanation of this word in *Moor*, *Forby*, *OED*, or *EDD*. G. L. Brook glosses *arrize oneself* as "to make up one's mind."[22] Nina Burgis demonstrates that this word "may well be mistake of Dickens's for 'avize' or 'awize', a word close in sound and which fits the context," and that the printer of the first volume edition of this book (1850), "puzzled by word, drew attention to it by underlining and writing 'qy' in the margin; but Dickens firmly crossed out the query."[23] I, however, claim that *arrize* is a dialectal variant of *arise* or *araise*, both of which are much closer in sound and fit the context much more than *avize* or *awize*.

---

[20] In this respect *Moor* is wrong. *Forby* (s.v. *afeard, adj.*) quotes "This wyf was nat *afered* nor *affrayed*," from "The Shipman's Tale" (l. 400) in *Canterbury Tales* and points out the difference between the significations of *afeard* and *afraid* in Chaucer's time from the origins of the two words.

[21] *EDD* (s.v. *afeard, adj.*) suggests that it is found throughout Sc., Irel. and Eng.

[22] G. L. Brook (1970) *The Language of Dickens*, p. 118.

[23] "Introduction" to the Clarendon Dickens edition of *David Copperfield*, 1981, p. lv.

There are three entries concerning *bahd's neezing* in *Moor*: one is in *bahd*, "A bird—'bahds-neezen' birds-nesting;" another in *neest*, "Nest—'bahds-neest;'" and the other in *neezen*, "or *bahd's-neezing*—seeking bird's nest." H. Kökeritz records [ˈbʌdznẹːzn] for the Suffolk pronunciation of the verb *bird's-nest*.[24] The meaning of this word is glossed into the text:

> "Unless my wits is gone a *bahd's neezing*"—by which Mr. Peggotty meant to say, bird's-nesting—"this morning, 'tis along of me as you a going to quit us." (*DC*, 619)

Moor (s.v. *beein*) defines *beein* as "A home—a place to *be in*," and quotes "If I could but git a *beein*, I can fisherate for myself," which is a good deal similar to the second citation below. *EDD* (s.v. *being, sb.*, 2.) cites the last example below as an example for Norfolk dialect.

> "... I shall have enough to do to keep a *Beein* for you" (Mrs. Gummidge meant a home), "again you come back—to keep a *Beein* here for any that may hap to come back, Dan'l." (Mrs. Gummidge, 391)
>
> "... my sister might ... find Missis Gummidge give her a leetle trouble now-and-again. Theerfur 'tan't my intentions to moor Missis Gummidge 'long with them, but to find a *Beein'* fur her wheer she can fisherate for herself." (A *Beein'* signifies, in that dialect, a home, and to fisherate is to provide.)(Mr. Peggotty, 625)
>
> "We was living then in a solitary place, but among the beautifullest trees, and with the roses a-covering our *Beein*[25] to the roof." (Mr. Peggotty, 743)

---

[24] "Glossary" to *The Phonology of the Suffolk Dialect*, Uppsala University Uppsala, 1932, p. 248.

[25] *Bein'* was selected in *Charles Dickens Edition* in 1867 (See, footnotes to p. 743). *The New Oxford Illustrated Dickens Edition* chose *Bein'*.

CHAPTER VI   PROVINCIALISMS AND AMERICANISMS   121

On 7 August 1849, Dickens received a letter from the Rev. George Frederick Hill, in which we can find Hill's suggestion of Dickens's misuse of *bo'* for *bor*.[26] The absence of its entry in *Moor* might have caused his misuse. The etymology of this term is OE *(he)búr* as in *neighbour*. *OED* (s.v. *bor*, n.) demonstrates that this is "an East Anglian form of address." Brook glosses it as "term of endearment to a child."[27] *Bor'* is always preceded by "Mas'r Davy" when Ham Peggotty addresses to David: "Mas'r Davy *bor'*" (88, 90, 121, 122); "Mas'r Davy *bor*" (266). *EDD* (s.v. *bor*, sb.) suggests that it is heard in Cmb., Nrf., Suf., and Ess.

The verb *to clicket*, according to *Moor* (s.v. *clicket*), "is applied to the garrulity and chattering of women and children." *EDD* (s.v. *clicket*, v.¹, 8) defines that it is used only in East Anglia.

> "... if I disturb you with my *clicketten*," she meant her chattering, "tell me so, Dan'l, and I won't." (Mrs. Gummidge, 391)

Mr. Peggotty uses *dodman* playfully and humorously in the following speech:

> "I'm a reg'lar *Dodman*, I am," said Mr. Peggotty; by which he meant snail, and this was in allusion to his being slow to go ... (Mr. Peggotty, 90)

EDD (s.v. *dodman sb*.) claims that the noun is used in n.Cy., Nhp., e.An., and s.Cy. Both *OED* and *EDD* cite the speech

---

[26] See K. J. Fielding (1949) "*David Copperfield* and Dialect," p. 288, and *Let V*, p. 590.

[27] G. L. Brook (1970) *The Language of Dickens*, p. 118.

above.

Mr. Peggotty uses *dyke* once[28], which means "a ditch." *Moor* (s.v. *dike*) illustrates that "We do not use this word as in Scotland, Holland, &c. in the sense of a wall or rampart, or any thing raised." *Forby* is silent for this word.

Mr. Peggotty uses *fare* always together with *feel* as in "I don't *fare to feel* no matters" (390). Mrs. Gummidge employs the same construction: "Maybe you'll write to me too, Dan'l, odd times, and tell me how you *fare to feel* upon your lone lorn journeys" (391). This verb signifies "to seem likely." *OED* (s.v. *fare*, v.[1], 5. b.) points out that "it is often little more than a periphrasis for the finite verb." and quotes "How do you *fare to feel* about it, Mas'r Davy?" (Mr. Peggotty, 576) as the first citation in this sense. *Moor* (s.v. *fare*) interestingly comments that "it is not lost to general usage—we retain it in Farewell."

Moor (s.v. *fisherate*) suggests that this means "provide for—probably officiate—" and "occurs in a phrase under *beein*." *EDD* (s.v. *fisherate*, v.) shows that this is heard in Yks., Nhp., and eAn. and quotes the following extract from Dickens:

> "... my sister might ... find Missis Gummidge give her a leetle trouble now-and-again. Theerfur 'tan't my intentions to moor Missis Gummidge 'long with them, but to find a Beein' fur her wheer she can *fisherate* for herself." (A Beein' signifies, in that dialect, a home, and to fisherate is to provide.)(Mr. Peggotty, 625)

---

[28] "If her uncle was turned out of house and home, and forced to lay down in a *dyke*, Mas'r Davy ..." (379)

CHAPTER VI PROVINCIALISMS AND AMERICANISMS   123

OED and *Forby* are both silent for this verb.

Moor (s.v. *hull*) defines *hull*[29] as "to throw" and takes up *hurl, cail, cop, ding,* and *sky* as its native synonyms. Mr. Peggotty said, "You doen't ought ... to take and *hull* away a day's work" (378). *EDD* (s.v. *hull, v.*[3]) suggests that *hull* is to be heard in Yks., Chs., Stf., Der., Not., Lin., Rut., Lei., Nhp., War., Shr., Bdf., Hrt., Hnt., e.An., Ken., Sus., Hmp., and Som.

The noun *inquiration* with the same meaning as *inquire* is employed only in Suf. and Ess., according to *EDD* (s.v. *inquiration, sb.*). *OED* (s.v. *inquiration*) labels this word as *dialectal.* and cites the latter quotation below:

> "I had my thowts o' coming to make *inquiration* for you, sir, tonight," (Mr. Peggotty, 497)
> "... she found ... a friend; a decent woman as spoke to her about ... making secret *inquiration* concerning of me and all at home, tomorrow ..." (Mr. Peggotty, 623)

Mr. Peggotty often uses *kiender* adverbially in his local speech, which denotes "in a way," "as it were," or "to some extent."[30] This modifier can be considered to be Mr. Peggotty's idiolect. *Moor* (s.v. *kiender*) comments that "it is a very common term, and often occurs among our examples of local phraseology." *EDD* (s.v. *kind, sb.1*, 3. (3)) gives *kiend-* as a dialectal form of Nrf. and Suf.

> "I'm *kiender* muddle ..." (Mr. Peggotty, 390)

Ham was just the same, "wearing away his life with

---

[29] It is pretty plainly a corruption of *hurl* (*Forby*, s.v. *hull*). *OED* (s.v. *hurl, v*) illustrates it is a nineteenth century dialectal form.

[30] See *OED* (s.v. *kind, n.* 14.d.), where the sixth example is quoted.

kiender no care nohow for 't ..." (Mr. Peggotty, 578)

"... my niece was *kiender* daughter-like to me." (Mr. Peggotty, 584)

"... she kneeled down at my feet, and *kiender* said to me, as if it was her prayers, how it all come to be ..." (Mr. Peggotty, 619)

"But, fear of not being forgiv ... turned her from it, *kiender* by force, upon the road ..." (Mr. Peggotty, 622)

"Theer's been kiender a blessing fell upon us," (Mr. Peggotty, 743)

"... *kiender* worn; soft, sorrowful, blue eyes;" (Mr. Peggotty, 743)

"Lone and lorn" is Mrs. Gummidge's repeated favourite phrase, which is considered as her idiolect. *EDD* (s.v. *lorn*, *adj.*) labels *lorn*, whose meaning is "forlorn," as *obsolete* and suggests that it is used in Sc., Yks., e.An., and Dev. There is no entry concerning *lorn*, but *lone-woman*[31] in *Moor*.

"I am a lone *lorn* creetur'." (Mrs. Gummidge, 33, 34^{2x}, 120, 125)

she was "a lone *lorn* creetur' ..." (Mrs. Gummidge, 33)

"I'm a lone *lorn* creetur' myself, and everythink that reminds me of creetur's that ain't lone and *lorn*, goes contrary with me." (Mrs. Gummidge, 125)

a lone *lorn* child (as Mrs. Gummidge might have said) ... (David, 132)

"Nothink's nat'ral to me but to be lone and *lorn*." (Mrs. Gummidge, 383)

"... How could I expect to be wanted, being so lone

---

[31] In this entry, E. Moor illustrates that "A widow, without children. A melancholy description of humanity. An aged single woman would similarly describe herself."

CHAPTER VI   PROVINCIALISMS AND AMERICANISMS   125

and *lorn*, and so contrary!" (Mrs. Gummidge, 383)

"... my lone lorn Dan'l ..." (Mrs. Gummidge, 387)

"... your lone *lorn* journeys." (Mrs. Gummidge, 391)

"... She's the faithfullest of creeturs. 'Tan't to be expected, of course, at her time of life, and being lone and *lorn*, as the good old Mawther is to be knocked about aboardship ..." (Mr. Peggotty, 625)

"... I know you think that I am lone and *lorn*; but, deary love, 'tan't so no more! ..." (Mrs. Gummidge, 633)

"... I have never know'd her to be lone and *lorn*, for a single minute ..." (Mr. Peggotty, 745)

EDD (s.v. *mavis, sb.*) gives *mavish*[32] as the form found in Sc., Ant., n.Cy., Bdf., and e.An. and defines it as "the songthrush." Mr. Peggotty uses this lovely noun in reference to David and Em'ly just when they come back into his boathouse from a long walk for breakfast:

"Like two young *mavishes*," Mr. Peggotty said. I knew this meant, in our local dialect, like two young thrushes, and received it as a compliment. (Mr. Peggotty, 32)

Mr. Peggotty addresses Mrs. Gummidge as "Mawther," whose meaning David glosses as "old girl" (Mr. Peggotty, 34). *Moor* (s.v. *mawther*) indicates that it is "used familiarly, or rather contemptuously: and generally applied to one just grown or growing to womanhood." *Mawther* is frequently preceded by adjectives, "old Mawther" (Mr. Peggotty, 34, 88, 625[33]), "pritty Mawther" (Mr. Peggotty, 383), and sometimes used without any modifiers as in "Mawther" (Mr. Peggotty, 120,

---

[32]   *OED* regards this form as the nineteenth century dialectal form and cites Mr. Peggotty's speech.

[33]   "the good old *Mawther*"

266).

A mort of, which is equal to *a lot of* in the meaning, is one of Mr. Peggotty's favourite phrases. *Mort* is in general dialectal use in Irel. and Eng., according to *EDD* (s.v. *mort, sb.*[1]). *OED* (s.v. *mort, n.*[6]) quotes, "We have had *a mort of* talk, sir," (Mr. Peggotty, 389), and comments on its origin as follows:

> The suggestion that it is derived from ON. *mart*, neut. of *margr* great, as in *mart manna* a great number of people, is not supported by the form, chronology, or locality of the Eng. word. It is possibly a dial. corruption of *mortal* used as an intensive (e.g. with such a *n.* as *deal*). The existence of the north. dial. *murth* (ON. *mergð*) in the same sense may have assisted its development.

The other examples are:

> "I've put the question to myself a *mort* o' times, and never found no answer." (Mr. Peggotty, 578)
> "Well, I've had a *mort* of con-sideration, I do tell you," (Mr. Peggotty, 624)
> "It's a *mort* of water ... fur to come across, and on'y stay a matter of fower weeks." (Mr. Peggotty, 742)
> "She might have married well, a *mort* of times," (Mr. Peggotty, 744)

Mr. Peggotty went out to wash himself in a kettleful of hot water, remarking that "cold would never get *his muck* off" (27). *Muck* here means "dirt." *OED* (s.v. *muck*, n.1, 3. a.) quotes the sentence above.

David is addressed only once as "my pretty *poppet*"[34] (52) by his beloved Peggotty through the keyhole when he was

---

[34] Here cited in *OED* (s.v. *poppet, n*, 1.).

CHAPTER VI PROVINCIALISMS AND AMERICANISMS   127

confined in his small room by Miss Murdstone. It is interesting enough that *Moor* (s.v. *poppet*)[35] suggests it is a term of endearment to a young girl, while both *EDD* (s.v. *poppet, sb.*[1], 2.) and *OED* (s.v. *poppet, n.* 1.) claim that it is a term of endearment for a child or a young girl.

Though *wimicking*, which is used by Mr. Peggotty[36], is undoubtedly an error for *winnicking*,[37] it is still in print on the modern editions and what is worse, it is listed in *OED* (s.v. *wim(m)ick, v.*) as a head word. *Winnick* is a dialectal form of *whinnock* as is mentioned in *EDD* (s.v. *whinnock, v.*). *Moor* (s.v. *winnick*) also records *winnick* with the meaning of "to cry."

Table 10 East Anglia provincialisms in *David Copperfield*

	Moor	Forby	OED	EDD
afeerd	*afeard*	*afeard*	*afeard*, ppl. a.	*afeard*, adj. In gen. dial. use throughout Sc. Irel and Eng.
arrize				
bahd's neezing	*bahdneest*	—	*bird's-nesting*, vbl. n. 1. a.	*bird, sb.*[1], 4. (12) *bird's-neezening*
Beein, Beein'	*beein*	*being, sb.*	—	*being, sb.* 2. Sc., Irel., Yks., Lan., e.Ang., Sus.

---

[35] *Moor* (s.v. *moppet*) records *moppet* for its synonym.

[36] "Betwixt you and me, Mas'r Davy—and you, ma'am—wen Mrs. Gummidge takes to *wimicking*,"—our old country word for crying, —"she's liable to be considered to be, by them as didn't know the old 'un, peevish-like ..." (624)

[37] K. J. Fielding (1949) "*David Copperfield* and Dialect," p. 288.

bor', bor	—	borh, bor, sb.	bor, n. dial.	bor, sb. Cmb. Nrf. Suf. Ess.
clicketten	clicket	clicket, v.	clicket, v., 2.	clicket, v.¹, 8. e.An.
dodman	dodman, hodman-dod	dodman, sb.	dodman Now dial.	dodman, sb. n.Cy. Nhp. e.An. s.Cy.
dyke	dike	—	dyke, n.¹, 2. a.	dike, sb., Var. dial. uses in Sc. Irel. and Eng.
fare	fare	fare, v.	fare, v.¹, 5. b. dial.	fare, v.², 5. n.Yks. Lin. e.An. Cmb. Ess.
fisherate	fisherate	—	—	fisherate, v. Yks., Nhp., and eAn.
hull	hull	hull	hurl, v., 3. (9 dial. hull)	hull, v.³, 1. Yks. Chs. Stf. Der. Not. Lin. Rut. Lei. Nhp. War. Shr. Bdf. Hrt. Hnt. e.An. Ken. Sus. Hmp. Som.
inquiration	inquiration	—	inquiration, dial.	inquiration, sb. Suf. and Ess.
kiender	kiender, local phraseology	kind o'	kind, n. 14. d. *Colloq.* vulgarly kinder	kind, sb.¹, 3. (3) kiend-, Nrf. Suf.
lorn	Cf. *lone*	—	lorn, ppl. a. 2.	lorn, adj. 1. *Obs.*, Sc. Yks. e.An. and Dev.
mavish	mavis	mavis, sb.	mavis, Now *poet.* and *dial.*	mavis, sb. Sc. Ant. n.Cy. Bdf. e.An.
Mawther	mawther	—	mother, n.¹, 4. a.	mawther, sb. Glo. Hrt. e.An. Wil.

mort	mort	mort, sb.	mort, n.⁶, dial.	mort, sb.¹, In gen. dial. use in Irel. and Eng.
muck	muck	muck, sb. 3.	muck, n.¹, 3. a. Now vulgar	muck, sb., 1. In gen. dial. use in Sc. and Eng.
poppet	poppet	poppet	poppet, n. 1.	poppet, sb.¹, 2., Yks. Lan. Chs. Midl. Der. Not. Lei. Nhp. War. Hrt. Hnt. e.An. Som.
wimick	winnick	whinnock, v.	wim(m)ick, v.	whinnock, v. 1., winnick, Cum. Lei. Brks. e.An. Ess. Hmp. Dev. Cor.

6.4 Kentish provincialisms in *Great Expectations*

When Pip asks Mrs. Joe Gargery about Hulks, she answers "Hulks are prison-ships, right 'cross th' *meshes*," and the omniscient narrator Pip explains "We always used that name for marshes, in our country" (*GE*, 15). According to *EDD* (s.v. *marsh, sb.*¹, 1.), *mesh* is a dialectal form of Nrf., Suf., w.Hmp., and Dev., while *OED* (s.v. *marsh*¹) does not record this form, but *mash* for a dialectal form in England and the United States from the 17th to the 19th century.

As we have already studied in Chapter I, Kent is so near to London and the Thames and the Old Roman Road have provided easy access to the capital. Consequently the difference between London and Kentish dialect had gradually become smaller from the beginning of early Modern English.[38]

---

[38] See J. Franklyn (1953) *Cockney*, p.34, and H. Hirooka (1965) *Dialects in English Literature*, p. 69, 73.

In addition to *meshes*, we can find only three words for Kentish provincialisms in *Great Expectations*: one is *afeerd*; another *afore*; and the other *oncommon*.[39]

Joe Gargery uses *afeerd* once in "I'm dead *afeerd* of going wrong in the way of not doing what's right by a woman" (50). *OED* (s.v. *afeard, ppl. a.*) illustrates that the word is "used more than 30 times by Shakespeare, but rare in literature after 1700, having been supplanted by *afraid*," and that "it survives everywhere in the popular speech, either as *afeard*, or *'feard*; and has again been used in poetry by W. Morris." *EDD* (s.v. *afeard, adj.*) suggests that it is found throughout Sc., Irel. and Eng.

Afore, whose place is now taken by *before* , can sometimes be found in the speech of Joe. *OED* (s.v. *afore, adv., prep.,* and *conj.*) comments that *afore* is "common in the dialects generally as well as, in 'vulgar' London speech, and in nautical language." *EDD* (s.v. *afore*) shows that the word is generally used in various dialects of Sc., Ir., and Eng. Joe uses it as a preposition, "sit me down *afore* a good fire" (47) and "she had wrote out a little coddleshell in her own hand a day or two *afore* the accident" (461); and as a conjunction, "Biddy giv' herself a deal o' trouble with me *afore* I left" (465). *OED* (s.v. *afore*, C. *conj.*) suggests that the use of *afore* as a conjunction is "elliptical use of the prep. of time, as *afore the time that* he came, *afore that* he came, *afore* he came."

Oncommon is sometimes found in Joe's speech. According to *OED* (s.v. *on-, prefix*[4]), *on-* is frequently found in ME. and

---

[39] T. Tanaka (1972) "Regional and Occupational Dialect of Joe Gargery," p. 154.

CHAPTER VI   PROVINCIALISMS AND AMERICANISMS   131

early Mod.E., and is the dialectal variant of *un-*[1], before adjes., pples., advbs. and their derivatives. *EDD* (s.v. *oncommon*) suggests that the term is used in Sc. Ire. Nhb. Dur. Cum. Wm. Yks. Lan. Der. Lin. and e.An. In the following extracts, *oncommon* is used as an adjective:

> "such a *oncommon* Bolt as that" (12)
> "You are *oncommon* in some things." (72)
> "Likewise you're a *oncommon* scholar." (72)
> "you must be a common scholar afore, you can be a *oncommon* one." (72)
> "Whether common ones as to callings and earnings," pursued Joe, reflectively, "mightn't be the better of continuing for a keep company with common ones, instead of going out to play with *oncommon* ones – which reminds me to hope that there were a flag, perhaps?" (72)
> "And the *oncommonest* workman can't show himself oncommon in a gridiron – for a gridiron IS a gridiron." (111)

and as an adverb:

> "... I'm *oncommon* fond of reading, too."
> "Are you, Joe?"
> "*On-common*. Give me," said Joe, "a good book, or a good newspaper ..." (47)
> "You're *oncommon* small." (72)
> "If you can't get to be *oncommon* through going straight, you'll never get to do it through going crooked." (72)
> "And the oncommonest workman can't show himself *oncommon* in a gridiron – for a gridiron IS a gridiron." (111)
> " But it took a bit of time to get it well round, the change come so *oncommon* plump; didn't it?" (146).

As is seen above, Joe's use of *oncommon* always occur in the dialogue with Pip and it is interesting that his use of the word is to be found only in the first stage of Pip's great expectations.

Table 11 Kentish provincialisms in *Great Expectations*

	OED	EDD
afeard	*afeard, ppl., a.* Everywhere in the popular speech.	*afeard, adj.* In *gen.* dial. use throughout Sc. Irel and Eng.
afore	*afore, adv., prep., and conj.* Arch. and *dial.*	*afore.* In var. dial. of Sc. Ir. and Eng.
mesh	*marsh*[1], 7-9 *Eng.* and *U.S. dial.*	*marsh.* Nrf. Suf. w.Hmp. Dev.
oncommon	*on-, prefix*4, *dial.* variant of *un-*[1], before adjs., pples., advbs. and their derivatives.	*oncommon*, Sc. Ire. Nhb. Dur. Cum. Wm. Yks. Lan. Der. Lin. and e.An.

6.5 Americanisms in *American Notes* and *Martin Chuzzlewit.*
As soon as he landed on Boston, he perceived the differences between British and American English, about which he wrote to Forster with his surprise:

> I will only say...that but for an odd phrase now and then—such as *Snap of cold weather*; a *tongue-y man* for a talkative fellow; *Possible?* as a solitary interrogation; and *Yes?* for indeed—I should have marked, so far, no difference whatever between the parties here and those I have left behind. (*Let. III*, 35-6)

However, Dickens had already been interested in American vocabulary, before he went over to the new world. In the letter to Daniel Maclise, his close friend, a painter and illustrator, he wrote, "Kate and Fanny have Raised the Standard of Rebellion this morning, and placed me in what the Americans would call '*a slantindicular fix.*'" (*Let. II*, 180)

While staying in the United States, he became interested in American English for its peculiarities in pronunciation, grammar, usage and vocabulary. Steven Marcus describes his first trip to America as "a six months' voyage into the English language."[40] Dickens frequently introduced many examples of these peculiarities in his letters to Forster. These examples helped him to refresh his memory when he later wrote *American Notes* and the American chapters of *Martin Chuzzlewit*. N. F. Blake observes that "Dickens is one of the first English writers to realize the potential of American speech, which no doubt came from his visits to America and his familiarity with American writings."[41]

In the following letter, Dickens, as Louise Pound points out, "is able to write the American language himself," and humorously introduces "pure Americanisms of the first water"[42] by describing the dreadful voyage on board "the Britannia" from Liverpool to Boston:

> ... you may have a pretty con-siderable damned good sort of a feeble notion that it don't fit nohow; and that it a'nt calculated to make you smart, overmuch; and that you don't feel 'special bright; and by no means first rate; and not at all tonguey (or disposed for conver-

---

[40] S. Marcus (1965) *Dickens from Pickwick to Dombey*, pp. 218-19.
[41] N. F. Blake (1981) *Non-standard Language in English Literature*, p. 159.
[42] L. Pound, L. (1947) "The American Dialect of Charles Dickens," p. 127.

> sation); and that however rowdy you may be by natur', it does use you up com-plete, and that's a fact; and makes you quake considerable, and disposed toe damn ĕngīne!—All of which phrases, I beg to add, are pure Americanisms of the first water. (*Let. III*, 89-90)

Tadao Yamamoto quotes this passage and says, "From this single quotation we may acquire a general notion of what American English is."[43] This passage makes Dickens's views on American English clear. On the same page, the scholar illustrates in detail his use of American English shown in the paragraph above as follows:

> In the first place we notice peculiarities in pronunciation such as 'natur'', 'com-plete', 'toe', and 'ĕngīne'. Secondly, we find some peculiar uses of words, such as 'to fit', 'smart', 'bright', 'rowdy', 'use up', &c. Thirdly, a few grammatical anomalies should be noticed, such as 'considerable' and '´special' used as adverbs. Lastly we cannot miss phraseological peculiarities such as 'a pretty con-siderable damned good sort', 'it don't fit nohow', 'that's a fact', &c.

We shall try to examine words or phrases peculiar to the United States, which are generally known as "Americanisms."[44] According to the comments and illustrations in the dictionaries and references, we shall classify words or phrase into four categories: (1) words or phrases whose meanings were obsolete or dialectal in mid-Victorian England but retained in the United States; (2) words or phrases whose meaning is

---

[43] T. Yamamoto (2003) *Growth and System of the Language of Dickens*, p. 201.

[44] *OED* (s.v. *Americanism*, 3.) defines the term as "A word or phrase peculiar to, or extending from, the United States."

originally or chiefly used in America; (3) slang words or phrases whose meaning is purely American origin; (4) words coined in America from the elements that are familiar separately in British English; and (5) words or phrases that are different in usage between British and American English.

6.5.1 Words or phrases whose meanings were obsolete or dialectal in mid-Victorian England but retained in the United States
Of all the words and phrases in this category, *fall*, the name of autumn is one of the best-known examples. *OED* (s.v. *fall*, *n.*[1], 2.) observes that this noun is "in N. Amer. the ordinary name for autumn; in England now rare in literary use, though found in some dialects," and *Century* (s.v. *fall*, *n.* 7.) also suggests that this word is "formerly in good literary use in England, but now only local there, and generally regarded as an Americanism." Dickens used this word in his letter to Forster and *American Notes*:

> Longfellow...will be in town "next *fall*." (*Let. III*, 96)
> "Ran away, negro Ben. Has a scar on his right hand; his thumb and forefinger being injured by being shot last *fall*..." (*AN*, 232-4)

The latter extract is one of the specimens of the advertisements of fugitive slaves in the public newspapers. H. W. Fowler gives us an interesting illustration of the word:

> *Fall* is better on the merits than *autumn*, in every way: it is short, Saxon (like the other three season names), picturesque; it reveals its derivation to every one who uses it, not to the scholar only, like *autumn*; and we once had as good a right to it as the Americans; but we have chosen to let the right lapse, and to use the word

now is no better than larceny.[45]

L. Pound takes up *I guess, I reckon, I calculate*, and *I expect* as Americanisms, all of which are equivalent in meaning to "I suppose."[46] The dictionaries and references used in this book allow us to discuss *I guess* and *I reckon* in this section, but we should treat *I calculate* in the following section. With respect to *I expect*, OED (s.v. *expect, v.* 6.) claims that "the misuse of the word as a synonym of *suppose*, without any notion of 'anticipating' or 'looking for', is often cited as an Americanism, but is very common in dialectal, vulgar or carelessly colloquial speech in England." *MEU* (s.v. *expect*) regards this idiom neither as American English nor British English, while Dickens seemed to consider it as an Americanism, which he put in the mouth of Colonel Diver (*MC*, 258, 265), Major Pawkins (*MC*, 269), La fayette Kettle (*MC*, 345, 359), General Choke (*MC*, 352), Elijah Pogram (*MC*, 533), a gaoler of "The Tombs" in New York (*AN*, 84), and the coachman (*AN*, 84).

Fowler brothers remark that "if any one were asked to give an Americanism without a moment's delay, he would be more likely than not to mention *I guess*."[47] This parenthetical phrase is one of the favourite expressions of Chaucer's, as in "the Prologue" to *the Canterbury Tales*, where he describes a young Squire: "Of twenty yeer of age he was, *I gesse*" (l. 82). *Century* (s.v. *guess, v.* 1.) argues that "this use is common in

---

[45] H. W. Fowler (1926) *A Dictionary of Modern English Usage*. Second edition, revised by Sir Ernest Gowers, 1965, p. 33.

[46] L. Pound (1947) "The American Dialect of Charles Dickens," p. 127.

[47] H. W. and E. G. Fowler (1906) *The King's English*, p. 33.

English literature from the first appearance of the word; but it is now regarded as colloquial, and, from its frequency in the United States, it is generally supposed by Englishmen to be an 'Americanism.'" According to *OED* (s.v. *guess*, *v.* 6.), this expression was used colloquially and originally in the northern United States. The captain of *The Screw*, who is "a genuine New Englander," says, "*I guess* there air a dozen if you want 'em, colonel." (*MC*, 259) In *American Notes*, this phrase is employed by a gaoler of "The Tombs" in New York (*AN*, 84), a coachman in western Pennsylvania (*AN*, 141), and Judge Jefferson (*AN*, 190). These persons except Jefferson clearly belong to the northern part of the United States.

In America there is a regional variation between *I guess* and *I reckon*. The former is used in the north and the latter in the south. *OED* (s.v. *reckon*, *v.* 6. b.) suggests that *I reckon* is "formerly in literary Eng. use; still common in Eng. dialects, and current in the southern States of America in place of the northern *I guess*," and *Century* (s.v. *reckon*, *v.* 6.) also states that *I reckon* "has by reason of its frequency in colloquial speech in some parts of the United States, especially in the South (where it occupies a place like that of *guess* in New England), come to be regarded as provincial or vulgar." Unlike *I guess*, there is no clear evidence that Dickensian characters using *I reckon* belong to the southern States of America. This phrase is employed by Colonel Diver (*MC*, 265), editor of *the New York Rowdy Journal*, Mr. Bevan, Massachusetts physician (*MC*, 292), Captain Kedgick, landlord of the National Hotel in fictitious American town through which Martin Chuzzlewit passes on his way westwards from New York (*MC*,

364, 536), and Mr. La Fayette Kettle, secretary of the Watertoast Association of United Sympathisers (*MC*, 344) in *Martin Chuzzlewit*; and by an American gentleman in a straw hat (*AN*, 190) in *American Notes*.

Mr. Bevan said, "I *was 'raised'* in the State of Massachusetts, and reside there still" (*MC*, 278). Putnam Smif wrote to Martin, "I *was raised* in those interminable solitudes where our mighty Mississippi (or Father of Waters) rolls his turbid flood" (*MC*, 363). In *American Notes*, Dickens described that "our host...was a handsome middle-aged man, who had come to this town from New England, in which part of the country he was *'raised.'*" (*AN*, 197) *DAE* (s.v. *raise*, v. 4.) illustrates that *to raise*, with the meaning of "to bring up (a person), was used in England from 1744 to 1795 and it states that this sense became obsolete in British usage about 1800, but has survived in the United States. *OED* (s.v. *raise*, v.¹ 10. a.) labels this sense as now chiefly *U.S.*

Dickens first introduced *tonguey* in his letter to Forster, saying, "a *tongue-y* man for a talkative fellow."[48] Scadder said to General Choke, "You air a *tongue-y* person, Gen'ral. For you talk too much" (*MC*, 352). *OED* (s.v. *tonguey*, a. 1.) and *Century* (s.v. *tonguey*, *tonguy*, a.) record that *tonguey*, which means "talkative, loquacious", was first used in John Wyclif's *Ecclesiasticus* in 1382: a *tungy* man (viii. 4: *OED*); a *tungy* woman (xxv. 27: *Century*). We cannot find any recorded instances of this epithet for about four hundred years until 1774 on both sides of the Atlantic. *OED* and *Century* regard it as

---

[48] *Let. III*, pp. 35-36.

"Now *U.S.* and *dial.*" and "Now *colloq.*" respectively, but *Webster, DAE, and DA* are silent with respect to the adjective.

Table 12 Americanisms I

	OED	Century	Webster	DAE	DA
expect	*Expect, v.* 6. See above.	*Expect, v.* 5. *Prov.* Eng., and *local* U.S.	—	*Expect, v.* See *OED*.	—
fall	*Fall, n.*¹, 2. See above.	*Fall, n.* 7. See above.	*Fall, n.* 12.	*Fall, n.* 4. a. & b. In Eng. now *local*.	—
guess	*Guess, v.* 6. *I guess. Colloq.*, orig. in the northern U.S.	*Guess, v.* 1. See above.	*Guess, v.* 5.	*Guess, v.* 3. In Eng. now *dial*.	—
raise	*Raise, v.*¹, 10. a. Now chiefly *U.S.*	*Raise, v.* 14. *Colloq.*	*Raise, v.* 3. d.	*Raise, v.* 4. See above	—
reckon	*Reckon, v.* 6. b. *I reckon.*	*Reckon, v.* 6. See above.	*Reckon, v.* 4. *Prov.* Eng. & *Colloq.* U.S.	*Reckon, v.* 2. See *OED*.	—
tonguey	*Tonguey, a.* 1. Now *U.S.* and *dial.*	*Tonguey, a.* Now *colloq.*	—	—	—

6.5.2 Words or phrases whose meaning is originally or chiefly used in America.

Century (s.v. *calculate, v.* 5.) explains that *I calculate* is used colloquially in New England, and *Webster* labels it as "Local

U.S." *OED* (s.v. *calculate*, v.¹, 7.) and *DA* (s.v. *calculate*, v. 1.), however, do not refer to its geographical feature, only to regard it as *colloq.* In *DAE* (s.v. *calculate*, v. 1.), there is an interesting example quoted from P. Paxton's *Yankee in Texas* (1853, p. 116), and it clearly suggests that this phrase is used in New England: "The Yankee *calculates*, and pretty shrewdly also, while the southron *allows*." We have only two instances: one is uttered from the mouth of Kedgick, "You're quite a public man, *I calc'late*" (*MC*, 314); and the other from that of an American gentleman in a straw hat, "*I calculate* you'll have got through that case of the corporation" (*AN*, 190).

According to *OED*, *DAE*, and *DA*, a noun *compensation* with the meaning of "salary, esp. of a public servant" is first recorded in *The Constitution of the United States* (1787, i. §6.): "The Senators and Representatives shall receive a *compensation* for their services to be...paid out of the Treasury of the U.S." Dickens used this term only in *American Notes*: I take it for granted that the Presidential housemaids have high wages, or, to speak more genteelly, an ample amount of "*compensation*:" which is the American word for salary, in the case of all public servants (*AN*, 125).

Scadder (*MC*, 353) twice uses *dander* with the meaning which *OED* (s.v. *dander*, n.⁴) defines as "raffled or angry temper": "But you didn't ought to have your *dander* ris with *me*, Gen'ral," and "I do my duty; and I raise the *dander* of my feller critters, as I wish toe serve..." *OED* (s.v. *dander*, n.⁴) labels it as *colloq.* (orig. *U.S.*) and *dial.* and states that it is "conjectured by some to be a fig. use of DANDER³, dandruff, scurf; but possibly fig. of DANDER², ferment."

Dickens observes that "by-the-way, whenever an Englishman would cry 'All right!' an American cries 'Go ahead!' which is somewhat expressive of the national character of the two countries" (*AN*, 131). *OED* suggests (s.v. *go. v.* 72.) that the phrasal verb was chiefly used in the United States until recently and defines it as "to go forward without pause or hesitation" or "to make rapid progress." *Century* (s.v. *ahead, adv.* 2.) argues that it is "an idiomatic phrase said to have originated in the United States, and sometimes converted into an adjective: as, a *go-ahead* person." We can find two quotations which support Dickens's observation. Firstly, *DAE* (s.v. *ahead, adv.*) quotes the illustration from Clapin's *A New Dictionary of Americanisms* (1902), which says, "*Go ahead* ... this idiomatic phrase is very characteristic of the restless and energetic progress of the American People." Secondly, *OED* (s.v. *go. v.* 72.) cites the following from *The National Encyclopaedia* (1818): "*Go-ahead* is of American origin, and is used ... where the British would say 'all right'."

Go-ahead is a compound adjective derived from the preceding phrasal verb and it also reflects the national character of the United States. In *American Notes*, an American passenger on board a railroad train says, "Yankees are reckoned to be considerable of a *go-ahead* people" (*AN*, 63). *OED* (s.v. *go-ahead, a.*) suggests that the adjective is used colloquially or originally in the United States and defines its meaning as "forward and energetic in undertaking; 'pushing', enterprising."

Dickens observed a counsel interrogated a witness and wrote down his answer, which read, "he was alone and had no '*junior*'" (*AN*, 54), when he visited the courts at Boston. *OED* (s.v. *junior*, B. *n.* 1. a.) suggests that the noun is chiefly used in America and that it denotes "a child, esp. a young boy", but we cannot find any comments on this noun in any other dictionaries.

Colonel Diver introduces Martin to Major Pawkins, saying, "Here is a gentleman from England ... who has concluded to *locate* himself here" (*MC*, 268). The verb is sometimes used reflexively with the meaning of "to settle down or establish residence in a place", as *DAE* (s.v. *locate*, *v.* 1. b.) claims. It is more frequently used in the passive voice, meaning (s.v. *locate*, *v.* 1. c.) "to live or be established in a place". We have four examples in the passive, and find two examples in General Fladdock (*MC*, 290), one in General Choke (*MC*, 347), and one in his letter to Forster (*Let. III*, 135).

General Choke remarks that "if her *location* was in Windsor Pavilion it couldn't be in London at the same time" (*MC*, 347). This noun, according to *OED* (s.v. *location*, *n.* 6.) and *Webster* (s.v. *location*, *n.* 3.), is used chiefly in the United States with the meaning of "place of settlement or residence". It is frequently spelled with a hyphen between first and second syllable, as *lo-cation* (*MC*, 345, 362, 533) and between every syllable, as *lo-ca-tion* (*AN*, 63), so as to convey the flavour of the peculiarity of American pronunciation.[49]

OED (s.v. *locofoco*, *n.*) conjectures that "*loco* was taken from *locomotive*, wrongly imagined to mean 'self-moving'; *foco* may be a jingling alteration of It. *fuoco* or Sp. *fuego* fire

---

[49] See Chapter III, §3.5.2, p. 38.

CHAPTER VI PROVINCIALISMS AND AMERICANISMS   143

(the inventor would hardly think of L. *focus* hearth, which is the source of the mod. Rom. words for 'fire')," and it (s.v. *locofoco, n.* 1.) defines the word as "a self-igniting cigar or match". *Century* (s.v. *locofoco, n.*) tells us why the noun is used in a political sense:

> In *U.S. hist.*, one of the equal-rights or radical section of the Democratic party about 1835; by extension, in disparagement, any member of that party. The name was given in allusion to an incident which occurred at a tumultuous meeting of the Democratic party in Tammany Hall, New York, in 1835, when the radical faction, after their opponents had turned off the gas, relighted the room with candles by the aid of locofoco matches. The Locofoco faction soon disappeared but the name was long used for the Democratic party in general by its opponents. Often in the abbreviated form *Loco* (pl. *Locos*).

We have two examples of the political use of the noun in *Martin Chuzzlewit*: an American news-boy cries out, "Here's all the New York papers! Here's full particulars of the patriotic *locofoco* movement yesterday, in which the whigs was so chawed up" (*MC*, 255); and Chollop pursues, "I shot him down...for asserting in the Spartan Portico, a tri-weekly journal, that the ancient Athenians went a-head of the present *Locofoco* Ticket" (*MC*, 521).

Both Colonel Diver (*MC*, 265) and Scadder (*MC*, 353) say, "They *rile up*..." This phrasal verb, according to *OED* (*rile, v.* 2. b.), means "to get angry." Interestingly enough, this phrase is uttered from the mouth of Martin (*MC*, 536), when his return to England is drawing near, partly because it was a colloquialism in both England and America at that time, and partly because several months had passed since he had came there, and he was quite familiar with American English.

Mrs. Hominy described her exhausting railway trip as "the jolting in the cars is pretty nigh as bad as if the rail was full of *snags* and *sawyers*" (*MC*, 367), but Martin did not seem to realize her meaning. Dickens (*AN*, 172) described the foul stream of the Mississippi and introduced *snags* and *sawyers* with a gloss into the text to English readers who did not understand the meaning of these words: "for two days we toiled up this foul stream, striking constantly against the floating timber, or stopping to avoid those more dangerous obstacles, the *snags*, or *sawyers*, which are the hidden trunks of trees that have their roots below the tide." *Century* (s.v. *sawyer*, *n*. 2.) comments that it is used in the Western United States. *DA* (s.v. *sawyer*, *n*. 2.) labels it as "now *hist.*", and *OED* (s.v. *snag*, *n*.[1] 1. b.) labels it as "orig. *U.S.*".

Dickens described *snap of cold* (*AN*, 185) and *snap of cold weather* (*Let. III*, 35-6) as Americanisms. *Webster* (s.v. *snap*, *n*. 7.) defines this noun as "a sudden severe interval or spell; —applied to the weather; as, *a cold snap*."

Dickens (*AN*, 185) used one of the Americanisms which he picked up during his stay in the United States: "as I had a desire to travel through the interior of the state of Ohio, and to '*Strike* the lakes,' as the phrase is, at a small town called Sandusky..." *OED* (s.v. *strike*, *v*. 68.) labels the verb as "orig. chiefly *U.S.* and *Colonial*" and defines it as "to come upon, reach (a hill, river, path, etc.) in travelling."

DA (s.v. *fact*, *n*.) states that *that's a fact* is "an assertive expression used for emphasis." This phrase is used by the captain of *The Screw* (*MC*, 259), Kettle (*MC*, 343, 347), a waiter on board *The Britania* (*AN*, 24), a gaoler of "The Tombs" in New York (*AN*, 84, 85), and a gentleman in a straw hat (*AN*, 190). It is also found in his letter to Forster (*Let. III*, 90). *OED* (s.v. *fact*, v. 6. d.) suggests that this phrase was originally used in the United States.

Table 13 Americanisms II

	OED	Century	Webster	DAE	DA
calculate	Calculate, v.[1] 7. *U.S.* colloq.	Calculate, v. 5. *Colloq.* New Eng.	Calculate, v. 4. *Local U.S.*	+[50]*Calculate,* v. 1.	Calculate, v. 1. *Colloq.*
compensation	Compensation, n. 2. d. *U.S.*	Compensation, n. 2.	—	+Compensation, n.	Compensation, n.
dander	Dander, n.[4] *Colloq.* (orig. *U.S.*) and *dial*.	Dander[2], n. 2. *Vulgar.*	Dander, n. 2. *Low.*	Dander, n. dial.	—
junior	Junior, B. n. 1. a. Chiefly *U.S.*	—	—	—	—
locate	Locate, v. 3. Chiefly *U.S.*	Locate, v. I. 1.	Locate, v. t. 1.	+Locate, v. 1. b. & c.	Locate, v. 7.
location	Location, n. 6. Chiefly *U.S.*	Location, n. 1.	Location, n. 3. *U.S.*	Location, n. 4.	Location, n. 4. a.
locofoco	Loco-foco, n. 2. *U.S.* Polit. Hist.	Locofoco, n. 3. *U.S.* hist.	Locofoco, n. 2. *U.S.*	+Locofoco, n. 2. Polit. Now *hist.*	Locofoco, n. 2. *U.S.*

[50] + indicates that the term or sense clearly or to all appearance originated within the present limits of the United States.

rile up	Rile, v. 2. b. Chiefly *U.S.* and *colloq.*	Roil², v. 2.*Colloq.*	Rile, v. 2. Prov. Eng. & Colloq. U.S.	Rile, v. Chiefly *U.S.* and *colloq.*	—
sawyer	Sawyer, n. 3. *U.S.*	Sawyer, n. 2. Western *U.S.*	Sawyer, n. 2.*U.S.*	+Sawyer, n. 3.	Sawyer, n. 2.Now *hist.*
snag	Snag, n.¹ 1. b. Orig. *U.S.*	Snag¹, n. 3.	Snag, n. 3.	+Snag, n. 1.	Snag, n. 1.
snap	Snap, n. 7. a. Orig. *U.S.*	Snap, n. a. cold snap. Colloq.	Snap, n. 7.	+Snap, n. 1.	—
strike	Strike, v. 68. Orig. chiefly *U.S.* and Colonial	Strike, v. II. 10. Chiefly *colloq.*	Strike, v. 17.	+Strike, v. 4.	Strike, v. 2. b.
That's a fact.	Fact, n. 6. d. (*and*) *that's a fact*, orig. *U.S.*	—	—	+Fact, n. 1. a. *That's a fact.*	Fact, n. *That's a fact.*

6.5.3 Slang words or phrases whose meaning is purely American origin.

One of the invading American conquerors at Pawkins's tells Mark Tapley that "Snakes more ... rattlesnakes ... there air some *catawampous* chawers in the small way too" (*MC*, 343). *OED* (s.v. *catawampous, a.*) regards this word as "a high-sounding word with no very definite meaning," while defining it as "fierce, unsparing, destructive," and quotes the following interesting extract from Bartlett's *A Dictionary of Americanisms* (1848): "to be *catawampously chawed up* is to be completely demolished, utterly defeated." *OED* (s.v.

catawampous, a.) and *Century* (s.v. *catawampous, a.*) label this word as *slang* and *U.S. DAE* (s.v. *catawampous, a.*) and *DA* (s.v. *catawampous, a.*) regard it as a colloquialism.

Dickens lets both an American newsboy and bystander use *to chaw up*, a slang phrasal verb employed in the United State, whose meaning is, according to *OED* (s.v. *chaw, v.* 3.), "to demolish, 'do for', 'smash'". The newsboy cried, "Here's full particulars of the patriotic of the patriotic locofoco movement yesterday, in which the whigs was so *chawed up*" (*MC*, 255), and the bystander told Martin "that he guessed he had now seen something of the eloquential aspect of our country, and was *chawed up* pritty small" (*MC*, 534). All the dictionaries but *Webster* consider this phrasal verb as American slang.

Scadder said, "P'raps he was a loafin' rowdy; p'raps *a ring-tailed roarer*" (*MC*, 357). *OED* (s.v. *ring-tailed, a.* 4.) defines *a ring-tailed roarer* as "a fanciful name for an imaginary animal; also applied to persons" and quotes the following from De Vere's *Americanisms* (1872): "a specially fine fellow of great size and strength is called *a ring-tailed roarer*." *DAE* (s.v. *ring-tailed, a.*) and *DA* (s.v. *ring-tailed, a.*) label this compound as slang.

An American gentleman in a straw hat said to a coachman, "we were a pretty *tall* time coming that last fifteen mile" (*AN*, 190). According to *OED* (s.v. *tall, a.* 8. d.), the meaning of *tall* in this sentence is "large in amount" and regarded as *slang* (orig. *U.S.*). This is the earliest quotation in *OED* and the only one collocated with *time*. The quotations in *OED* show that from 1893 we can find five examples of *tall order* which means "something expected to be hard to achieve or fulfil."

148 Charles Dickens and Literary Dialect

Table 14 Americanisms III

	OED	Century	Webster	DAE	DA
Catawampously	Catawampous, a. Slang, chiefly *U.S.*	Catawampous, a. Slang, *U.S.*	—	+Catawampous, a. *Colloq.*	Catawampous, a. *Colloq.*
Chaw up	Chaw, v. 3. *Slang*, chiefly *U.S.*	Chaw, v. 2. chaw up, *U.S. slang.*	—	+Chaw, v. 1. b. *Slang.*	Chaw, v. 2. *Slang.*
Ring-tailed roarer	Ring-tailed, a. 4. *U.S.*	Ring-tailed, a. 2. ring-tailed roarer.	—	+Ring-tailed roarer, *Slang.*	Ring-tailed roarer, *Slang.*
Tall	Tall, a. 8. d. *Slang*, orig. *U.S.*	Tall², a. 4. *Colloq.*	Tall, a. 3. *Obs.* or slang.	+Tall, a. 1. *Colloq.*	Tall, a. and adv. 1. a. *Colloq.*

6.5.4 Words coined in America from the elements that are familiar separately in British English

The following type of Americanisms consists of, as G. L. Brook suggests, "words coined in America from the elements that are familiar separately in British English."[51] We shall treat only two words in this category: one is *to eventuate* and the other *slantindicularly*, both of which appear in *Martin Chuzzlewit*.

Both Colonel Diver and Zephaniah Scadder use *to eventuate* with the meaning of "to turn out": the former tells Martin that "her passage either way, is almost certain to *eventuate* a spanker!" (*MC*, 259); and the latter says, "No matter how it did *eventuate*. P'raps he cleared off, handsome,

---

[51] G. L. Brook (1970) *The Language of Dickens*, p. 134.

with a heap of dollars; p'raps he wasn't worth a cent" (*MC*, 357). *A Dictionary of Contemporary American Usage*[52] suggests that it "seems to be an American coinage," and *OED* (s.v. *eventuate*, *v.*) points out that this verb was "first used in U.S., and still regarded as an Americanism, though it has been employed by good writers in England."[53]

Brook notes that "*slantindicularly* is a blend-word."[54] Both *OED* and *DAE* (s.v. *slantindicular*, *a.* and *adv.*) illustrates that *slantindicular* is formed from *slanting* and *perpendicular*, and the former labels this word as "orig. *U.S.* and chiefly colloq. or humorous." General Choke uses this term:

> "if, sir, in such a place, and at such a time, I might venture to con-clude with a sentiment, glancing—however *slantindicularly*—at the subject in hand, I would say, sir, may the British Lion have his talons eradicated by the noble bill of the American Eagle, and be taught to play upon the Irish Harp and the Scotch Fiddle that music which is breathed in every empty shell that lies upon the shores of green Co-lumbia!" (*MC*, 346)

In the letter, as I have mentioned, Dickens had used *slantindicular* as one of the examples of an Americanism, before he went across the Atlantic:

> Kate and Fanny have Raised the Standard of Rebellion this morning, and placed me in what the Americans would call "a *slantindicular* fix" — swearing that I promised to bring them to see your picture to day; being

---

[52] B. Evans and C. Evans (1957) *A Dictionary of Contemporary American Usage,* (s.v. *eventuate*).

[53] According to *MEU* (s.v. *eventuality, eventuate*), "the words are much used in OFFICIALESE and also to be found in flabby journalese."

[54] G. L. Brook (1970) *The Language of Dickens*, p. 134.

at the moment inflamed with wine and "the Mazy". (*Let. II*, 180)[55]

Brook regards *tongue-y* and *to opinionate* as examples of this category[56], but judging from the evidence the dictionaries references offer, the former should be treated in 6.5.1, and the latter is not an Americanism.

Table 15 Americanisms IV

	OED	Century	Webster	DAE	DA
eventuate	Eventuate, v. 1.	Eventuate, v. 2.	Eventuate, v.	+Eventuate, v. a.	Eventuate, v. 1.
slantin-dicularly	Slantin'-dicularly, adv. Orig. U.S. and chiefly colloq. or humorous.	Cf. Slantin-dicular, a. Humorous slang	—	+Slantin-dicularly, adv. Slang.	—

6.5.5 Words or phrases that are different in usage between British and American English

Next we shall turn to the discussion of Dickens's views on the use of Americanisms described in *American Notes*, *Martin Chuzzlewit*, and his letters sent from America and study the differences in usage of vocabulary between British and American English which Dickens introduced to Forster in his letters and to his British readers in *American Notes* and *Martin Chuzzlewit*. Moreover we need to examine whether his views

---

[55] According to the footnote, "Portmanteau word from "slanting" and "perpendicular"; fig., "indirect" (slang, 1840).

[56] G. L. Brook (1970) *The Language of Dickens*, p. 134.

on these differences are correct in the light of the evidence with which references and dictionaries provide us.

At the end of the letter dated 28th March, 1842 (*Let. III,* 172), Dickens first introduces, with obvious amusement, various uses of the verb *to fix* to Forster, saying, "I told you the many uses of the word 'fix.'" In *American Notes,* he writes almost the same passage as in the letter above, beginning with the sentence, "There are few words which perform such various duties as this word 'fix'" (145). In these passages Dickens sometimes glosses the meanings of the verb for Forster and his readers in Britain as well as he explains the various uses and duties of it. We quote the passage from *American Notes*:

> There are few words which perform such various duties as this word "*fix*." It is the Caleb Quotem of the American vocabulary. You call upon a gentleman in a country town, and his help informs you that he is "*fixing himself*" just now, but will be down directly: by which you understand that he is dressing. You inquire, on board a steamboat, of a fellow-passenger, whether breakfast will be ready soon, and he tells you he should think so, for when he was last below they were "*fixing the tables:*" in other words, laying the cloth. You beg a porter to collect your luggage, and he entreats you not to be uneasy, for he'll "*fix it presently:*" and if you complain of indisposition, you are advised to have recourse to Doctor So-and-so, who will "*fix you*" in no time. (*AN,* 145)

Dickens called *to fix* "the Caleb Quotem of the American vocabulary" in the passage above. Caleb Quotem[57] is an eccentric and loquacious jack-of-all-trades in George Colman

---

[57] We can gather the information of this character from *The Century Dictionary, Vol. VI* (q.v. *Quotem, Caleb*).

the Younger's farce, *The Review, or the Wags of Windsor*, first performed on 1st September, 1800. Captain Marryat in his *A Diary in America*, 1839 (II. 35) claims that the verb 'fix' is "universal" and means "to do anything."[58] According to *OED* (s.v. *fix. v.* 14. a. and b.), sense (14. a.), "To adjust, make ready for use (arms, instruments, etc.); to arrange in proper manner" has wider sense (14. b.) in the United States. This semantic change in America makes Dickens and Marryat consider the word to be "the Caleb Quotem" and "universal" respectively.

G. L. Brook remarks that "his comments on the word *fix* show that he had the instincts of a lexicographer."[59] We enumerate the various meanings of the verb *to fix* employed by Dickens according to the best definition selected from the dictionaries used for the present book:

(a) To tidy up or make trim (the hair, the dress, one's person, etc.). (*DAE*)
(b) *To fix the tables*: To prepare (food or drink). (*OED*)
(c) *To fix it*: To arrange matters. (*OED*)
(d) To improve the physical condition: RESTORE, CURE. (*Webster*)
(e) *To fix* (a person): To 'do for' (a person); to kill (a person). (*OED*)

We have an example for the last definition above in *American Notes*:

There were some fifteen or twenty persons in the

---

[58] This is quoted from *DAE*. (q.v. the illustration of *fix, v.*).
[59] G. L. Brook (1970) *The Language of Dickens*, p. 131.

CHAPTER VI PROVINCIALISMS AND AMERICANISMS   153

room. One, a tall, wiry, muscular old man, from the west; sunburnt and swarthy; with a brown white hat on his knees, and a giant umbrella resting between his legs; who sat bolt upright in his chair, frowning steadily at the carpet, and twitching the hard lines about his mouth, as if he had made up his mind "*to fix*" the President on what he had to say, and wouldn't bate him a grain. (*AN*, 124)

Judging from Table 16 below, all the examples of *to fix* found in *OED*, *Century*, *Webster*, and *DAE* are to be classified as American English, because they are written by native Americans, uttered from the mouths of American characters which American or British writers create, or described as Americanisms by such British writers as Dickens.

As has been mentioned in "Introduction," Dickens suggests that Americans employ "*Yes?* for indeed" (*Let. III*, 36). This has various tones in itself when it is used interrogatively. With respect to one of its tones, *OED* (s.v. *yes, adv.* 3. d.) illustrates that it is usually used interrogatively "as a mere expression of interest (= 'indeed?' 'is it so?')." On the other hand, *OED* does not mention whether this use and tone of 'yes?' are American or British usage, and moreover *Century*, *DAE*, and *DA* are silent for all of them. Although *OED* quotes three examples for this usage, there is little evidence that this usage shows the peculiarity of English in America.

Dickens describes the use of "Yes?" illustrated by *OED* in the dialogue between a supposed British and American passenger on a railroad train with the illustration for the tones of "Yes?" in round brackets:

Everybody talks to you, or to anybody else who hits his

fancy. If you are an English man, he expects that that railroad is pretty much like an English railroad. If you say "No," he says "*Yes?*" (interrogatively), and ask in what respect they differ. You enumerate the heads of difference, one by one, and he says "*Yes?*" (still interrogatively) to each. Then he guesses that you don't travel faster in England; and on your replying that you do, says, "*Yes?*" again (still interrogatively), and it is quite evident, don't believe it. After a long pause he remarks, partly to you, and partly to the knob on the top of his stick, "that Yankees are reckoned to be considerable of a go-ahead people too;" which you say "*Yes*," and then *he* says "*Yes*" again (affirmatively this time). (*AN*, 63)

We have another example of this use, which occurs in the speech of Colonel Diver, unscrupulous editor of *The New York Rowdy Journal*, when Martin first met him on board the ship named *Screw*:

>The gentleman nodded his head, gravely; and said, "What is your name. sir?"
>Martin told him.
>"How old are you, sir?"
>Martin told him.
>"What is your profession, sir?"
>Martin told him that, also.
>"What is your destination, sir?" enquired the gentleman.
>"Really," said Martin, laughing, "I can't satisfy you in that particular, for I don't know it myself."
>"*Yes?*" said the gentleman.
>"No," said Martin. (*MC*, 258)

Dickens wrote to Forster, "One of the most amusing phrases in use all through the country, for its constant repetition, and adoption to every emergency is "Yes, sir." Let me give you a specimen," but the specimen is omitted by Forster. According to the footnote to this omission, "the specimen, Forster interpolates, was the dialogue used in *American Notes* (Ch. 14) between 'Straw Hat' and 'Brown Hat' during the coach-journey to Sandusky."[60] The following long passage is supposed to be the omitted specimen:

> Whenever the coach stops, and you can hear the voices of the inside passengers; or whenever any bystander addresses them, or any one among them; or they address each other; you will hear one phrase repeated over and over and over again to the most extraordinary extent. It is an ordinary and unpromising phrase enough, being neither more nor less than "*Yes, sir;*" but it is adapted to every variety of circumstance, and fills up every pause in the conversation. Thus:—
>
> The time is one o'clock at noon. The scene, a place where we are to stay and dine, on this journey. The coach drives up to the door of an inn. The day is warm, and there are several idlers lingering about the tavern, and waiting for the public dinner. Among them, is a stout gentleman in a brown hat, swinging himself to and fro in a rocking-chair on the pavement.
>
> As the coach stops, a gentleman in a straw hat looks out of the window:
>
> STRAW HAT. (To the gentleman in the rocking-chair.) I reckon that's Judge Jefferson, an't it?
>
> BROWN HAT. (Still swinging; speaking very slowly; and without any emotion whatever.) *Yes, Sir.*
>
> STRAW HAT. Warm weather, Judge.
>
> BROWN HAT. *Yes, Sir.*
>
> STRAW HAT. There was a snap of cold, last week.
>
> BROWN HAT. *Yes, Sir.*
>
> STRAW HAT. *Yes, Sir.*
>
> A pause. They looked each other, very seriously.

---

[60] The two quotations in the paragraph are from *Let. III*, p. 233.

STRAW HAT. I calculate you'll have got through that case of the corporation, Judge, by this time, now?
BROWN HAT. *Yes, Sir.*
STRAW HAT. How did the verdict go, Sir?
BROWN HAT. For the defendant, Sir.
STRAW HAT. (Interrogatively.) *Yes, Sir?*
BROWN HAT. (Affirmatively.) *Yes, Sir.*
Both. (Musingly, as each gazes down the street.) *Yes, sir.*
Another pause. They looked each other again, still more seriously than before.
BROWN HAT. This coach is rather behind its time to-day, I guess.
STRAW HAT. (Doubtingly.) *Yes, Sir.*
BROWN HAT. (Looking at his watch.) *Yes, Sir*; nigh upon two hours.
STRAW HAT. (Raising his eyebrows in very great surprise.) *Yes, Sir!*
BROWN HAT. (Decisively, as he puts up his watch.) *Yes, Sir.*
STRAW HAT. (Doubtingly.) *Yes, Sir.*
ALL THE OTHER INSIDE PASSENGERS. (Among themselves.) *Yes, Sir.*
COACHMAN. (In a very surly tone.) No, it an't.
STRAW HAT. (To the coachman.) Well, I don't know, Sir. We are pretty tall time coming that last fifteen mile. That's a fact. (*AN*, 189-190)

Dickens describes various uses and tones of "Yes, sir." as well as those of "Yes?" in (2). According to him, it is used without any emotion whatever, interrogatively, affirmatively, musingly, or doubtingly.

OED and *Century* illustrate that "Yes, sir." is chiefly used in the United States, and *OED* and *DA* label it "colloquial," as Table 16 below shows. *OED* also observes that it represents "an emphatic assertion." *OED* and the other dictionaries have

CHAPTER VI PROVINCIALISMS AND AMERICANISMS 157

no quotation or illustration for its interrogative use, while Dickens uses it both affirmatively and interrogatively in the preceding dialogue. Judging from his frequent reference to its tones, Dickens seems to be more interested in its various tones which are not familiar with him rather than its emphatic use. On the other hand, its interrogative use seems to result from caricature Dickens sometimes falls into.

Differences in use between British and American English sometimes convey misunderstanding each other. In the following passage Dickens humorously describes his confusion and misunderstanding of "Right away." At the end of the passage he realises that "Right away" and "Directly" are one and the same expression:

> "Dinner, if you please," said I to the waiter.
> "When?" said the waiter.
> "As quick as possible," said I.
> "*Right away?*" said the waiter.
> After a moment's hesitation, I answered, "No," at hazard.
> "*Not right away?*" cried the waiter, with an amount of surprise that made me start.
> I looked at him doubtfully, and returned, "No; I would rather have it in this private room. I like it very much."
> At this, I really thought the waiter must have gone out of his mind: as I believe he would have done, but for the interposition of another man, who whispered in his ear, "*Directly.*"
> "Well! and that's a fact!" said the waiter, looking helplessly at me: "*Right away.*"
> I saw now that "*Right away*" and "*Directly*" were one and the same thing. So I reversed my previous answer, and sat down to dinner in ten minutes afterwards; and a capital dinner it was. (*AN*, 23-24)

The first example of this phrase recorded in both *OED* and *DAE* is from H. B. Fearon's *Sketches of America* (1818), in which American English is sometimes described from the standpoint of the British writer. *OED* illustrates that this phrase is used originally in the United States (s.v. *right, adv.* 3. b.), and colloquially in both America and England (s.v. *away, adv.* 8.). *OED* shows that this phrase is first used in Britain in 1903. Judging from the evidence, British people might have known about it, but it was not used until the beginning of the twentieth century.

Other examples of "right away" are found in his letter and in the speech of Zephaniah Scadder, American fraudulent land agent and Hannibal Chollop, American frontiersman in *Martin Chuzzlewit*:

> I had a design of going from Charleston to Columbia in South Carolina, and there engaging a carriage, a baggage-tender and negro boy to guard the same, and a saddle-horse for myself—with which caravan I intended going *"right away,"* as they say here, into the west, through the wilds of Kentucky and Tennessee, across the Alleghany-mountains, and so on until we should strike the lakes and could get to Canada. (*Let. III*, 88)
>
> "You know we didn't wish to sell the lots off *right away* to any loafer as might bid." (*MC*, 353)
>
> "You bought slick, straight, and *right away*, of Scadder, sir?" (*MC*, 522)

As is seen in the first citation, Dickens sometimes uses double quotation marks to alert readers to the presence of Americanisms or apologise for it.

One American passenger on board a railroad train says,

CHAPTER VI PROVINCIALISMS AND AMERICANISMS   159

"Yankees are reckoned to be considerable of a *go-ahead* people" (*AN*, 63). In the later chapter Dickens observes that "By-the-way, whenever an Englishman would cry '*All right!*' an American cries '*Go ahead!*' which is somewhat expressive of the national character of the two countries" (*AN*, 131).

The original and literal meaning of this phrase is "to go forward without pause or hesitation" or "to make rapid progress" as *OED* (s.v. go. v. 72) defines. In connection with the meaning, *DAE* (s.v. *ahead, adv.*) quotes the illustration from S. Clapin's *A New Dictionary of Americanisms* (1902), which says, "*Go ahead* ... This idiomatic phrase is very characteristic of the restless and energetic progress of the American People." This comment is paralleled in Dickens's observation.

According to *OED*, the first example for the original and literal meaning is dated 1831, and this phrase is chiefly used in the United States until the end of nineteenth century. On the other hand, apart from the original and literal meaning, this phrase is used instead of British "All right" in America from 1841 as *DAE* (s.v. *go-ahead, adv.* 2.) suggests. The evidence tells us that Dickens came to know about this phrase used instead of "All right" and perceive the national character of American people implied in this phrase.

Dickens claims that "Possible?" is used as "a solitary interrogation" (*Let. III*, 35-6). We have a similar example in another letter and *American Notes*:

> "In England, if a man is under sentence of death even, he has a yard to walk in at certain times."
> "*Possible?*" (*Let. III*, 103)

160   Charles Dickens and Literary Dialect

> "In England, if a man be under sentence of death, even he has air and exercise at certain periods of the day."
> "*Possible?*" (*AN*, 84)

All the dictionaries used in this book are silent for the solitary interrogative use of "possible," but *DAE* (s.v. *possible, interj.*) and *DA* (q.v. *possible, adj.*) give two examples of "possible" used as an interjection. One of them is quoted from Todd's *Notes upon Canada and the United States of America* (1835): "O my! with *Possible!* [is] universal interjection [in America]." We have one example of 'possible' used as an interjection in *Martin Chuzzlewit*:

> "But stay!" cried Mr. Norris the father, taking him by the arm. "Surely you crossed in the Screw, general?"
> "Well! so I did," was the reply.
> "*Possible!*" cried the young ladies. "Only think!"
> (*MC*, 291)

Table 16 Americanisms V

	OED	Century	Webster	DEL	DA
Fix, v. (a)	*Fix, v.* 14. b. Chiefly *U.S. colloq.*	*Fix, v.* 10. <A>[61]	*Fix,v.*4a.(1)	*Fix, v.* 5. b. <B>[62]	—
Fix, v. (b)	*Fix, v.* 14. b. Chiefly *U.S. colloq.*	*Fix,v.* 10. <A>	*Fix,v.*4a.(1)	*Fix, v.* 5. c., 8. <B>	—
Fix, v. (c)	*Fix, v.* 14. c.	*Fix, v.*	*Fix, v.* 4b.	*Fix, v.* 5. e.	—

[61] This signifies that though not common in England, this use is regarded as an Americanism.

[62] This denotes the word or sense clearly or to all appearance originated within the present limits of the United States.

CHAPTER VI PROVINCIALISMS AND AMERICANISMS

	Orig. and chiefly U.S.	11.Chiefly U.S.		<B>		
Fix, v. (d)	Fix, v. 14. b. Chiefly U.S. colloq.	Fix, v. 10. <A>	Fix, v. 4a. (1)	—	—	
Fix, v. (e)	Fix, v. 14. c. Orig. and chiefly U.S.	Fix, v. 11. Chiefly U.S.	Fix, v. 4b.	Fix, v. 6. <B>	—	
Yes, adv.	Yes, adv. 3. d.	—	Yes, adv. 5.	—	—	
Yes, sir	Sir, n. yes, sir. 8. c. Chiefly U.S. colloq.	—	Yes, adv. 2.	Yes, adv. 3. b. <B>	Yes, adv. 2. Colloq.	
Right away	Away, adv. 8. U.S. & Eng. colloq.	Away, adv. 3.	Right away	Right away, adv. <B>	—	
Go ahead	Go, v. 72. Until recently chiefly U.S.	Ahead, adv. 2. <C>[63]	Go ahead, 2.	Ahead, adv. 1.	Ahead, adv. 2. Colloq.	
Possible	—	—	—	Possible, interj. <B>	Possible, adj. Colloq.	

Dickens's descriptions of American speech in *American Notes* and *Martin Chuzzlewit* are so derisive and offensive that R. W. Emerson protests that "no such conversations ever occur in this country in real life, as he relates," and that "he has picked up and noted with eagerness each odd local phrase that he

---

[63] This means an idiomatic phrase said to have originated in the United States.

met with, and when he had a story to relate, has joined them together, so that the result is the broadest caricature."[64] Louise Pound, who has the same nationality as Emerson, supports Dickens's observations and states thus:

> They are caricatures embodying certain characteristics, as is so often to be expected from this novelist. But they are no more eccentric and little more addicted to dialect than are his English characters, such as Mrs. Gamp...or Sam Weller. One can understand, however, that they made contemporary American readers restive. Dickens tends to picture our countrymen as offensive, conceited, bad-mannered, and ignorant, but he does so humorously. Even a hundred years later his pictures seem to me richly entertaining, to Americans themselves as well as to their critics.[65]

Dickens's observations sometimes seem to tend to be fallen into caricatures as both of the Americans suggest, but it is not right that "no such conversations ever occur in this country in real life" because our philological studies have shown that the words or phrases which Dickens considered Americanisms are all listed and illustrated as Americanisms in the references. They are clearly classified into four categories according to the labels and illustrations in the references.

Dickens, however, paid little attention to the regional variation between the northern and southern part of the United States in the case of northern *I guess* and *I calculate,* and southern *I reckon*, all of which are equivalent in meaning to "I suppose". He was merely interested in the English of both sides

---

[64] This extract (*Journal*, Nov. 25, 1842) is taken from H. L. Menken's *The American Language*, 1957, p. 27.

[65] L. Pound (1947) "The American Dialect of Charles Dickens," p. 126.

of the Atlantic and he did not regard the language spoken in the United States as the American language, but as the English language in America. He frequently wrote to Forster about the queer words and phrases he encountered with "the one-fourth serious and three-fourths comical astonishment," which he described on the opening page of *American Notes*, and it was from these letters that he later refreshed his memory to create *American Notes* and *Martin Chuzzlewit*.

Dickens perceived the differences between the British and America varieties of English soon after he landed on the native soil of United States. He described the various uses of the verb *fix* with the instincts of a lexicographer. In America this verb has wider sense than in Britain. He observed that Americas used "Yes?" and "Yes, sir." with various tones. He seems to have had more interest in the tones than in the use and meanings.

The differences between the British and American usage sometimes cause misunderstanding and confusion between them. Dickens humorously and amusingly introduced "Right away" instead of "All right" to Forster and his readers in Britain.

Dickens claims that "Go ahead!" and "All right!" express the national characters of the two countries, and thinks Americans' "Go ahead!" represents the restless and energetic progress of the American People, which is deeply connected with its original and literal meaning.

Dickens marked a solitary interrogative use in "possible," but the dictionaries used in the book are silent for this use. They give such examples for the interjectional use as that in *Martin Chuzzlewit*.

Judging from the evidence of this study, Dickens's views on

the use of Americanisms are correct and to the point. He introduced these interesting differences in use between two countries to Forster in his letters and to his readers in Britain in *American Notes*. In *Martin Chuzzlewit*, he practised them in the speech of American characters to help the readers to identify their nationality, and to colour the real life in the United States.

CONCLUSION

In Introduction we have made sure that there lies a clear difference between dialectology and dialectism. The main object of the latter is not dialect itself but the author's use of dialect. Therefore our primary concern has always been concentrated on literary dialect which Dickens created.

In chapter I, we strictly restricted the regional dialects for this book and determined their provenance and sources for making the dialect approach to the reality. Dickens would often visit the place which later became one of the main scenes in his novel with his friend or his illustrator, sometime before he began to write the novel. He was eager to collect provincial glossaries: Edward Moor's *Suffolk Words and Phrases* for *David Copperfield* and John Collier's *A View of the Lancashire Dialect* for *Hard Times*.

In Chapter II, we have studied inconsistency between spoken and written language and we testify that it is very difficult or almost impossible to render spoken language in writing. We took a close look at Dickens's endeavour to make written dialect accurate in the emendation of *nighbut* in *Hard Times* and in three various forms of *prairie* in American speech.

It may be the literary and linguistic art to manage to convey a true flavour into the text by using various devices: some of which are conventional and others innovative or experimental.

Chapter III has shown that phonetic spellings are made good use to represent John Browdie's broad Yorkshire accents; apostrophes are so much rendered to represent Stephen Blackpool's quick and short ways of Lancashire speech; capital letters and italics are employed to show the shifting of the stress; the use of hyphens and diacritic marks are Dickens's innovative and experimental devices to describe the peculiarities of American pronunciation.

The time of tone-down or termination of his experimental use of a rhetorical style of punctuation is paralleled with that of his experimental or innovative use of typographical devices. This fact also coincides with the literary criticism that Dickens's attitude toward writing his novels completely changed from *Dombey and Son* (1846-8).

Chapter IV has demonstrated the relation between realism and verisimilitude. Dickens had keen ear for regional dialects as well as Cockney. In addition to this natural gift, his eagerness to collect linguistic materials made his novels more real. Critics of Dickens sometimes stigmatise Dickens's application of standard English to the speech of Oliver Twist, although he was born and bred in a workhouse and received no proper education at all. This artificial speech is called "heroic speech" or "dialect suppression." Dickens, however, re-examined himself on the unnatural and far-fetched representations of Oliver's speech by the time when he wrote *Great Expectations*. His linguistic penance is to be found in Pip's letter to Joe written on a slate with his own hand. *H*-droppings in *hope* and an *h*-adding in *able* clearly suggests that Pip belongs to the lower-class as well as Joe.

Another discussion has been made in Chapter IV. Many of the dialectal pronunciations are to be found in *MW* and *DSL* and paralleled to the illustrations of the references, but the following phonetic descriptions are not to be assumed as Lancashire dialect: *anoother, discoosed, soombody, toother, t'oother, awlung, heer, Gonnows, a'toogether, faw'en, sma'est, wi'in,* and *wi'out.* In the case of *weel* for *well,* Dickens strictly followed its dialectal usage except one example and used the standard form at the beginning of the sentence. Due to some examples that are not to be recognized as Lancashire dialect and a few inconsistencies of spellings, the dialect Dickens tried to describe in *Hard Times* has been subject to the most caustic criticism by both literary and linguistic scholars.

In chapter V, our concern is chiefly on the stylistic point of view. We have studied David's role as a first person omniscient glossarist, secondly Dickens's splendid use of *drowndead* for *drownded* which testified the power of written words, and lastly interesting is ebullient style from his energy of youth as in the reproduction of Browdie's Yorkshire dialect, however, much more attractive and skilful is condensed style from his mutuality as in Mr. Peggotty's use of *drowndead* and Estella's reference to Pip's vulgar habit of "calling the knaves, Jacks".

It is very important for a writer who works for a serial instalment system of publication to typify the speech of class society or local society by scattering a large number of the instances of class and regional dialects here and there as we have already seen in Browdie's Yorkshire speech in Chapter

III. However, after the publication of *The Cricket on the Hearth* (1845), except for rendering Lancashire dialect in Blackpool's speech in *Hard Times*, Dickens's way of representing both class and regional dialect became condensed and foregrounded.

The elision of the vowel sound of the definite article occurs in the speech of Mr. and Mrs. Joe Gargery, *"th'meshes"* (*GE*, 15, 225), not in that of Pip, *"the meshes"* (*GE*, 19), while Kentish provincialism *meshes* is found in the speech of Pip as well as in that of Mr. and Mrs. Gargery. Dickens allows Pip to use regional dialect but never to employ class dialect.

There must have been many people among the readers of *Great Expectations* who was shocked to realize that "calling the knaves, Jacks" made them belong to the lower and vulgar society. G. L. Brook asserts that "if the author's works are widely read, his linguistic habits are likely to exert an important influence on others who use the language."[1] Pip's use of *Jacks* instead of *the Knaves* is considered as one of the best examples of Brook's remark. I think it no exaggeration to say that a word is enough to the reader when he or she enjoys and appreciates Dickens's use of literary dialect.

Grammatical anomalies in the speech of his American characters are closely parallel with that of both British low-life characters and dialect speakers. On the other hand, judging from the present survey, the use of *ris* and *rose* instead of "raised" as past particple, of *ought* with periphrastic *didn't*, and of *alarming, complete, considerable, moderate* and

---

[1] G. L. Brook (1970) *The Language of Dickens*, p. 13.

'special as flat adverbs represent salient features of American English clearly. All of them are deeply connected with earlier stage of the English language. This phenomenon has a good deal in common with the fact that archaic or obsolete English remains in substandard and dialectal speech in Britain. As the titles of their books imply, G. P. Krapp considers American English as one of the dialects of the English language, and H. L. Mencken, on the contrary, regards it as one indigenous and independent language. All things considered, the grammatical anomalies of American English Dickens describes combine many features of both substandard and dialectal British English. In this respect Krapp's view on the English language in America is much more persuasive.

Chapter VI has been used to discuss English provincialisms in *Nicholas Nickleby*, *Hard Times*, *David Copperfield* and *Great Expectations*; and Americanisms in *American Notes* and *Martin Chuzzlewit*. In contrast to *David Copperfield* and *Hard Times*, Dickens did not possess any glossarial references for Yorkshire provincialisms when he wrote *Nicholas Nickleby*. Consequently we seldom encounter Yorkshire words and phrases, while his keen ear for the dialect helped him to reproduce Yorkshire accents.

With respect to Lancashire provincialisms in *Hard Times*, *fair faw, haply, nighbut, nigh 'bout* are not regarded as Lancashire dialect vocabulary by the fact recorded by *EDD* and *GLD*. Besides *DSL* and *GLD*, *MW* is silent about *nighbut* and *nigh 'bout*, which made Dickens so much confused when he decided its form, because *MW* was major source for his creating Lancashire dialect. Many of the terms, however, are to be considered as Lancashire dialect from the evidence shown by the dictionaries and references.

The accurateness of the use of the dialectal vocabulary in *David Copperfield* is due to Moor's *Suffolk Words and Phrases* and some useful suggestions from his readers. I consider it very regrettable that *wimmicking* has not been emended. It is no doubt that its correct form is *winnicking*. As for *arrize*, we have decided that it is the variant form of *arise* or *araise*.

Due to the geographical closeness to London, Kent has lost its local peculiarities in its language use, In addition to *meshes*, we can find only three words for Kentish provincialisms in *Great Expectations*: one is *afeerd*; another *afore*; and the other *oncommon*.

Dickens perceived the difference between British and American English, when he first landed the United States. He sent many letters to his friend Forster in which he recorded the peculiarities of their pronunciation, grammar, and vocabulary in order to refresh his memory when he wrote *American Notes* and *Martin Chuzzlewit*.

The editors of the third revised edition of T. Yamamoto's *Growth and System* made it public that "*Dickens Lexicon* is expected to be published on CD-ROM within a few years"[2], which is "the ultimate aim in Yamamoto's Dickens studies". The present writer is one of the compilers of the *Lexicon*. I hope this lexical study will make some contributions to it.

---

[2] T. Yamamoto (2003) *Growth and System of the Language of Dickens*. The 3rd edition, p. 588.

SELECT BIBLIOGRAPHY

A. Texts
Charles Dickens
Dickens, C. (1833-1836) *Sketches by Boz*. The New Oxford Illustrated Dickens. Oxford University Press: Oxford, 1957.
Dickens, C. (1836-1837) *The Pickwick Papers*. The Clarendon Dickens. Edited by James Kinsley. The Clarendon Press: Oxford, 1986.
Dickens, C. (1837-1839) *Oliver Twist*. The Clarendon Dickens. Edited by Kathleen Tillotson. The Clarendon Press: Oxford, 1966.
Dickens, C. (1838-1839) *Nicholas Nickleby*. The Oxford World's Classics. Edited by Paul Schlicke. Oxford University Press: Oxford, 1998.
Dickens, C. (1840-1841) *Master Humphrey's Clock*. The New Oxford Illustrated Dickens. Oxford University Press: Oxford, 1958.
Dickens, C. (1840-1841) *The Old Curiosity Shop*. The Clarendon Dickens. Edited by Elizabeth M. Brennan. The Clarendon Press: Oxford, 1997.
Dickens, C. (1841) *Barnaby Rudge*. The New Oxford Illustrated Dickens. Oxford University Press: Oxford, 1954.
Dickens, C. (1842) *American Notes*. The New Oxford Illustrated Dickens. Oxford University Press: Oxford, 1957.
Dickens, C. (1843-1844) *Martin Chuzzlewit*. The Clarendon Dickens. Edited by Margaret Cardwell. The Clarendon Press: Oxford, 1982.
Dickens, C. (1843-1848) *Christmas Books*. The New Oxford Illustrated Dickens. Oxford University Press: Oxford, 1954.
Dickens, C. (1846-1848) *Dombey and Son*. The Clarendon Dickens. Edited by Alan Horsman. The Clarendon Press: Oxford, 1974.

Dickens, C. (1849-1850) *David Copperfield*. The Clarendon Dickens. Edited by Nina Burgis. The Clarendon Press: Oxford, 1981.
Dickens, C. (1852-1853) *Bleak House*. The New Oxford Illustrated Dickens. Oxford University Press: Oxford, 1948.
Dickens, C. (1854) *Hard Times*. The New Oxford Illustrated Dickens. Oxford University Press: Oxford, 1955.
Dickens, C. (1855-1857) *Little Dorrit*. The Clarendon Dickens. Edited by Harvey Peter Sucksmith. The Clarendon Press: Oxford, 1979.
Dickens, C. (1859) *A Tale of Two Cities*. The New Oxford Illustrated Dickens. Oxford University Press: Oxford, 1949.
Dickens, C. (1860) *The Uncommercial Traveller*. The New Oxford Illustrated Dickens. Oxford University Press: Oxford, 1958.
Dickens, C. (1860-1861) *Great Expectations*. The Clarendon Dickens. Edited by Margaret Cardwell. The Clarendon Press: Oxford, 1993.
Dickens, C. (1864-1865) *Our Mutual Friend*. The New Oxford Illustrated Dickens. Oxford University Press: Oxford, 1952.
Dickens, C. (1870) *The Mystery of Edwin Drood*. The Clarendon Dickens. Edited by Margaret Cardwell. The Clarendon Press: Oxford, 1972.

Other writers

Brontë, E. (1836-1837) *Wuthering Heights*. The Clarendon Edition of the Novels of the Brontës. Edited by Hilda Marsden and Ian Jack. The Clarendon Press: Oxford, 1976.
Chaucer, G. (1987) *The Riverside Chaucer*. The third edition. Edited by L. D. Benson. Houghton Mifflin Company: Boston.
Mayhew, H. (1851) *London Labour and the London Poor*. 3 vols. George Woodfall: London. Reprinted in 4 vols. by Frank Cass: London, 1967.
Shakespeare, W. (1986) *The Complete Works*. Original Spelling Edition. Edited by S. Wells, G. Taylor, J. Jowett, and W. Montgomery. The Clarendon Press: Oxford.
Shaw, G. B. (1916) *Pygmalion*. The Bernard Shaw library. Under the editorial supervision by Don H. Laurence. Penguin Books:

London, 2000.

B. Letters and Periodicals

Dickens, C., cond. (1850-1859) *Household Words*. Bradbury and Evans: London. Reprinted in 19 vols. by Hon-no-tomosha: Tokyo, 1989.

Dickens, C., cond. (1859-1870) *All the Year Round*. C. Whiting: London. Reprinted in 20 vols. by Hon-no-tomosha: Tokyo, 1991.

House, M. and G. Storey, eds. (1965) *The Letters of Charles Dickens*. Volume One 1820-1839. The Pilgrim Edition. The Clarendon Press: Oxford.

House, M. and G. Storey, eds. (1969) *The Letters of Charles Dickens*. Volume Two 1840-1841. The Pilgrim Edition. The Clarendon Press: Oxford.

House, M., G. Storey, and K. Tillotson, eds. (1974) *The Letters of Charles Dickens*. Volume Three 1842-1843. The Pilgrim Edition. The Clarendon Press: Oxford.

Storey, G. and K. J. Fielding, eds. (1981) *The Letters of Charles Dickens*. Volume Five 1847-1849. The Pilgrim Edition. The Clarendon Press: Oxford.

Storey, G., K. Tillotson and N. Burgis, eds. (1988) *The Letters of Charles Dickens*. Volume Six 1850-1852. The Pilgrim Edition. The Clarendon Press: Oxford.

Storey, G., K. Tillotson and A. Easson, eds. (1993) *The Letters of Charles Dickens*. Volume Seven 1853-1855. The Pilgrim Edition. The Clarendon Press: Oxford.

Storey, G. ed. (1997) *The Letters of Charles Dickens*. Volume Nine 1859-1861. The Pilgrim Edition. The Clarendon Press: Oxford.

Storey, G. ed. (1999) *The Letters of Charles Dickens*. Volume Eleven 1865-1867. The Pilgrim Edition. The Clarendon Press: Oxford.

C. References

Abbott, E. A. (1869) *A Shakespearian Grammar*. The third edition. Macmillan: London, 1883, rpt. 1929.

Adamson, S. (1998) "Literary Language". Chapter 7 of *The*

Cambridge History of the English Language, Vol. IV. 1776-1997. Edited by Suzanne Romaine. Cambridge University Press Cambridge. 589-692.
Bamford, S. (1850) *Dialect of South Lancashire*. John Heywood: Manchester.
Bentley, N., M. Slater, and N. Burgis, eds. (1988) *The Dickens Index*. Oxford University Press: Oxford.
Berrey, L. V. and M. Van Den Bark. eds. (1942) *The American Thesaurus of Slang*. The second edition. George G. Harrap & Co.: London, 1954.
Blake, N. F. (1979) "The Northernisms in The Reeve's Tale," *Lore and Langauge*, Vol. 3, No. 1. The Centre for English Cultural Tradition and Langauge, University of Sheffield, 1-8.
Blake, N. F. (1981) *Non-standard Language in English Literature*. André Deutsch: London.
Booth, W. C. (1961) *The Rhetoric of Fiction*. University of Chicago Press: Chicago.
Brilioth, B. (1913) *A Grammar of the Dialect of Lorton*. Uppsala University: Uppsala.
Brook, G. L. (1963) *English Dialects*. The third edition, André Deutsch: London, 1978.
Brook, G. L. (1970) *The Language of Dickens*. André Deutsch: London.
Brook, G. L. (1973) *The Varieties of English*. Macmillan: London.
Bryson, A. B. (1929) "Some Texas Dialect Words," *American Speech*, Vol. IV, 330-31.
Burchfield, R. ed. (1998) *The Cambridge History of the English Language*, Vol. V. English in Britain and Overseas. Cambridge University Press: Cambridge.
Carter, R. ed. (1982) *Language and Literature: An Introductory Reader in Stylistics*. Geroge Allen and Unwin: London.
Cercignani, F. (1981) *Shakespeare's Works and Elizabethan Pronunciation*. The Clarendon Press: Oxford.
Chapman, R. (1973) *Linguistics and Literature: An Introduction to Literary Stylistics*. Edward Arnold: London.
Chapman, R. (1984) *The Treatment of Sounds in Language and Literature*. Basil Blackwell: Oxford.

Chapman, R. (1994) *Forms of Speech in Victorian Fiction*. Longman: London & New York.
Chapple, J. A. V. and A. Pollard, eds. (1966) *The Letters of Mrs. Gaskell*. Manchester University Press: Manchester.
Chesterton, G. K. (1908) *All Things Considered*. Methuen: London. Re-set and published by Darwen Finlayson: Henley-on-Thames, 1969.
Collier, J., 'Tim Bobbin'. (1818) *The Miscellaneous Works of Tim Bobbin, Esq*. T. and J. Allman: London / Wilson and Sons: York.
Collins, P. ed. (1971) *Dickens: The Critical Heritage*. Routledge and Kegan Paul: London.
Craigie, W. A. (1938) "Dialect in Literature," *Essays by Divers Hands*, Vol. XVII. Edited by E. H. W. Meyerstein. Oxford University Press: London, 69-91.
Craigie, W. A. and J. R. Hulbert, eds. (1938-44) *A Dictionary of American English on Historical Principles*. 4 vols. The University of Chicago Press: Chicago.
Crystal, D. (1995) *The Cambridge Encyclopedia of the English Language*. Cambridge University Press: Cambridge.
Crystal, D. (2004) *The Stories of English*. Allen Lane: London.
Dean, C. (1960) "Joseph's Speech in *Wuthering Heights*". *Notes and Queries* (New Series) Vol. 7, No.1, 73-6.
Dobson, E. J. (1957) *English Pronunciation 1500-1700*. 2 vols. The second edition. The Clarendon Press: Oxford, 1968.
Easson, A. (1976) "Dialect in Dickens's *Hard Times*," *Notes and Queries*, 23, 412-413.
Ellis, A. J. (1869-89) *On Early English Pronunciation*. 6 vols. Early English Text Society: London. Reprinted by Haskell House Publishers: New York, 1969.
Evans, B. and C. Evans, eds. (1957) *A Dictionary of Contemporary American Usage*. Random House: New York.
Fielding, K. J. (1949) "*David Copperfield* and Dialect," *The Times Literary Supplement*. 30 April 1949, 288.
Forby, R. (1830) *The Vocabulary of East Anglia*. 2 vols. J. B. Nichols and Son: London. Reprinted by David & Charles: Newton Abbot, 1970.

Ford, G. H. (1955) *Dickens and his Readers.* Princeton University Press: New Jersey.
Ford, M., ed. (1999) *Nicholas Nickleby.* Penguin Classics Edition. Penguin Books: Harmondsworth.
Forster, J. (1893) *The Life of Charles Dickens,* first published in three volumes, 1871-74. Chapman & Hall: London.
Fowler, H. W. and E. G. Fowler (1906) *The King's English.* The third edition, 1931, reprinted, 1970. The Clarendon Press: Oxford.
Fowler, H. W. (1926) *A Dictionary of Modern English Usage.* Second edition. Revised by Sir Ernest Gowers, 1965. The Clarendon Press: Oxford.
Fowler, R. (1971) *The Language of Literature: Some Linguistic Contributions to Criticism.* Routledge and Kegan Paul: London.
Fowler, R. (1977) *Linguistics and the Novel.* Methuen: London.
Franklyn, J. (1953) *The Cockney: A Survey of London Life and Language.* André Deutsch: London.
Franz, W. (1889) "Die Dialektsprache bei Ch. Dickens," *Englische Studien* Vol. XII, 197-244.
Gaskell, The Rev. W. (1854) *Two Lectures on the Lancashire Dialect.* Chapman and Hall: London.
Gerson, S. (1967) *Sound and Symbol in the Dialogue of the Works of Charles Dickens.* Almqvist and Wiksell: Stockholm.
Golding, R. (1985) *Idiolects in Dickens.* Macmillan: London.
Grove, Lady A. G. (1907) *The Social Fetich.* The second edition. Smith Elder: London, 1908.
Grove, P. B. et. al. (1964) *Webster's Third International Dictionary of the English Language, Unabridged.* G. & C. Merriam Company: Massachusetts.
Hayward, A. (1924) *The Dickens Encyclopædia.* Routledge & Kegan Paul: London.
Hardwick, Michael and Mollie Hardwick, eds. (1973) *The Charles Dickens Encyclopedia.* Osprey: London.
Hargreaves, A. (1904) *A Grammar of the Dialect of Adlington.* Carl Winter: Heidelberg.
Hedevind, B. (1967) *The Dialect of Dentdale in the West Riding*

of Yorkshire. Studia Anglistica Upsaliensia 5. Uppsala University: Uppsala.
Hirooka, H. (1965) *Dialects in English Literature*. Shinozaki Shorin: Tokyo.
Hori, Masahiro (2004) *Investigating Dickens' Style: A Collocational Analysis*. Palgrave Macmillan: Basingstoke.
Horwill, H. W. ed. (1935) *A Dictionary of Modern American Usage*. The second edition. The Clarendon Press: Oxford, 1944.
House, H. (1941) *The Dickens World*. The second edition. Oxford University Press: London, 1942.
Ichikawa, S. (1912) *Studies in English Grammar*. The new edition. Kenkyusha: Tokyo, 1948.
Imahayashi, O. (1998) "Grammatical Anomalies of American English in Dickens." *ERA, New Series*, Vol. 16, No. 2. 31-48.
Imahayashi, O. (1999) "Dickens's Use of American Pronunciation." *Journal of Kibi International University*, No. 9. 67-74.
Imahayashi, O. (2001) "Dickens on the Use of Americanisms." *A Festschrift for Professor Norihisa Matsumoto*. Hiroshima. 35-50.
Imahayashi, O. (2001) "Americanisms in Dickens." *Originality and Adventure: Essays on English Language and Literature In Honour of Masahiko Kanno*. Edited by Y. Nakao and A. Jimura. Eihôsha: Tokyo. 159-181.
Imahayashi, O. (2003) "Lexical Studies on the Regional Dialect in *Hard Times*." *Ful of Hy Sentence*. Edited by Masahiko Kanno. Eihôsha: Tokyo. 193-206.
Imahayashi, O. (2004) "Dialectal Features of Stephen Blackpool's Pronunciation." *English Philology and Stylistics: A Festschrift for Professor Toshiro Tanaka*. Edited by O. Imahayashi and H. Fukumoto. Keisuisha: Hiroshima. 153-166.
Imahayashi, O. (2005) "'A Word to the Reader': Dickens on the use of Literary Dialect," read at the 25th PALA, Huddersfield University, England.
Imahayashi, O. (2006) "A Stylistic Approach to Pip's Class-consciousness," read at the 26th PALA, Joensuu University, Finland.

Ingham, P. (1986) "Dialect as 'Realism': *Hard Times* and the Industrial Novel," *The Review of English Studies*, 37, 518-27.
Jespersen, O. (1909) *A Modern English Grammar on Historical Principles*, Vol. I. Ejnar Munksgaard: Copenhagen. Reprinted by Meicho-Fukyukai: Tokyo, 1983.
Jespersen, O. (1940) *A Modern English Grammar on Historical Principles*, Vol. V. Ejnar Munksgaard: Copenhagen. Reprinted by Meicho-Fukyukai: Tokyo, 1983.
Jimura, A. (2005) *Studies in Chaucer's Words and His Narrative*. Keisuisha: Hiroshima.
Johnson, E. (1952) *Charles Dickens: His Tragedy and Triumph*. 2 vols. Simon and Schuster: New York.
Kaplan, F. and S. Monod, eds. (2001) *Hard Times*. The Norton Critical Edition. The third edition. W. W. Norton & Co.: New York.
Kökeritz, H. (1932) *The Phonology of the Suffolk Dialect*. Uppsala University: Uppsala.
Krapp, G. P. (1925) *The English Language in America*. 2 vols. The Century Co.: New York.
Labov, W. (1966) *The Social Stratification of English in New York City*. Center for Applied Linguistics: Washington D. C.
Latham, R. G. (1841) *The English Language*. The second edition. Taylor and Walton: London, 1848.
Latham, R. G. (1851) *A Hand-Book of the English Language*. The fourth edition. Walton and Maberly: London, 1860.
Langton, Robert (1912) *Childhood and Youth of Charles Dickens*. Hutchinson and Co.: London.
Leech, G. N. (1969) *A Linguistic Guide to English Poetry*. Longman: London.
Leech, G. N. and M. H. Short. (1981) *Style in Fiction: A Linguistic Introduction to English Fictional Prose*. Longman: London.
Lohrli, A. (1962) "Dickens's *Household Words* on American English." *American Speech*. Vol. XXXVII, No. 2. 83-94.
Lodge, D. (1966) "The Rhetoric of *Hard Times*" in *Language of Fiction*. Routledge and Kegan Paul: London, 144-163.
McCrum, R., W. Cran, and R. MaCneil (1986) *The Story of*

English. Faber and Faber: London.
Marcus, S. (1965) *Dickens from Pickwick to Dombey*, Chatto and Windus: London.
Mathews, M. M. ed. (1951) *A Dictionary of Americanisms on Historical Principles*. The University of Chicago Press: Chicago.
Matthews, W. (1938) *Cockney Past and Present: A Short History of the Dialect in London*. Routledge and Kegan Paul: London.
Melchers, G. (1978) "Mrs. Gaskell and Dialect". *Studies in English Philology, Linguistics and Literature: Presented to Alarik Rynell 7 March 1978*. Edited by Mats Rydén and Lennart A. Björk. Almqvist and Wiksell International: Stockholm. 112-124.
Mencken, H. L. (1919, 1957) *The American Language, Supplement One* (1945, 1956), and *Supplement Two* (1948, 1956). Reprinted by Senjo Publishing Co.: Tokyo, 1962.
Moor, E. (1823) *Suffolk Words and Phrases*, R. Hunter: London.
Mugglestone, L. (1998) *'Talking Proper': The Rise of Accent as Social Symbol*. The second edition. Oxford University Press: Oxford, 2003.
Nall, J. G. (1866) *Guide to Yarmouth and Lowestoft*. George Nall: Great Yarmouth.
Nodal, J. H. and G. Milner. *A Glossary of the Lancashire Dialect*. Part I - Words from *A* to *Eysel* (1875). Part II - Words from *Ettle* to *Yoi* (1882) Alexander Ir. and Co.: Manchester / Trübner and Co.: London.
Orton, H. and E. Dieth, eds. (1962-71) *Survey of English Dialects*. 13 vols. E. J. Arnold & Son Ltd.: Leeds.
Page, N. (1969) "'A Language Fit for Heroes': Speech in *Oliver Twist* and *Our Mutual Friend*". *The Dickensian*. Vol. 65, Part 2. 100-107.
Page, N. (1970) "Convention and Consistency in Dickens's Cockney Dialect". *English Studies*. Vol. 51, No. 4. 339-344
Page, N. ed. (1984) *The Language of Literature*. Macmillan: London.
Page, N. (1988) *Speech in the English Novel*. The second edition.

Macmillan: London. First published by Longman: London, 1973.
Paroissien, D. (2000) *The Companion to* Great Expectations. Helm Information: London.
Partridge, E. (1937) *A Dictionary of Slang and Unconventional English*. 2 vols. The fifth edition. Routledge & Kegan Paul: London, 1979.
Petyt, K. M. (1976) "The Dialect Speech in *Wuthering Heights*." Appendix VII to *Wuthering Heights*. The Clarendon Edition of the Novels of the Brontës. Edited by H. Marsden and I. Jack. The Clarendon Press: Oxford, 1976. 500-513.
Petyt, K. M. (1980) *The Study of Dialect: An introduction to dialectology*. André Deutsch: London.
Phillipps, K. C. (1984) *Language and Class in Victorian England*. Basil Blackwell: Oxford.
Pound, L. (1947) "The American Dialect of Charles Dickens", *American Speech*. Vol. XXII., 124-130.
Quirk, R. (1959) *Charles Dickens and Appropriate Language*. The University of Durham: Durham.
Quirk, R. (1961) "Some Observations on the Language of Dickens". *A Review of English Literature*. Vol. II. No. 3. 19-28.
Quirk, R. (1974) "Charles Dickens, Linguist". Chapter 1 of *The Linguist and the English Language*. Edward Arnold: London,
Ross, A. S. C. (1956) "U and Non-U." *Noblesse Oblige: An Enquiry into the Identifiable Characteristics of the English Aristocracy*. Edited by Nancy Mitford. Hamish Hamilton: London. 11-36.
Saxe, J. (1936) *Bernard Shaw's Phonetics: A Comparative Study of Cockney Sound-Changes*. Levin & Munksgaard: Copenhagen.
Schlicke, P., ed. (1999) *Oxford Reader's Companion to Dickens*. Oxford University Press: Oxford.
Schilling, K. G. (1906) *A Grammar of the Dialect of Oldham*. Dissertation. Darmstadt.
Simpson, J. and E. S. C. Weiner, eds. (2004) *The Oxford English Dictionary*. The second edition. CD-ROM, Version 3.1. Oxford University Press: Oxford.

Sivertsen, E. (1960) *Cockney Phonology*. Oslo Studies in English, No. 8. Oslo University Press: Oslo.
Slater, M., ed. (1971) "A Note on the Text and Annotation" to *The Christmas Books*. Vol. 1. Penguin Classics Edition. Penguin Books: Harmondsworth.
Sørensen, K. (1985) *Charles Dickens: Linguistic Innovator*. Acta Jutlandica LXI, Humanistisk serie 58. Arkona: Aarhus.
Sørensen, K. (1989) "Dickens on the Use of English". *English Studies*. Vol. 70, No. 6. 551-559.
Stone, H. (1959) "Dickens and Interior Monologue," *Philological Quarterly*, Vol. XXXVIII, No. 4, 52-65.
Stonehouse, J. H. (1935) *Reprints of the Catalogues of the Libraries of Charles Dickens and W. M. Thackeray etc*. Piccadilly Fountain Press: London.
Tanaka, T. (1972) "Regional and Occupational Dialect of Joe Gargery" (in Japanese). *Literature and Language of Dickens*. Edited by Michio Masui and Masami Tanabe. Sanseido: Tokyo. 153-187.
Tanaka, T. (1973) "Regional Dialect of Abel Magwitch". *Eibungaku-Ronshu*. No. 11. The English Literary Society of Kansai University: Osaka. 44-59.
Tolkien, J. R. R. (1934) "Chaucer as a Philologist: *The Reeve's Tale*," *Transactions of the Philological Society*, 1-70.
Trudgill, P. (1974) *Sociolinguistics: An Introduction to Language and Society*. The fourth edition. Penguin: London, 2000.
Trudgill, P. (1990) *The Dialects of England*. Basil Blackwell: Oxford.
Wagner, T. (1999) "John Collier's 'Tummus and Meary': Distinguishing Features of 18th-Century Southeast Lancashire Dialect–Morphology," *Neuphilologische Mitteilungen*, 2 C. 191-205.
Wakelin, M. F. (1972) *English Dialects: An Introduction*. The Athlone Press: London.
Wales, K. (1990) *A Dictionary of Stylistics*. The second edition. Longman: London, 2001.
Webb, L. K. (1983) *Charles Dickens*. Evergreen Lives. Tonsa: San Sebastian.

Wells, J. C. (1982) *Accents of English.* 3 vols. Cambridge University Press: Cambridge.
Wentworth, H. and S. B. Flexner. (1960) *Dictionary of American Slang.* Thomas Y. Crowell Co.: New York.
Whitney, W. D. *et al.* (1889-91) *The Century Dictionary.* 7 vols. Century Co.: New York. Reprinted by Meicho-Fukyukai: Tokyo, 1980.
Wilson, A. (1960) "Charles Dickens: A Haunting," *Critical Quarterly,* Vol. II, 101-08.
Wright, E. M. (1913) *Rustic Speech and Folk-lore.* Oxford University Press: London.
Wright, J. ed. (1898-1905) *The English Dialect Dictionary.* 5 vols. Henry Frowde: London. Reprinted by Oxford University Press: Oxford, 1981.
Wright, J. (1892) *A Grammar of the Dialect of Windhill in the West Riding of Yorkshire.* Trübner: London.
Wright, J. (1905) *The English Dialect Grammar.* Henry Frowde: Oxford.
Wright, J. and E. M. Wright (1924) *An Elementary Historical New English Grammar.* Oxford University Press: London.
Yamamoto, T. (1950) *Growth and System of the Language of Dickens: An Introduction to A Dickens Lexicon.* The third edition. Keisuisha: Hiroshima, 2003.

INDEX

A

A, indef. article 31, 32
a-, prep. 92, 93; *a begging* 92; *a-biling* 93; *a coming* 93; *a dying* 93; *a goin* 93; *a going* 93; *a having* 93; *a printing* 93; *a waitin'* 93
a-, pref 38; *a-dopted* 38; *a-larming* 38; *a-live* 38; *a-mazing* 38
Abbott, E. A. 96
able 50
aboot 28
aboove 61, 65
accent 26
accusative 67
ac-quire 38
ac-tive 36
ac-Tive 31, 36
adding [d] 76
adjective 104, 107, 111, 118, 131; adjectives 95
adverb 64, 102, 106, 113, 114, 131; adverbs 95, 96
afeard 102, 104, 118, 119, 127, 132; *'feard* 102, 119; *afeared* 102; *afeerd* 118, 127, 130, 170; *afered* 119
affirmative 118
affrayed 119
afore 102, 104, 106, 116, 130, 132, 170; *ofore* 106, 116
agean 26
ahind 106, 116; *ahint* 106, 116

ain't for "am not" 86; *ain't* for "hasn't" 87; *ain't* for "isn't" 86
alarming, adv. 97, 99, 168; *a-larming* 97
all 56
All is True (*Henry VIII*) 96
All right. 159, 163; *All right!* 141, 163
almost 55
along 63, 116; *along of* 107, 116; *along o'* 107; *alung* 116
America 15, 16, 22; American dialect 6; American English 3, 5, 6, 8, 15, 16, 71, 82, 83, 96, 99, 100, 132, 133, 134, 135, 136, 144, 150, 157, 158, 169, 170; American language 163; American pronunciation 21, 31, 33, 34, 39, 142, 166; American slang 147; American speech 16, 37, 133, 161, 165; American usage 83; American vocabulary 151
American Notes 3, 6, 8, 15-17, 22, 38, 39, 40, 83, 8-86, 90, 97, 99, 132, 133, 135, 136-138, 140, 141, 144, 145, 147, 150-152, 155, 157, 159, 161, 163, 169, 170
Americanism 94, 137, 149, 150, 160; Americanisms v, 8, 101, 132, 133, 134, 136, 144, 162, 164, 169
among 62, 63
amoong 30, 61, 65

183

An, indef. article 31
an (=and) 54, 59; *an'* 59, 54, 55
analogy 64, 118
anaptyxis 22
anoother 28, 61, 65, 70, 167
another 62
an't for "am not" 84; *an't* for "aren't" 85; *an't* for "isn't" 84
apostrophes 7, 26, 27, 29, 166
araise 119, 170
archaic 83
arise 119, 170
arrize 119, 127, 170
as, rel. 90; *as for "which" or "that"* 91; *as for "whom" or "that"* 91; *as for "who" or "that"* 91
as-TONishin 31; *as-TONishing* 38
Askey, Arthur 33
'soizes (=*assize*) 28
aught 67
autumn 135
auxiliary 57, 112
avize 119
aw 60
awa' 29
awful, adv. 97, 99
awize 119
awlung 63, 66, 70, 116, 167; *awlung o'* 116, 106, 107; *awlúng* 116
awmost 55, 59; *awmust* 55, 59
a' 27, 29
a'toogether 55, 59, 70, 167

B

bahds-neest 120; *bahds-neezen* 120; *bahd's neezing* 73, 120; *bahd's-neezing* 120; *birds-nesting* 120; *bird's-neezening* 127; *bird's-nesting* 127
Barkis, Mr. 12
Barnaby Rudge 33

Barnard Castle 10
Barnes, Richard 10
bars 39
Bartlett, John 146
Battle of Life, The 39
Bayham Street 46
BBC 79
Beak 74
Beein 72, 120, 127; *beein* 120, 127; *Beein'* 73, 120; *be-índ* 116
behint 116; *be-índ* 116; *behund* 116; *behunt* 116; *behínt* 116; *behúnd* 116; *behúnt* 116
being 127
betther 26, 27
Bevan, Mr. 137, 138
Blackpool, Stephen 4, 12, 13, 23, 24, 29, 40, 52-55, 57, 58, 61, 63, 63, 67-69, 84, 88, 90-93, 103, 106-114, 166, 168
Blake, N. F. 16, 133
blend-word 149
Blunderstone 10, 12
Blundeston 11, 12, 18
Bo' 41; *bo'* 11, 42, 121; *Bor* 41; *bor* 11, 42, 121, 128; *bor'* 41, 42, 128
boan 26
Bobbin, Tim 14, 24, 105
boddy 26
boost 28
Booth, W. C. 71
bootuns 28
borh 128
Boston 34, 132, 133, 142
Boswell, James 16
Boucicault, Mr. 14
Bounderby, Mr. 12, 108, 111
Bowes 10, 18
Boz 26, 27, 48
brak' 26, 28
brig 69, 70; *brigg* 69, 70
British English 8, 15, 36, 37, 71, 82,

96, 100, 132, 135, 136, 148, 150, 157, 169, 170
broid 28
brokken 28
Brontë, Anne 2
Brontë, Charlotte 2, 47
Brontë, Emily 2, 47
Brook, G. L. 1, 5, 20, 26-28, 35, 36, 41, 49, 52, 53, 63, 64, 70, 71, 80, 82, 84, 88, 93, 94, 99, 105, 119, 121, 148, 150, 152, 168
Browdie, John 4, 10, 18, 26-28, 40, 101-104, 107, 109, 166, 167
Browne, H. K. 9
Bryson, Artemisia Bear 22, 23
Bumble, Mr. 91
Bung, Mr. 98
Burgis, Nina 3, 119
Burnett, Fanny 13
Burnett, Mrs. 13
Butt, John 40
butther 27

C
cail 123
Camden Town 46
Canada 18
Canterbury Tales, The 96, 119, 136
capital letters 7, 26, 31, 40, 166
catawampous 146, 148; *catawampously* 148
ca's 26
central vowel 21
-cg 69
Chapman and Hall 16
Chapman, R. 1, 21
characterisation 7
Chatham 17, 18
Chaucer, Geoffrey 96, 119, 136
chaw up 147, 148
Cheke, John 20

Chesterton, G. K. 20
chilt 69, 70
Chimes, The 39
Chitling, Tom 83
Choke, General 16, 18, 83, 92, 136, 142, 149
Chollop, Hannibal 16, 18, 83, 87, 88, 91, 92, 93, 98, 143
Christmas Carol, A 39
Clapin, S. 159
class dialect 1, 2, 6, 8, 71, 79, 168
clicket 121, 128
clicketten 72, 121, 128
Co-lumbia 38
coarse hands 79, 81, 82
Cockney 3, 5, 19, 21, 166; Cockney speech 21; Cockneys 83
coinage 149
*coin*cidence 33
Coketown 12, 14, 110
Collier, John 14, 18, 29, 53, 105, 165
Collins, P. 48
colloquial 94, 137, 156; colloquial idioms 4; colloquial speech 87, 136; colloquialism 79
Colman, George the Younger 151
colons 39
com- 37; *Com-mittee* 38; *com-pete* 38; *com-plete, adv.* 97
common boots 81
common labouring boy 79
compensation 140, 145
complete, adv. 97, 99, 168
compound adjective 110, 141
con- 37; *con-ceive* 37; *con-clude* 37; *con-cluded* 37; *con-sider* 38; *con-siderable* 38; *con-siderin* 38
condensed style 167
conjunction 102, 103, 106, 107, 108, 114, 130
considerable, adv. 97, 99, 168

consonant 29; consonants 53, 54, 58, 69
conventional use 7, 26
Cooke, Thomas 47
Cooling 17, 18
coom (pp.) 61, 65, *coom (pr.)* 26, 61, 65; *cooms* 26, 30, 61, 65
coomfortable 28
coompany 61, 65
coop 61, 65
coot 28
coover 61, 65
cop 123
Cornwall 47; Cornwall dialect 47
corrected proof 23, 109
Court Magazine 48
Crackit, Toby 83
Cricket on the Hearth, The 39
Crystal, David 20

D
daark 26
daft 105
dander 140, 145
dashes 39, 72
David Copperfield 10, 11, 41, 71, 72, 73, 75, 77, 125, 167
David Copperfield 3, 6, 8, 10, 12, 41-44, 71, 76, 77, 84, 86, 87, 90-95, 98, 99, 101, 103, 107-119, 120-126, 169, 170
-*dead* 76, 77
-*ded* 76
definite article 29, 30
delimitable units 4
di-rection 38
diacritic marks 7, 26, 33, 39, 40, 166
dialect 1, 2, 4, 6, 9, 13, 19, 26, 50, 52, 53, 101, 119, 165; dialects 2, 7, 8, 55, 58, 101, 102, 130, 169; dialect glossarist 71; dialect speakers 83, 84, 94, 99, 103; dialect suppression 166; dialect vocabulary 105; dialectal deviation 7; dialectal form 55, 61, 63, 69, 78, 107, 123, 125, 129; dialectal forms 61, 106; dialectal pronunciation 67, 68; dialectal pronunciations 70, 167; dialectal speech 29, 45, 169; dialectal varieties 26; dialectal vocabulary 115
dialectism 1, 2, 165
dialectology 1, 2, 165
Dickens, Charles v, 2-17, 19, 21, 22, 25, 26, 28-31, 33-35, 38, 40, 41, 45, 46, 48, 50, 52, 53, 63, 70, 71, 75, 77, 79, 83, 90, 96, 101, 103, 105, 106, 115, 119, 132, 133, 136, 141, 149, 152, 153, 157, 159, 165, 167, 168
Dickens Lexicon 170
didn't ought 94, 168
Dieth, Eugen 1
ding 123
"Dinner at Poplar Walk, A" 45
diphthong 38, 67, 68; diphthongs 27, 38, 68
directly 157
discoosed 61, 65, 70, 167
disyllabic words 35, 36, 37, 38
Diver, Colonel 16, 18, 34, 83, 98, 136, 137, 142, 143, 148, 154
do-minion 38
Dodger, The Artful 84, 86, 91, 92, 93
dodman 72, 121, 128
doen't ought 94, 95
Dombey and Son 33, 34, 40, 166
done 62
Doolittle, Eliza 47
doon 27, 28, 61, 65
doonstairs 26, 28
Dorsetshire dialect 2

INDEX

Dotheboys Hall 10
dreadfo' 60, 56
dreadful, adv. 97, 99
dree 107, 116; *dree rain* 107; *dree road* 116; *dreely* 107
droonk 28
droonken 61, 65
drown 76
drownd 76
drowndead 75-77, 78
drownded 75, 76, 77
dry 107
dull 97
dun 61
dwelling'ouse 51
dyke 122, 128; *dike* 128

E
-e 95
e- 38; *e-mo-tion* 38; *e-tarnal* 38
early Modern English 18
Easson, Angus 6, 14, 105
East Anglia 3, 12, 46, 118; East Anglia dialect 5, 6, 11, 12, 41, 44, 71, 84, 103; East Anglia provincialisms 43, 118, 127
easy, adv. 98, 99; *easie, adv.* 96
ed (=head) 50
Ees 26
efther 26, 27
Eliot, George 2
elision 54, 78
elliptical use 102
elsewheer 68, 69
elth 50
Emerson, R. W. 161, 162
Em'ly 11, 76, 77, 125
en- 37; *en-gine* 36; *ĕn-gīne* 36, 39; *en-tirely* 37
ĕngine 33, 39; *ĕngīne* 39
ene-mies 36

English Research Association of Hiroshima vi
English schoolboy 94
rican 15
equall, adv. 96
ere 107; *ere ever* 108, 116
'special 98, 99, 169
Estella 79, 81
Eu-rope 37
Evans, B. 149
Evans, C 149
evening school 81
eventuate 148, 150
ex- 37; *ex-alted* 37; *ex-cited* 37; *ex-citement* 37; *ex-clusiveness* 37; *ex-pect* 37; *ex-pression* 37
excellent, adv. 96

F
Fagin, Bob 83, 98
fair fall 116; *fair faw* 108, 115, 116, 169; *fair fo* 116; *fair-faw* 116
faithfo' 60, 56
fall 56, 135
fare 122, 128
fare to feel 122
faw 56, 60
fawn 56
fawt 55, 56, 59
faw'en 55, 59, 70, 167
fearfo 56, 60; *fearfo'* 60, 29, 56; *feerfo* 56
Fearon, H. B. 158
Fechter, Charles 14
fesTIval 31
fewtrils 108, 116
Fielding, Henry 3, 4, 11, 41, 71, 121
finite verb 122
fisherate 73, 122, 128
fix, v. 151, 153, 160, 161; *fix it presently* 151; *fix you* 151; *fixing*

188   *Charles Dickens and Literary Dialect*

himself 151; *fixing the tables* 151
Fladdock, General 142
flat adverbs 96
flats 11, 41
fo 56, 60; *fu'* 60
foco 142
focus 143
fogels 75
foind 28
fok, great 108
Forby, Robert 3, 118
Ford, George H. 25
Ford, M. 9
Ford, Richard 48
Forster, John 3, 10, 15, 16, 21, 22, 45, 82, 132, 133, 135, 138, 142, 145, 150, 151, 154, 155, 163, 164, 170
Fowler, H. W. 135
fra 108, 109, 116; *fra'* 116, 29, 109, 108; *fro* 108, 109, 116; *fro'* 116, 109, 108; *frá* 108
fram 108
Franklyn, Julian 18, 21, 78
Franz, Wilhelm 2
fratch 108, 116
frightful, adv. 98, 99
fuego 142
fuoco 142

G
Gad's Hill 47; Gad's Hill Place 17
Gamp, Mrs. 93, 97, 162
gan 105
gane 26
gang 103
Garden of England 18
Gargery, Joe 5, 17, 50, 51, 78, 79, 82, 84, 86, 87, 91, 94, 97, 98, 103, 130, 132, 168
Gargery, Mrs. Joe 17, 73, 78, 79, 129, 168
garthers 27
Gaskell, Elizabeth 2, 6, 15
Gaskell, The Rev. William 6, 15, 24, 30, 105, 106, 107
General Choke 138
Gerson, Stanley 4, 27, 36, 37, 39, 54, 55
Gibson, Milner 12
gin 103, 105
Go ahead! 141, 161, 163
go-ahead, adj. 141; *go-ahead people* 159
Gŏ-lāng 39
gold 55
Gonnows 54, 59, 70, 167
gowd 55, 56, 59
gown 76; *gownd* 76
Gradgrind, Mr. 111
Gradgrind, Tom 111
grammar 3, 4, 15, 41, 133, 170
grammatical anomalies 83, 99, 168, 169
gratful 28
Great Expectations 6-8, 17, 45, 50-52, 71, 73, 78, 80, 81, 86, 87, 90, 91-94, 98, 99, 103, 129-131, 166, 168-170
Great Vowel Shift, the 20
Greta Bridge 10
Grose, Francis 115
Gummidge, Mrs. 11, 42, 44, 107, 118, 120, 121, 122, 124, 125
guttural vowel 56

H
h-adding 50
h-addings 51
h-droppings 50
ha 60; *ha'* 60, 29, 30, 57
'air (=hair) 51

INDEX

han 57
haply 109, 115, 116, 169
happly 109, 116
Hard Times 4, 6, 8, 12-14, 23, 24, 29, 47, 52-56, 58, 62, 67-70, 84, 88, 90-93, 99, 101, 103, 105-110, 112, 113, 115, 116, 165, 167, 168, 169
Hardwick, Michael 13
Hardwick, Mollie 13
Hardy, Thomas 2
Hargreaves, A. 55
'arm (=harm) 51
'armony (=harmonry) 30
'at (=hat) 51
Haunted Man, The 40
Havisham, Miss 79, 81, 82
Haworth dialect 48
'eating (=heating) 51
heer 30, 68, 69, 70, 118, 167
heerd 26, 27, 30, 118
heroic speech 7, 49, 166
heroine 50
hetter 109, 110, 117
Hexam, Lizzie 49, 50
hey-go-mad 110, 117; *heigh-go-mad* 117
Hill, The Rev. George Frederick 11, 41, 121
him for "he" 90
Hirooka, Hideo 18
hodman-dod 128
hold 55
Hominy, Mrs. 16, 18, 83, 86, 144
h*onour* 33; h*nour* 34; h*onors* 33; h*onourable* 33
hoo 28; *hoo'* 28
Hoo Peninsula 17
hoold 26
hoonger 28; *hoongry* 28
hoorly-boorly 26
hope 50
hotter 117; *hottering mad* 110;

hottering-mad 117; *hotterin'-mad* 117
House, Humphry 52
housebreakers 84
Household Words 13, 23, 30, 63, 112, 113
HOUT 51, 52
howd 56, 59
Hulks 73, 129
hull 123, 128
hummabee 117; *hummobee* 110, 117
hurl 123, 128
hyphen 31, 36, 142; *hyphens* 7, 26, 33, 34, 35, 40, 166; *hyphenated word* 38

I

I calculate 136, 140, 145, 162
I expect 136
I gesse 136
I guess 104, 136, 137, 162
I reckon 104, 105, 136, 137, 162
Ichikawa, Sanki 3
identification 41
idiom 13
Ikey 97
illiterate speech 87
imperative 103
implied author 71
indefinite article 31
indicative 57
individualisation 41, 44
Industrial Revolution 79
infinitive 103, 112
Ingham, Patricia 6, 14, 15, 105
inquiration 123, 128
inquire 123
insertion of semi-vowel [j] 58
instalment 33, 41, 63, 167
interjection 160
International Copyright 15

invariable plural noun 108
't (=it) 30
italics 7, 26, 33, 166
i' (=in) 60, 57; i' th' (=in the) 57

J
jack-of-all-trades 151
Jacks 79, 80, 81, 82, 168
japanning his trotter-cases 74
Jerk the tinkler 74
Jespersen, Otto 22, 31, 34, 54, 57, 76
Jimura, Akiyuki v
Johnson, Edgar 9, 13
Johnson, Samuel 16
Jonson, Ben 13
Joseph 48
junior 142, 145

K
Katou, Kenji vi
Kaplan, Fred 23, 109
Kawai, Michio v
Kedgick, Captain 16, 18, 83, 87, 88, 91, 93, 94, 137, 140
Kent 18, 78, 103, 170; Kentish dialect 6, 18, 84, 129; Kentish provincialism 79, 130, 168, 170
Kettle, La Fayette 16, 18, 83, 86, 97, 136, 138, 145
kiender 43, 44, 123, 124, 128; kind o' 128
Kimura, Itsushi vi
Knaves 79-82, 168
know'd, pp. 88
Krapp, G. P. 35, 87, 88, 100, 169
Kökeritz, H. 22, 120

L
Labov, William 1

lad 110, 111, 117
Lancashire 12, 14, 18, 24, 29, 46, 52, 53, 55, 115; Lancashire accent 29; Lancashire accents 40; Lancashire dialect 4, 5, 6, 8, 12, 29, 52, 53, 70, 84, 103, 105, 115, 167, 168, 169, 170; Lancashire Dialect Society 5; Lancashire provincialisms 116; Lancashire speech 166
Langton, Robert 52
lass 111, 117
Latham, R. G. 96
latthers 27
le-Vee 31, 36; lĕ-vēe 36, 39
Leech, G. N. 2, 49, 50
Leech, John 10
leefer 112, 117
leetsome 111, 117
Lemon, Mark 10, 47
lesser breeds 80
level stress 31, 33, 36, 37, 38
lexicographer 152, 163
-līc 95
-līce 95
lief 111; liefer 112, 117; liever 117
lightly-stressed syllable 31, 36
lightsome 111
linguistic characterisation 2, 7, 43, 44
linguistic experiments 39
linguistic habits 80
linguistic symbols 33
linguistic typification 40
literary art v, 165
literary dialect 2, 6, 71, 165, 168;
literary piracy 15
literary text 2; literary texts 20
Liverpool 13, 133
lo-ca-tion 38, 142; lo-cation 38, 142
local accent 26; local phraseology 123

INDEX

locate 142, 145; *location* 142, 145
loco 142
locofoco 142, 143, 145
locomotive 142
loight 26; *loit* 28
loike 28
London 9, 18, 19, 45-47, 129, 170; London dialect 3, 18; London English 99; London speech 102, 130; London underworld 73
lone 128; *lone and lorn* 42-44, 124, 125; *lone lorn* 42, 43; *lorn* 124, 125, 128
long vowel 37, 38, 67; long vowels 38
looder 28
look'ee 30
loonching 28
loove 28
loss of [d] 76; loss of [v] 57; loss of *d* 54; loss of final *l* 56; loss of final *n* 57; loss of *h* 58; loss of medial [ð] 58; loss of medial *l* 55
loude, adv. 96
low-life London characters 5, 83, 84, 90, 94, 99, 103
lower-class 2, 48, 50, 79, 167
Lowestoft 11
-ly 95

M
Mackin, Mrs. 90
Maclise, Daniel 132
Maeda, Emi vi
Magwitch, Abel 5, 84, 90, 92, 93
mak 28; *mak'* 28; *mak'st* 28
Manchester 13, 14, 18
manuscript 23
Marcus, Steven 15, 133
Marryat, Captain 152

marsh 132
Martin Chuzzlewit 34, 137, 142, 143, 154
Martin Chuzzlewit 3, 6, 8, 15-17, 22, 31, 33, 34, 36, 38, 40, 83, 84, 86-94, 97-99, 132, 133, 136-138, 140, 142-144, 147, 148, 150, 158, 160, 161, 163, 169, 170
Mary Barton 6, 15, 106
Master Humphrey's Clock 33
Mas'r Davy 41
Mas'r Davy bor 121; *Mas'r Davy bor'*, 44, 41, 121
matther 27
mavis 128; *mavishes* 72, 125
Mawther 72, 125, 128
McCrum, Robert 80
ME 28, 63, 64, 76; Middle English 20, 57
me for "I" 90
Meary 14, 54, 105
measther 27
Medway, The 17, 78
Mencken, H. L. 95, 96, 100, 169
mesh 132; *meshes* 73, 78, 79, 129, 130, 168, 170
Midland dialect 64, 111; Midland dialects 63
Misther 27
moderate, adv. 98, 99, 168
Modern English 20, 95
monger 63; *mongrel* 63
monig 64
monny 64, 66
Monod, Sylvère 23, 109
monosyllables 69
Monsther 27
monthly instalments 9
Monthly Magazine, The 45
mooney 30
moonths 28
Moor, Edward 3, 11, 18, 71, 76, 118,

124, 165, 170
mooth 28
moothers 28
morphology 3
Morris, W. 102, 119, 130
mort 129; *mort o'*, *a* 43, 126; *mort of*, *a* 43, 44, 126
moydert 112, 117; *moider* 117; *moither* 117
moŭntaĭnoŭs 39
Mr. Bounderby 110
"Mr. Minns and his Cousin" 45
muck 126, 129
muddled 112
Mugglestone, Linda 50
mun 112, 113, 117; *munt* 117
My 31, 32

N
Nakagawa, Ken v
Nakao, Yoshiyuki v
na-tive 36
narrator 77
nasal drawl 34
nautical language 102, 130
-nd 76
negative 118; negative form 87; negative sentence 102
neologisms 25
New Inn, the 10
New York 34
Newcomes, The 34
Nicholas Nickleby 4, 6, 8-10, 26, 27, 33, 71, 101-104, 107, 109, 169
nigh 23, 113, 117; *nigh about* 113; *nigh 'bout* 115, 169; *nigh-abouts* 114; *nigh-bout* 113; *nighbout* 23; *nighbut* 21, 23, 24, 113-115, 117, 165, 169; *nighb't* 23; *nightbut* 23; *nigh 'bout* 117
Noakes, Percy 98

nobbut 114, 118; *nobbo* 118
noice 28
nominative 67
non-U 80
noo 28
Norfolk 11, 12, 18, 41; Norfolk dialect 120
North and South 6
north-country speech 52
northern dialect 69, 111; northern dialects 53, 57; northern form 64; northern speech 54, 55
Norwich 41
noun 108, 143
nowt 67; *naught* 67

O
o' 61, 29, 30, 57; *o* 61
o-ration 38
objective case 90
OE 64, 69, 89
OF 76
Of 31, 32
Old English 20, 92, 95
Old Roman Road, The 18, 129
Oliver Twist 45, 49, 50, 166
Oliver Twist 39, 49, 73, 75, 84-88, 90-93, 98, 99, 103
omniscient narrator 71, 72, 129; omniscient narrator, the first person 71
on- 130, 132
oncommon, adj. 130, 131, 132, 170; *oncommonest* 131
oncommon, adv. 98; *on-common* 131
onny 64, 66; *onny way* 66; *onnythin* 64, 66; *onnything* 64, 66; *onnyway* 64; *onnyways* 64, 66
oop 26, 28
oot 26, 28

oother 61, 65
ootside 29
opinionate 150
orthography 48
Orton, Harold 1
Oshimo, Tomoko vi
ought 67, 94; *ote* 30; *owt* 67
Our Mutual Friend 49
ouse (=house) 51
owd 55, 56, 60

P
Page, Norman 5, 6, 13-15, 19, 24, 26, 49, 101, 105
parasitic 22;
Paroissien, David 17
past participle 88
pasthry 27
Pawkins, Major 136, 142, 146
Paxton, P. 140
Peggotty, Clara 11, 118
Peggotty, Daniel 3, 11, 12, 41, 43, 44, 72, 75-77, 84, 86, 87, 90, 91-95, 103, 107, 118-127
Peggotty, Ham 11, 41, 44, 77, 84, 94, 98, 103, 118, 121
Pegler, Mrs. 110, 111
penultimate accent 35
periphrastic auxiliary *did* 94
perpendicular 150
personal pronoun 30; personal pronouns 90
Petyt, K. M. 48
Phillipps, K. C. 80
philologist 35; philologists 13, 52
philology v
phonetic alphabet 19, 47; phonetic descriptions 70, 167; phonetic spelling 7, 20, 26; phonetic spellings 7, 21, 26, 27, 30, 70, 166

phonology 3
phrasal verb 141
Pickwick Papers, The 45, 83, 8-88, 90-93, 98, 99, 103
Pip 17, 50, 71, 73, 78-82, 129, 132, 166, 168
po-session 38
poetic archaism 57
Poetics and Linguistics Association, The v
Pogram, Elijah 16, 18, 22, 83, 87, 136
point of view 75
pooder 29
poppet 126, 129
portmanteau word 150
Possible? 15, 132, 161
Pound, Louise 3, 35, 83, 133, 136, 162
prairie 21, 22, 23, 165; *paraaer* 22; *paraarer* 21, 22; *paraarer* 22; *pararie* 22; *parearer* 21, 22; *parearer* 22; *paroarer* 21, 22; *paroarer* 22; *perearers* 22
pre- 38; *pre-diction* 38
preju-dice 36; *prĕjŭ-dīce* 36, 39
preposition 57, 102, 106, 130
prescriptive grammarians 96
Present-day English 20
Present-day Standard English 21
Preston 13, 14, 18, 23, 29
preterite 88
Price, Miss 107
primary stress 37
Pro-fessor 38
pronunciation 4, 13, 15, 23, 26, 27, 35, 36, 64, 170
proodest 29
protraction 37
provenance 7, 9, 165
provincial dialect v, 1, 24, 27; provincial glossaries 165; provincial glossary 47, 71; provincial

words and phrases 72
provincialisms 8, 11, 41, 101, 105
public reading 15
Pumblechock, Mr. 81, 82
punctuation 39, 40
Pygmalion 19, 21, 47

Q
quarther 27
Queen's English 80
Quirk, Randolph 25, 26, 40, 41, 44
Quotem, Caleb 151

R
Rachael 12, 52, 108, 109, 110, 111
Rackheath 41
raised 138
-rās 89
rational spelling 20
re- 38; *re-ceive* 38; *re-quest* 38; *re-quire* 38; *re-quires* 38; *re-tard* 38
real life 45
real sound 20
realism 7, 45
reduced form 54
reduction 29, 53, 54, 59
reformed spellings 20
regional accents 53
regional dialect 1, 2, 7, 8, 26, 41, 52, 70, 71, 79, 168; regional dialects 4, 5, 12, 21, 83, 165, 166
regius professor 48
relative pronoun 90
reverse psychology 82
rhetorical punctuation 39; rhetorical style of punctuation 166
Right away! 157, 161, 163
rile up 143, 146; *roil* 146
ring-tailed roarer 147, 148

ris, pp. 89, 168; *-risen* 89
Rochester 18, 78, 103
room 28
roon 28; *roonaway* 28
rose, pp, 89, 168
Ross, A. S. C. 80
rural community 2

S
sands 11, 41
Satis House 79, 82
sawyer 146; *sawyers* 144
Saxon 135
Scadder, Zephaniah 16, 18, 83, 86, 89, 91, 94, 97, 138, 140, 143, 147, 148, 158
Schilling, K. G. 55
schoolmeasther 26, 27
schwa 19
Scottish 64
second person pronoun 67
semantic generalisation 79
semi-autobiographical novel 71
semi-colons 39
shak 28
Shakespeare, William. 96, 102, 119, 130
Shang, William vi
Shaw, George Bernard 19-21, 47
Shaw, William 10
Shipman's Tale, The 119
sholl 30
short vowel 67; short vowels 27, 28, 61
Short, Michael 49, 50
Sikes, Bill 84, 87, 88, 90, 98, 103
Simpson, M. 12
sin 114, 118; *sin'* 118; *sinn* 118; *sithen* 114
Sketches by Boz 83, 86, 90, 91, 93, 97, 98, 99

sky, v. 123
Slackbridge 109, 110
slang 47, 48
slantindicular 133; *slantindicularly* 148, 149, 150; *Slantin'dicularly*, 150; *slanting* 150; *perpendicular* 150
Slater, Michael 39
Sleary 47, 106
slurs 39
sma'est 55, 60, 70, 167
Smith, H. L. 89
Smith, Thomas 20
snag 146
snags 144
snap 146; *snap of cold* 144; *Snap of cold weather* 15, 132
snoog 28
social dialect 1
social status 79
sociolinguistics 1, 7, 71
soight 28
soizable 28
soobjact 28
soodden 26, 28
sooffer 28
soom (= 'some') 28, 61, 66
soom (= 'sum') 61, 66
soomat 28; *soom'at* 28; *soom'ut* 28
soombody 61, 66, 70, 167
soop 28
sooper 28
soun 76
sound change 37
source 7, 9; sources 165
sōplīc 95
sōplīce 95
special negative forms 84
speech 2, 5, 13, 19, 25, 27-29, 35, 40, 47, 49, 52-55, 58, 75, 76, 78, 79, 93, 99, 101, 103, 107, 108, 114, 158, 164, 167, 168

spelling reformer 20; spelling system 20
sploiced 28
spoken language 7, 165; spoken standardisation 80; spoken word 21
spok'n 28
Squeers, Wackford 10, 49
stan 54, 59
Standard English 49, 76-79, 166; standard form 63; standard norm 25; standard speech 45
steddy 26
Stone, Harry 25
Stonehouse, J. H. 105
stress 31, 38; stressed syllables 39
strike, v. 144, 146
Strike o' day 115, 118
strong form 37; strong forms 31
strong verbs 89
stylistics 7, 71
subjective 111; subjective case 90
substandard speech 4, 5, 78, 83, 169; substandard British speech 89; substandard English 88
Suffolk 10, 12, 18
Sulliwin, Mrs. 91
supposed narrator 71
synonyms 123
syntax 4
Sørensen, Knud 25

T
tak 28; *tak'* 26; *takken* 28; *takkin* 28
Takahashi, Masami vi
tall 147, 148
Taming of the Shrew, The 96
Tanaka, Toshiro v, 5, 130
Tapley, Mark 93, 146
Taylor, F. E. 115

Texan accent 23
Thackeray, William Makepeace 34
Thames, The 1, 78, 129
That's a fact. 146
theer 68, 118; *thee-er* 68
them for "they" 90
thick boots 79, 82
thieves' cant and slang 73
thot 26
thowt 67
Thrale, Mrs. 16
threat 27
thried 27
th' 59, 53, 57, 78
tickers 75
Tillotson, Kathleen 39, 40
Todd 160
Toe 31, 32, 33
toight 28
tongue-y 15, 36, 132, 138, 150; *tonguey* 138; *tungy* 138
tooches 61, 66
toon 29
toother 61, 66, 70, 167
towd 55, 56, 60
Tragedie of Macbeth, The 96
Trager, G. L. 89
trisyllabic words 35, 36, 37, 38
troifling 28
tumblers 47
Tummus 14, 54, 105
typification 44
typographical devices 21, 40, 166
t' (=to) 59, 30, 53, 54
t'oother 28, 61, 66, 70, 167
t'other 27

U
U (vs. Non-U) 80
Ueki, Kensuke v
U-nited 38

umlaut 39
unaspirated *h* 34
Uncommercial Traveller, The 17
uncommon, adv. 98, 99
understand 54; *understood* 54; *unnerstan'in* 54, 59
underworld 49; underworld lingo 73
unit-ed 38
United States, The 3, 15, 18, 21, 46, 89, 133, 134, 137, 141, 142, 145, 160, 163, 170
unstressed prefix 37, 38; unstressed syllable 31, 38; unstressed syllables 39
urban dialects 1
usage 15, 133; usage, American 153; usage, British 153
use 150, 154, 157, 164, 165

V
verisimilitude 7, 45, 70
Victorian England 79
visual effect 75
vocabulary 3, 4, 15, 25, 133, 150, 170
vowel 36, 37, 38, 54, 58; vowels 37, 39, 53, 58; vowel lengthening 68; vowel sound 38
vulgar 94, 102, 130, 136; vulgar society 80, 168; vulgar speech 57, 79, 92; vulgarisms 49; vulgarity 48

W
waither 27
wakken 26, 28
Wakuda, Hideaki vi
Walker, Mrs. 93
Warden, Mr. 86
warking 26
warn't 26

Warwickshire dialect 2
wa' 27, 60, 56, 27
Wa'at's 26
weak forms 31
Webb, L. K. 16, 52
weel 64, 66, 70, 167; *wele* 64; *wiel* 64; *well* 64, 70, 167
Weller, Sam 83, 84, 86, 90, 91, 92, 93, 98, 162
Weller, Tony 83, 84, 87, 88, 98, 103
wheer 68, 69, 118; *wheerever* 68, 69
wi 58; *wi'* 61, 26, 58
Wilson, Angus 46
wimicking 73, 127; *winnick* 129; *whinnock* 129; *winnicking* 170
wishfo' 60, 56
Wister, O. 89
wi'in 58, 61, 70, 167
wi'out 58, 61, 70, 167
Wopsle, Mr. 81
working-class 78
Wright, Elizabeth 63
Wright, Joseph 63, 64
written language 7, 165; written standardisation 80; written word 21
Wuthering Heights 48
Wyclif, John 138

Y

Yamamoto, Tadao 4, 134, 170
Yarmouth 3, 10, 11, 12, 18
year (=hear) 58, 61
Yes 161; *Yes, Sir.* 155, 156; *Yes, sir.* 154, 161
Yes? 15, 132, 153, 154; *Yes, Sir?* 156
yo 67, 68; *yo'* 68, 67
yoong 28, 61, 66; *yunger* 62, 66; *yoongster* 28; *yungster* 62
Yorkshire 5, 9, 10, 18, 46; Yorkshire accent 26, 27; Yorkshire accents 40, 101, 166, 169; Yorkshire dialect 2, 4, 5, 6, 21, 48, 109; Yorkshire provincialisms 101, 169; Yorkshire speech 167
yoursel' 30